W9-AIA-589

CAMILLA

She had said she was not of his world . . .

If he closed his eyes from looking at the sea to see her lovely face and her golden hair against the blue, he could feel again the thrill of that kiss, like no kiss he had ever given or received before. It made all other kisses seem common and unclean. This was something quite holy and apart . . . something spiritual that he could not understand.

GRACE
LIVINGSTON
HILL

WHITE ORCHIDS

A NATIONAL GENERAL COMPANY

*This low-priced Bantam Book
has been completely reset in a type face
designed for easy reading, and was printed
from new plates. It contains the complete
text of the original hard-cover edition.*
NOT ONE WORD HAS BEEN OMITTED.

WHITE ORCHIDS

*A Bantam Book / published by arrangement with
J. B. Lippincott Company*

PRINTING HISTORY
Lippincott edition published 1935
Bantam edition published July 1971
2nd printing
3rd printing

*All rights reserved.
Copyright 1935 by Grace Livingston Hill.
This book may not be reproduced in whole or in part, by
mimeograph or any other means, without permission.
For information address: J. B. Lippincott Company,
East Washington Square, Philadelphia, Pennsylvania 19105.*

Published simultaneously in the United States and Canada

*Bantam Books are published by Bantam Books, Inc., a National
General company. Its trade-mark, consisting of the words "Bantam
Books" and the portrayal of a bantam, is registered in the United
States Patent Office and in other countries. Marca Registrada.
Bantam Books, Inc., 666 Fifth Avenue, New York, N.Y. 10019.*

PRINTED IN THE UNITED STATES OF AMERICA

WHITE ORCHIDS

CHAPTER I

THE LIGHT FLASHED RED AND CAMILLA JAMMED ON HER brakes. The shabby little roadster came to a frightened, screeching stop just as a great truck came smashing down the crossroad, full power, striking the little flivver with a mighty impact, neatly removing a wheel, and sending the car spinning straight into the air in a series of somersaults. It landed in the opposite ditch with crumpled fenders, broken bumpers, a twisted axle and a fatal injury to its internal organs.

Back of the flivver a big shining car had stopped just in time, and a good looking young man in evening dress and a rich fur-trimmed overcoat stepped out into the road and came over to see the wreck. He was tall, with a nice face, a firm mouth and pleasant eyes. Just now they were filled with concern, as he peered across the ditch into the darkness where the shabby little broken car lay upside down.

The driver of the truck lay across the road with a broken leg, only partly sobered.

Camilla lay huddled inside the little broken roadster, stunned from the shock, unable for the moment to cope with the happening.

"Anybody hurt?" asked the young man from the sedan in a voice that matched his fine face. The traffic cop was approaching excitedly from across the road.

"They sure oughtta be!" said the officer. "Truck driver drunk as a fish, don't know what it's all about! Fool girl driving a flivver! She tried to pass my light, didya see her? They all do. Girls think they can get by with anything!"

"But she stopped the instant the light went red. I was

right behind her and I saw. Didn't you see her? Didn't you hear her brakes?"

"Oh yeah? Sure! I heard! I hear everything! All the same she was tryin' ta get by, an' now she's probably done for herself! Well, it happens every day, an' I gotta get her outta here. Traffic gettin' all balled up!"

He turned his flashlight onto the dark little crumpled car and the young man caught a glimpse of a white face and a huddled slender form.

The door was jammed shut, and it was some seconds before their united efforts got it open. The stalwart policeman lifted out the girl with strong accustomed movements. These things happen every day! Just another fool girl! He poised her on his arm and looked about for a place to lay her until the ambulance came.

"Put her in the back seat of my car!" said the young man graciously. "It's too cold and wet to lay her down by the roadside."

There was a genuineness about him that even the hurried traffic cop respected, and that in spite of the gardenia in his lapel.

"Aw right!" said the officer with an eye already across the road dealing with the drunken driver. He turned and took a step toward the big beautiful car.

It was then Camilla opened her eyes and came to an understanding of things. Her eyes were large and dark and her hair which had fallen down around her face was like fine spun gold.

"I'm—all right!" she murmured breathlessly. "Put me down, please!—I'll be all right! I can stand, myself."

She slid to her feet, steadying herself with her hand on the officer's arm and looked about her, dazed. She felt for her hat which had fallen on the ground, and the young man from the sedan picked it up and handed it to her.

"Thank you," she said, taking an uncertain step toward her car, blinking her eyes to discern its dark unshapely outlines in the ditch.

She looked at it dazedly and swayed, almost falling. The young man put out a steadying arm.

"I'm all right," she said again, straining her eyes toward her car, "if you'll—just please—help me to get my car back—on the road—" she gasped out the words, struggling desperately now to stop trembling.

"Can't be done, lady!" said the policeman. "That car has travelled its last road! It ain't nothin' but a bunch a' junk, now!"

Camilla's great troubled eyes looked in horror at the officer and then turned to the young man with an appeal in her young frightened eyes that instantly enlisted his sympathy.

"Oh, but it's got to go!" she said desperately. "I've got to get on. I'm in a great hurry!"

"So I saw, lady, afore you decided ta put on yer brakes. Yer brakes are no good anyhow. Guess ya ain't had yer car inspected yet, hev ya? Them brakes would never get by an inspector. Ef ya hadn't a ben in such a hurry, ya mighta been goin' on by this time instead o' bein' all but killed yerself, an' yer car dead entirely."

The officer eyed her coldly. Now that she wasn't dead it was his business to rub in the lesson she was learning.

"But it must go!" said Camilla frantically. "Please try to set it up for me! This is an emergency! I think it will go! It—always does—!" she urged hopefully. "It's old—but—it always comes back again—and goes on!"

"Well, it won't never do that again, lady!" said the officer dryly. "What's yer name an' *ad*dress? I gotta have them before ya can go anywheres," he added, getting out a pencil and notebook.

"Oh, but I must go!" cried Camilla frantically. "I can't wait for *anything!* My mother is dying and the doctor sent me to his office for some medicine that he needs at once!"

"Sorry, lady, but y'll havta go some other way. That car won't carry nobody nowhere! An' I gotta have yer *ad*dress 'fore I can let ya go."

"But what shall I do? I must get that medicine!"

Camilla was trembling from head to foot now, her lips trembling too, and tears of which she was wholly unaware were streaming down her cheeks.

The young man from the sedan stepped closer and took off his hat deferentially.

"I will take you wherever you need to go," he said politely. "My car will travel as fast as any."

Camilla lifted terrified eyes to his face, liked his clean-cut jaw and the lean pleasant line of his cheek, gave a comprehensive glance at the expensive car behind her, glanced back into his eyes and knew she could trust them.

"But—it is a long way—" she said with shaking voice, "it must be almost seven miles from here!—And—I have to get back again right away to the city with the medicine!"

"That's all right with me!" said the young man pleasantly. "Just step back here. Wouldn't you like to lie down in the back seat? You were pretty well shaken up you know."

"No, I'm all right!" she said eagerly. "Let's go quick! Every minute counts. My mother is dying. This medicine is the only hope!"

"I gotta get that *ad*dress, lady. I can't let ya go without that *ad*dress!" said the policeman insistently.

The young man watched her as she gave the address. Camilla Chrystie, and a street he did not know, down in the lower part of the city. He studied her trim slender young figure, her refined, delicate profile.

"I ought to do something about my car but I mustn't stop now," said Camilla breathlessly as the stranger helped her into his car.

"Look after that car, will you, officer, till I can get back and see to it?" said the young man, tossing a bill across to the officer behind Camilla's back.

When they were safely out of the thick of it he turned to Camilla, noting her strained white face, the horrible anxiety that burned in her dark brown eyes.

"Now," said the young man pleasantly, "my name's Wainwright, Jeffrey Wainwright. Which way do we go?"

She gave him brief crisp directions as if she had learned them by heart, and added:

"You're very kind. I ought not to let you, I'm afraid. I'm probably hindering you a lot. But— You know what your mother is to you. There is nobody like your mother, and—" with a quiver of her breath, "and—she's all I have in the world!"

"Of course!" said Wainwright with tender understanding in his tone, although he did not know. The conjured picture of his own mother showed her as he knew she probably was at that moment, elaborately gowned and playing bridge with a placid fierceness that was habitual to her. She had never been very close to him. He had known his nurses and his governesses, and later his tutors better than his mother. Yet there was something wistful in his glance as he furtively watched the lovely girl by his side.

"We must get back to her as soon as possible," he added, speeding up his car.

"I can't ever thank you enough!" quavered Camilla.

"Don't try, please. I'm just glad to be doing something worth while for once."

"But I'm probably keeping you from some important engagement," she said, coming out of her own troubles for an instant and giving a quick comprehensive glance at his handsome face, immaculate evening attire and the white gardenia in his buttonhole.

Wainwright stared ahead for an instant silently, and then answered her deliberately, thoughtfully.

"No, I don't think it was important. In fact it wasn't really an engagement at all, and I shouldn't be surprised if it turns out to be a good thing that you have kept me from it!"

Camilla stared at him perplexedly, faintly perceiving that there were problems and crises in other lives as well as her own.

"I am sure," she said contritely, "that I am taking you far out of your way."

"On the contrary," said Wainwright, "you are taking me in exactly the direction I was thinking of going before I saw your car."

"Oh," moaned Camilla, "but you are having to take me away back again!"

"But you see, my way leads back also," smiled the young man playfully, hoping to relieve the girl's evident strain. "And you know, it is queer, but somehow since decisions about the evening are taken out of my hands for a time I am strangely relieved. I wasn't at all certain about what I ought to do before, but now I am. And I don't think I ever before had a chance to help save somebody's life. I somehow think we're going to win out, don't you?"

The girl's eyes in her white face were startling as they looked at him through the darkness.

"Oh, I—hope—! I—I've been praying—all—the—way!"

Wainwright gave her a sudden quick glance.

"Well, I've never done much praying myself," he said almost embarrassedly, "but I'll drive and you pray! Perhaps it'll take them both. But we are out to win. Let's set our minds to that. Now, is this where we turn?"

They drove on silently for some distance, sitting alertly

watching the road. Wainwright gave her a furtive glance now and then.

"Why don't you lean back and relax?" he asked suddenly. "You've had a shock and you need to rest."

But Camilla remained tense.

"Oh, I can't rest now," she said with a catch in her breath like a suppressed sob. "I must get back to Mother!"

"But we'll get back just as quickly if you relax, you know," he reminded her sympathetically. "It seems hard that you should have had to come away at such a time. I can't understand how the doctor allowed you to do it! There surely must have been someone else to go. I should think he would have gone himself, or sent a special messenger."

"He couldn't," said Camilla, lifting her strained face to his. "He couldn't leave my mother. And there wasn't anybody else who could be trusted to go. You see his office is locked and there was nobody at home to find the medicine and the instruments he wanted. He had to tell me exactly how to find everything he wanted. He is a very wonderful doctor. He saved my mother's life once before, you see. He ought to have been called sooner. She wouldn't let me send for him at first. She thought she was soon going to be better, and she felt we ought not to get in his debt again. He has always been so kind."

Wainwright considered that. There were people in the world then, well educated, cultured people, who couldn't afford a doctor when they were desperately ill!

"But there surely must have been somebody else in the house he could have trusted without taking you away from your mother when she was so ill," he protested.

"No, there wasn't anybody in the house but a woman who rooms on the floor above us, and she's rather stupid. She's staying there to wait on the doctor if he needs anything while I am gone. She can bring hot water and answer the telephone if I have to call him."

There was desperation in the girl's voice again, and he put on more gas and drove fast, but he could see her white face strained and tense in the darkness, and her suffering eyes watching every bit of the way.

"This is the street!" she announced at last. "It's in the middle of the next block, the fourth house on the right hand side."

"But there's no light in the house!" said Wainwright as they drew up to the curb. "Is there nobody there at all?"

"No," said Camilla breathlessly, "the doctor's assistant won't be back until midnight, and his family are away in the south for a few weeks."

"Well, you're not going in there alone, that's certain!" said Wainwright in a firm voice as if he had been used to protecting this girl for years.

But Camilla was not waiting for protection. Before the car had fully come to a halt she was out, fairly flying up the steps of the house and was fitting a key into the lock of the door. As Wainwright followed her he was relieved to see a dignified bronze sign on the door. The girl hadn't made a mistake in the house then. It was a doctor's office.

Camilla's excited fingers had just succeeded in getting the key into the key hole as he arrived, and putting his hand over hers he turned the key and threw open the door.

"The switch is at the right hand!" said Camilla crisply. "The first three buttons he said would light the hall and offices."

Wainwright found the switch and instantly a spacious hall and doors to the left appeared, and Camilla drew a free breath.

"It's all right!" she said eagerly. "I was afraid I might have made a mistake in the house or something. But there's his wife's picture on the desk, and his little girl and boy on the wall. And there's the package on his desk where he said it would be. You see it's some special medicine he had sent away for, that might have come after he left this morning. He wasn't quite sure it had arrived."

Her voice choked with excitement, and Wainwright looked at her, for the first time seeing her face clearly by the bright light, and beholding that she was lovely.

"Is that all you had to get?" he asked, giving a quick interested glance about the office that gave so many evidences of culture and refinement.

"No," said Camilla, "there's a leather case, a black leather case on the desk in the back room, or perhaps on the floor by the desk. I'm to bring that. And a big bottle on the highest shelf of the cabinet in the other room. If it isn't there it may have been put on the inner closet shelf. He may have to be with Mother all night and not have time to get back to his office before he goes to an operation."

There was a quick catch in her breath at the thought of the possiblilities the night might bring forth, but she controlled herself bravely.

They found the bottle and the case without any trouble.

"Now, do we go?" asked Wainwright.

"No," said Camilla, "I'm to call up first, to make sure there is nothing else he needs."

Her eyes grew suddenly dark with anxiety and her hand trembled as she reached for the telephone.

Wainwright watched her again with admiration. The delicate flush that had been on her face as she hunted for the bottle and case had drained away, and her face was white with anguish again as she waited for the doctor's voice.

"It's Camilla, Dr. Willis," she said with that catch like a sob in her voice again. "How is she?"

Wainwright as he stood near her could hear the quiet voice of the doctor:

"No worse, Camilla. I think her pulse is a trifle steadier. Did you find everything?"

"Yes, everything."

"Well, hurry back. I hate to think of you driving all that way and going into an empty house alone!"

"But I'm not alone," said Camilla shyly, with the shadow of a smile on her lips, "I—found—a—a—kind friend on the way, who came with me!" Her eyes sought Wainwright's gratefully, and he smiled back at her and somehow comradeship seemed suddenly to be cemented between them. It was queer! Two strangers who never expected to meet again after that evening, and yet they seemed somehow well acquainted all at once.

When they had turned out the lights and locked the door Wainwright drew her arm through his with a possessive comforting grasp as they walked back to the car.

When he put her into the car she sat back with a breath of relief.

"She's no worse!" she said, looking up at him radiantly as he took the wheel again, and now that he knew how she really looked in the light it seemed a lovely glimpse of her inner self.

"Isn't that great!" he breathed fervently in almost the same tone of rejoicing she had used. Being glad with someone gave him a new thrill. He had seldom been called upon to experience unselfish joy. In his world you got and you gave mostly for your own pleasure. Now it seemed that he was touching deeper, more vital matters. Sin and danger and trifling with doom could give thrills. He had hovered near enough to each one to understand. But this was new and sweet. He looked at her almost tenderly through the darkness and then he laid his hand gently for just an instant over her small, gloved one.

"I'm so glad for you!" he said gravely.

"Thank you," she said brightly. "You've been just wonderful! I don't know how I should have gone through this awful evening without you."

Then she was silent a minute, thoughtful.

"Was that all true, what the policeman said about my car?" she asked presently. There was a hint of anxiety in her voice, yet her manner was strong, controlled, practical, ready to accept the worst quietly.

"Well, it's hard to say exactly," he answered with a quick reserve in his voice. "It did look rather badly beaten up, didn't it? But usually a good mechanic can do something with almost any car, you know." He tried to say it cheerfully although his better sense told him that the little car was beyond help. "Suppose we wait for daylight and expert advice before we try to think about it."

Camilla sighed.

"Yes, but expert advice costs a great deal, and I simply couldn't afford anything just now I'm afraid. I shall want to use every cent to make Mother comfortable."

"Of course!" he seconded her heartily, "but your insurance will cover all that you know. You had insurance of course, didn't you?"

"No," said Camilla sadly, "I couldn't. I bought the car for fifty dollars, and it took all I had saved to get the licenses and one second-hand tire it needed." She ended with a brave little attempt at a laugh.

He was appalled at such details, but he did not let her know it. "Oh, well, it will be up to the owner of this truck anyway," he said with more assurance than he felt. "Sometimes of course they try to slide out of such moral obligations, but you let me handle this. I'll make it a point to call upon him tomorrow and put the thing before him in the right light. Don't you worry."

"Oh, but I couldn't let you do anything more!" said

Camilla in a frightened voice. "You have already done more than any stranger could possibly be expected to do."

"Is that the way you rate me?" he said reproachfully with a twinkle in his voice. "Only a stranger after we've gone on an errand like this? I thought we were friends now."

Camilla gave him another look in the darkness, of mingled pleasure and surprise.

"You have certainly taken more trouble than any friend I have would have taken," she said earnestly. "The truth is I haven't many friends in this city anyway. We haven't been here long, only about nine months. I haven't had time to make friends."

"Then you'll let me count as a friend?" he asked gravely. "At least until your mother gets well and you have time to look me over?"

He smiled down at her through the darkness, and she felt a comforted sense of being taken care of in a sort of brotherly way.

"You certainly do not need any special looking over," said Camilla gravely, "after the way you have befriended me tonight."

There was a weary strain in her tone that made him look anxiously at her. It occurred to him that perhaps she had been more hurt in the collision than she would own.

"Are you sure you are all right?" he asked earnestly.

"Oh, yes," she said rousing again and putting on that forced attention she had worn since they started on their errand.

"Well, we'll get you home as quickly as possible," he said and began to question her as to where her street was located.

He purposely avoided the scene of the accident and took a short cut, for fortunately he knew the city well. He tried to talk cheerfully, as he furtively watched her droop in her corner. It was all too evident that she had been keeping up on her nerve and now that her errand was almost completed she was beginning to feel the reaction.

It was with great relief that he presently drew up at the house she indicated and helped her out, following her with the case and bottle. She took the little package of medicine and fairly flew up the steps and into the house.

CHAPTER II

IT WAS A SMALL, HIGH, OLD-FASHIONED BRICK HOUSE WITH white marble steps of a long-ago vintage, in an unfashionable quarter of the city, invaded now by business on every hand. The other houses on either side and across from it bore signs in the windows, "Vacancies," "Apartments to let," "Boarding." It was a sordid dreary street. But Wainwright did not wait to examine the surroundings. He hurried into the house, finding a strange anxiety at his own heart for the sick mother whom he had never seen.

The hall was of the dark narrow type with steep narrow stairs mounting straight up to a darker hall above. It seemed gloomy beyond description. But at the right, one half of a double door stood open, and there the gloom ceased, for the room into which it opened was surprisingly cosy and homelike. Soft lamplight rosily shaded played over some handsome pieces of old furniture and a good picture or two on the walls. A soft-toned rug covered the floor. There was even a speck of a fireplace with a log smoldering flickeringly, and an easy chair placed beside it, and there were low bookshelves running across the room on either side of the fireplace, and bits of good bric-a-brac here and there on the top shelf. It looked a pleasant place to live.

Between the front windows was a long old-fashioned mirror in a quaint gilt frame and in that he saw reflected the room beyond, which in the parlance of other days would have been called a back parlor.

The double doors between the rooms were open and he caught a glimpse of a wide old-fashioned bed, too large for the room, and a delicate face on the pillow framed in silver white hair. It was a face strangely sweet and filled with a great peace. He held his breath. Was she dead already? He could see Camilla touching her lips to the white brow with a caress as soft as a breath and then dropping quietly to her knees beside the bed. The doctor stood there with his back to the door, his hand on the frail wrist of the sick woman.

Wainwright hesitated in the hall, wondering whether it would be intrusion to step inside the front room and put down the doctor's case and bottle.

Then the doctor turned and saw him, his quick eye noting what he carried, and he stepped quietly out into the hall.

"What more can I do here?" asked Wainwright in a low tone handing over the doctor's case. "I'm at your service as long as I can help."

The doctor gave him a keen glance.

"Thank you," he said, "I'll be glad to accept that offer. We need a nurse at once. Could you go and bring her? I don't want Camilla to leave her mother any more. I can't tell how things are coming out yet. Besides that woman who rooms upstairs is so stupid she can't even boil water."

"I'll go," said Wainwright quickly. "Have you one in mind, or do I hunt one up?"

"Miss York," said the doctor briefly. "I phoned. She's free. She'll be ready when you get there. Here's the address."

"All right," said Wainwright taking the slip of paper the doctor handed him. "But before I go I must tell you, for I'm afraid Miss Chrystie won't think of it. You'd better look her over a little. She's been in a bad accident. Her car was all smashed up. She's very brave. She insists she's all right, but she's just keeping up on her nerve."

The doctor gave him a quick look.

"You don't say!" he exclaimed. "I somehow felt I ought not to let her go alone."

"She didn't get far alone," said the young man, "I happened along and saw it all. We picked her up for dead, but she snapped out of it wonderfully and was only anxious to get on with her errand. I'm afraid though that she's about all in, with the shock and anxiety together."

He gave the details briefly and then went out after the nurse.

It was not a long trip and the nurse was waiting when he reached her lodgings, so that they were soon back at the house again.

Camilla was lying on the couch in the front room when they entered the house, her eyes were closed and her face was wan and white. But the eyes flew open as they came in and she sat up at once.

Wainwright went toward her and gently pushed her back to the pillow again.

"Please!" he said in a whisper. "You'll need your strength you know. You must save yourself. Here's Miss York. She'll attend to everything. And I'm here to help her as long as I'm needed. I'm a friend tonight you know," and his face lit up with a sweet, gentle smile. Camilla felt again that sense of being protected and cared for in a peculiar way.

"But I must get a room ready for her," said Camilla anxiously as she yielded to his persuasive hand and lay still on her pillow.

"I can do that," asserted Wainwright firmly as though he were quite accustomed to getting rooms ready for people. "What you need is a little rest, or there'll be two patients here instead of one. That wouldn't be so good you know."

He smiled again with a flash of his perfect teeth and she succumbed.

"But you don't know where things are," said Camilla weakly with a worried pucker on her white brow.

"I can learn, can't I? Where were you planning to put her?"

"Oh, I don't know," said Camilla in a troubled voice. "She'll have to have the dining room I suppose. We'll eat in the kitchen. I wasn't planning. I didn't know she was coming. Oh, why did you bring her here? She will be so crowded here! We really haven't need for a nurse now I am back."

"It was the doctor's orders, I only went after her," said Wainwright serenely. "He had already phoned for her before we got back. He thought you ought not to be alone when he has to leave. He said there ought to be someone here who knows what to do in an emergency."

"Oh!" said Camilla with a little sharp breath like a moan, paling at the word emergency.

"Of course there may not be any emergency. We hope there won't be," went on Wainwright with a calm steady voice and another quieting smile, "but it is always best to provide against one you know. Now, could you just tell me what needs doing and where to find things? You must promise to lie still and wait till I come for instructions and not get up and run around or I'll have to lock you in here till we have things in order."

There was a twinkle in his eye as he said it, but somehow his firm chin looked as if he really might do it if he were disobeyed. Camilla resigned herself for the moment at least.

"Well, there's a cot in the third story back storeroom. There's an eiderdown quilt there and two blankets. A pillow, too."

She glanced at his immaculate evening attire and gave a little moan.

"Oh, you oughtn't to be doing things like that! Not with that beautiful coat on!" She put her hands together with a little helpless motion. "Oh, please! It distresses me!"

"My coat will come off," said Wainwright with a grin, and quickly whipped off, first his handsome overcoat, then his formal evening coat.

She had to smile he was so like a nice big boy oblivious to the whiteness of his shirt front.

"Now!" he said, "that's better! Keep that expression on till I get back. I'm all set for the storeroom on the third floor!"

The words were very low. They did not penetrate to the sick room although the door was open. Turning swiftly he went up the stairs with an incredibly soft tread. Even the creaky stairs were unbelievably silent under his careful strides. It was not long before he was moving down again bearing a light cot under one arm and an eiderdown quilt in the other.

She was standing in the hall when he returned, holding clean sheets, blankets, and a pillow in a case which she had taken from the shelves in the hall closet. She motioned him to follow her to the dining room and walked lightly as a feather.

He followed her as quietly, but when he had put down the cot and taken the bedclothing from her, laying it on the table, he stooped and picked her up in his arms, as if she had been a blanket, and bore her back to the couch in the front room.

"You are a naughty child!" he whispered. "You must be good or I shall be forced to stay here and hold you down."

She looked up and saw a pleasant grin upon his face, but there was something in his eyes and the firm mouth that made her lie back again and relax.

"I'm really quite all right," she protested in pantomime.

He stooped and whispered softly in her ear:

"If you will not do it for yourself, won't you do it for her sake?" He mentioned with his head toward the sick room.

This had an instant effect in the look of fear that came into her eyes. Then after an instant's quiet she said soundlessly:

"If you'll just let me get up and make that bed, then I can rest."

"I can make beds!" he declared earnestly. "I went to military school and learned how!" He grinned, and she succumbed.

He slipped off his shoes and disappeared into the dining room. She heard soft little swishing sounds of a hand on the smooth sheets, but for the most part it was very still. Only the creak of a board in the floor now and then. She raised her head and tried to look through her mother's room into the dining room to the left. She could see the foot of the cot and a hand tucking the blanket in with military precision, a nice white well-groomed hand that did not look as if it had made up a bed in many a day. Then she heard soft footsteps and lay down quickly lest he would return and find her disobeying orders.

The doctor was speaking to the nurse in low professional growls. The nurse on her rubber-shod feet went swiftly to the kitchen. She could hear running water. Wainwright had gone out into the kitchen. She could hear him talking softly to the nurse. Then the doctor went out and the nurse came back. Camilla lay there staring up at the ceiling, glancing now and then into the dimness of her mother's room, longing to be in there watching the doctor's face to know just what he was thinking at every passing minute about the possibilities of fear or hope.

Wainwright came back presently. His hair was tossed up over his forehead and again she thought how much he looked like a nice boy.

He stooped and murmured to her like a friend of years:

"I'm going out to the drug store for something the doctor wants. I won't be gone long. I'll phone about your

car and see that it's cared for. The doctor wants you to lie
still unless he calls you. He says you must rest so you can
help the nurse when he has to go. I'll be back very soon
and do anything that's needed."

She tried to protest, but he stepped into his shoes,
swung on his beautiful overcoat over his vest, and was
gone before she could do so. She lay there still staring at
the empty doorway where he had stood for an instant before he closed the front door so carefully after him. Then
she turned her gaze back to the room, to the handsome
evening coat that lay slumped across a chair as if it were
perfectly at home. She thought of the strange happenings
of the evening, like a dream, with a great fear standing
grimly in the background, and Wainwright like a strong
angel dominating everything. She thought how queer it was
for his coat to be lying there across their shabby little arm
chair; he a stranger from another world than theirs! How
kind he was! How like a tried friend! And he was an
absolute stranger. She didn't know a thing about him except his name, a name she had never heard before! What
would her mother say to it all? Would she live to know
about it?

Then fear came back and held her heart again till it
quivered and she prayed an agonized wordless prayer.

She must have closed her eyes while she prayed for
when she opened them again it was with a sense of a
strong breath of air from outdoors having blown in her
face. The light was turned out in the front room where she
lay and it seemed a long time afterwards. But when she
looked in affright toward her mother's room she could see
the nurse coming in with a glass in her hand, and then she
sensed Wainwright standing near her looking down at her.
Their eyes met in the dimness of the room and he smiled.
He had a kind look in his eyes and he stooped over her and
put two fingers gently on her wrist for a moment.

"Oh, yes," she stirred softly and tried to rise. "I am quite
rested now! I must go to Mother! And you should go home
and get some sleep. You have been so good!"

He shook his head and stooped to speak in her ear.

"Your mother is resting comfortably now. The doctor
thinks there has been a shade of improvement. I'm staying
awhile out there in the hall. If you want me just give a soft

little cough and I'll come. And don't worry about your car. They're taking care of it. It's gone to a garage."

He drifted away like one of the shadows in the room. She stared about her and wondered if he too had been a dream. Then she noticed the big chair was gone and his evening coat was slung across the top of the piano as if it had been a day laborer's coat. Still marvelling, between wakefulness and sleeping she fell asleep. She did not even hear the milkwagons when they began their rounds, nor the bread wagons a little later when they went clop, clop, clopping down the icy street. It was broad daylight when she woke with a start and heard the water running in the kitchen sink. She threw aside the coverings and got up quickly, thoroughly awake now and alive to duty and anxiety.

She hurried out into the hall softly with a fearsome glance toward her mother's room where the shades were drawn, keeping out the brightness of the morning. She could not see into the dim darkness of the room, her eyes were not yet accustomed to the light of day.

She wondered as she crossed the room how her shoes came to be off and where they were, and then she came into the dimness of the hall and saw Wainwright slumped down in the old Morris chair, his overcoat about him and his hair tossed back in disorder. He was asleep and his face looked white and tired and boyish. He had stayed all night! How wonderful! But what an obligation to have to a stranger!

But before she could pass him he had roused and caught her hand as she would have gone by.

"Good morning!" he whispered. "Are you all right, Camilla?" He did not seem to speak her name as if he felt himself a stranger.

She caught her breath softly.

"I'm fine," she answered, "but—my mother! How is she? Oh, I *shouldn't* have gone to sleep!"

"She's better!" he said with a light of eagerness in his eyes almost as if she might have been *his* mother. "Sleep was just what you should have done. Come out in the kitchen where we can talk."

He took her hand and led her through the dining room, and she did not realize that they were walking hand in hand until they came sharply upon the nurse washing a cup and plate. But she did not seem to think it strange. She said good morning in a business-like tone, and then, "Well, your mother is better, Miss Chrystie!"

"Oh!" Camilla caught her breath and closed her eyes for an instant, a light coming into her face. "Could I go to her?"

"No, she's sleeping quite naturally now, and the doctor said she shouldn't be disturbed. He's gone to another operation and he'll be back again in about two hours to see how we're getting on."

"Oh, I should have been here to get him some breakfast!" said Camilla aghast.

"Oh, no you shouldn't!" said the nurse capably. "I made him some coffee and toast and scrambled him some eggs. Now you can get yourself and Mr. Wainwright some breakfast. I've had all I want. Mr. Wainwright has been invaluable. I don't know what we should have done without him."

Camilla turned to Wainwright with gratitude and apology in her eyes.

"Oh, how terrible it was for me to sleep through everything and you a stranger doing it all."

Wainwright ran his fingers through his hair and turned about on her sharply, blinking at her through big blue pleasant eyes.

"What did you say I was, young lady?" he asked catching hold of her wrists and looking her straight in the eyes.

Camilla, her heart suddenly light, looked up with a shamedly sweet smile on her white young face.

"I said you were a—*friend*," she said shyly.

He gave her hand a quick warm clasp.

"Thank you for those kind words!" he said. "Remember I'm a young fellow taking his tests, and mighty anxious to pass muster."

Then he let her go, but not without another look that seemed somehow to cement a friendship that she knew no way to prevent.

It was when they were sitting across from each other at the white enameled kitchen table eating scrambled eggs and drinking amber coffee together cosily, that she summoned words again to protest gratefully at all he had done for her, and to deplore the fact that he had been up all night.

"This isn't the first time I've eaten scrambled eggs in a kitchen at an early hour in the morning," he said gravely. "I've often danced all night and ended up with scrambled eggs in the morning, but I can't say they ever tasted so good as these do. And I can tell you truly that I've had more satisfaction out of this night than I ever had out of any of those other nights. I'm so very glad your mother is better!"

She looked at him startled as his words gave her evidence of even more differences between them than she had visioned. Yes, of course he would belong to a world like that! A fashionable world with all it stood for today! His coat might have told her that, and the gardenia in his buttonhole. There was a strange little uneasy twinge as she took that in, and put it away for future thought.

And yet, it was all the more wonderful that he had stayed and been so fine, and worked so hard, when he came of an entirely different world! She would not let his kindness and friendship for that one night be spoiled or discounted in the least by any differences there might be in their worlds. Whatever he was or had been or was to be, he had been great tonight, and had a right to be called a friend.

He even helped her wipe their few dishes, as if he had been her playmate from childhood. She knew it couldn't last of course. It would be over like a dream—with this difference, it was a dream that she never would forget.

When he went away at last, after the doctor had returned and pronounced the mother out of immediate danger, he had his overcoat well buttoned up to hide his evening attire. But he came back immediately from his car with a big long white box in his hand and a nice grin on his face.

Camilla, from the window, had been watching him away, and hurried to the door as she saw him return.

"Won't you relieve me of these flowers?" he asked, with a funny wry smile. "The occasion for them is past and I wouldn't know how to dispose of them. Perhaps your mother will enjoy them."

"Oh," said Camilla, with a conscience-stricken look. "I've kept you from so much!" And then as the box was put in her hands, "And somebody has been missing you, and missing these, and wondering! I do hope you telephoned and explained."

She lifted her eyes and saw a queer puzzled look on his face.

"No," he said thoughtfully, "I didn't explain. I don't know that I shall. And I wasn't sure that I was going to use those flowers when I bought them. I think it was a good thing that I didn't!"

Then with a smile he was gone.

Camilla watched his car glide out from the curb where it had stood through the night, saw his lifted hand in adieu, and turned back to the house with wonder in her eyes and thoughtful mien. She went out to the kitchen with the big box to be alone and think this out.

But when she opened the box, there were great white orchids! And suddenly her problem was complicated by the vision of a third person, the girl for whom these strange white flowers had been bought! What was she? Who was she? His friend? His sweetheart? His wife perhaps!

The distance between her world and the world of the erstwhile stranger who had befriended her in her need was widening fast, and daylight was upon her. There was no more time for dreams.

Then suddenly the nurse called her, and she left the white flowers in water hastily drawn in the bread bowl, and went to meet the doctor.

White orchids in a yellow bread bowl!

CHAPTER III

JEFFREY WAINWRIGHT DROVE OUT INTO THE MORNING, BACK into the commonplace of his life, and remembered what had happened a little more than fifteen hours ago, before the accident.

He had been driving away from Stephanie Varrell's apartment to which he had just brought her home from a matinee they had been attending that afternoon, and as he turned the corner and glanced back down the street something in the swing of a figure approaching from the other direction brought a familiar wrath to his consciousness. Was that his old enemy, Myles Meredith? It certainly was. No other man could walk like that, with that insolent swagger, described in Jeffrey Wainwright's imaginative language as "walking delicately." How he despised him! Not because he was in a way a rival for Stephanie Varrell's smiles, for Wainwright had an honest fair mind, and liked to play the game squarely and take his medicine if things didn't go his way. But the man was a sneak, a snake in disguise, a double-crosser, an unprincipled rotter. In fact there wasn't a word in Wainwright's vocabulary of despicable adjectives that he hadn't at some time used in reference to Meredith, either in his own mind, or to Stephanie, and once to Meredith himself.

Wainwright was on his way home to dress for a dinner Stephanie was giving that night, and he had supposed himself to be in a hurry, but he brought his car to an abrupt stop on the crossing and watched Myles Meredith swing on affectedly down the street to the door of the big apartment house which sheltered Stephanie's charming abode, and enter.

For a second he sat there staring at the empty space on the sidewalk which Meredith had just vacated. Then he became aware of an automobile horn blowing viciously just behind him, and a traffic officer's whistle in the offing, and started his car with a sudden jerk that sent it shooting down the street at a frantic pace. His usually nice pleasant face was a study in frowns.

What was that villain doing here? He had supposed him to be on his way to Europe. He was to have sailed last Friday! Sneak! Had he dared to return after the affair of last week? And would Stephanie receive him, knowing he had been criminally involved with a girl of notorious character? Fool he had been that he had not stayed about to watch if she sent him away. If Stephanie let him hang around her after what had happened he was done with her!

And yet, she was the girl he had about decided to marry!

Well, he must get this thing cleared up before he went any farther! He would go back and find out if Meredith was there, and if so he would demand that Stephanie choose between them.

He was so angry that he turned corners on two wheels, and brought up speedily before the big apartment house again.

There was no sign of Meredith in either direction. He had not had time as yet to get far away. Likely he was just coming down in the elevator, if Stephanie had really refused to see him. But he found himself doubting whether Stephanie would do that. Stephanie loved to trifle with dangerous things.

He decided to stay there for a few minutes and wait for Meredith. This was as good a time as any for a showdown. He could dress quickly afterward. What matter if he was late when so important a circumstance was in the balance?

So he drew up within the latitude for parking and waited with his frowning gaze fixed upon the entrance from which he had just a few minutes ago come out so happily.

Perhaps it was the thought of his own evening garb which he was expecting to assume hastily that recalled the glimmer of white shirt front between the richly furred lapels of Myles Meredith's top coat. Myles Meredith, then, was dressed for the evening and had been unfastening the outer coat as he entered the apartment house door, as if he was sure of an entrance, and was going in to stay.

Could it be possible that Myles Meredith was invited to Stephanie's dinner? Or had even dared to call her up and ask if he might call? Either possibility was an insult to Stephanie, whom Jeffrey Wainwright wanted with all his heart to respect. Surely, surely, after all she knew, after all she had promised him, Stephanie would not involve herself again with that contemptible creature!

He waited for ten long minutes and still there was no sign of Meredith. Then he went into the office of the apartment house, sought out a booth and telephoned up to Stephanie's apartment.

He was told that Miss Varrell was busy just now and not able to come to the telephone. He might leave a message or call later, but at his insistence he finally heard her slow drawl mingled with annoyance.

"For sweet pity's sake, Jeff, what can be the matter with you? You haven't been away from here ten minutes. You can't have reached home yet. Have you been in a smash-up or anything?"

Wainwright's tone was hard and insistent as he demanded to know:

"Is Meredith there with you, Stephanie?"

There was an instant's silence. Evidently she had not expected that question. Her voice was vexed as she replied at last:

"Why in the world should you ask that, Jeff?" She was stalling for time to think. He could feel her hesitation over the wire.

"Because I saw him going in there just as I turned the corner!" said Wainwright. There was a grim indignation in his tone.

"Well," said Stephanie, adopting her haughtiest tones, full of resentment, "and suppose he is? What is that to you? Haven't I a right to have anyone call at my apartment? Is it your business to keep espionage over me?"

"You told me that Meredith sailed for Europe last Friday!" he accused her.

"Well, so he did. At least he went on board the ship, but found a message delaying him another week. Really, Jeff, you are most trying. You promised me that you would go home and dress and get back as soon as possible. Please hurry! You'll delay everything if you don't get back when I asked you."

"Is that bounder going to be at your dinner, Stephanie?" The grim voice was not to be placated.

"Jeff, you are simply *impossible!* What right have you to hold up my dinner while you ask tiresome questions?"

"The right of the man who has asked you to marry him, and who won't do it again until he knows where he stands."

"That's not enough to make you the censor of my list of dinner guests!" she said angrily. "I invite whom I will to my apartment. We're not married yet, remember. The question is merely under consideration. I'm sure you're not doing much just now to help your side of the case."

"Your list of dinner guests!" repeated Wainwright thoughtfully, ignoring her last remark. "Then he was an invited guest! Not a chance unexpected caller! Then you knew this afternoon that he was coming?" His voice was accusatory, condemning.

"Well, suppose I did?" said the woman vexedly. "What is that to you?"

"A good deal!" said Wainwright. "I like to know how far I can trust my friends. Thanks for letting me know in time!"

"What do you mean, in time, Jeff? You certainly aren't going to stage a scene at my dinner, are you?"

"No," said Wainwright coldly with a finality in his voice, "I shall not be there!"

"Infant!" she cried furiously. "Jealous infant, that's what you are! Just because poor Mylo was held up a day or two you are fussing. I declare I didn't know you were such a child!"

"This is not a matter of jealousy, Stephanie! You know my reasons. You know he is not fit to be around you. You know what he is and yet you ask him to one of your most intimate affairs!"

"Oh, nonsense! Don't be so extravagant in your denunciation! How hard men are on one another! Of course Mylo isn't an angel, but I like him. I always have. I asked him. Yes, I asked him because he is good company. I like to have him around. It doesn't matter to me what he has done, nor what he is. I enjoy an evening in his company."

"Then you'll not mind dispensing with mine of course!" said Wainwright.

"Oh, you child, you!" mocked the girl with a forced laugh. "You know you haven't the slightest intention of staying away. You know you would come just out of curiosity if for nothing else, to see what Myles Meredith is up to next. Go home, Jeff darling, as fast as you can get dressed and hurry back. Don't let's have any more child's play about it. You're going to sit beside me you know," her tone was low and insinuating as if she wished to guard it from being heard by a possible listener, "and remember," there was intimate caressing in the tone now, like patting a small boy on the back after reproof, "Remember, white orchids, darling!"

As Jeffrey Wainwright reviewed that conversation on the way through the next morning's traffic, it seemed to him that he was reading it or dreaming it about someone else. It couldn't be that he, Jeffrey Wainwright had been sap enough after that, knowing that Myles Meredith was there with her, waiting for that dinner, to go on home and get dressed, and actually plan to go back to that dinner.

Oh, he remembered that he was undecided about it. He had raged within himself all the time he was dressing, told himself that he wouldn't go a step, that she deserved to be let severely alone until she came around and saw how she was treating him, decided to do half a dozen different things instead of going to Stephanie Varrell's dinner.

But then he had reflected that that course would only please Meredith. It would only leave the coast clear for Meredith to play the lover to Stephanie. It would leave himself a prey to his angry imagination. He should at least be there and block the fellow's plans, sit a death's head at the feast, and show his disapproval, courteously of course, so that only his hostess should understand.

Yet even so she would have triumphed! Had she not told him he would not stay away for anything? Had she not challenged him to stay away if he dared? The real way to show her would be to stay away of course, and he would do it!

A dozen times he had changed his mind, till he was ready to go. Nor did he hasten in his preparation. If he was late it would not matter. It rather pleased him to keep her waiting. To make her think he was not coming.

"No, he would not go," he told himself. Of course he would not go. He fairly despised himself for his hesitancy.

And after all that vacillating he had gone and bought those white orchids.

"Infant!" Yes, infant! She had been right to call him that! In the clearness of the morning it seemed impossible that he should have been contemplating even for a moment, going to that dinner with the man whom he despised, and whom Stephanie not so long ago had promised to strike off her list of acquaintances.

Well, he had stayed away. Quite without his own planning. The matter had been taken out of his hands. Although he was dressed and ready and on his way with his white orchids in the back seat of his car, he had been stopped on the road and sent in an entirely different direction. And the strangest thing about it all was that he had not once thought about it the whole night through.

His mind went slowly back over his experiences since the shabby little car in front of him had suddenly stopped with screeching brakes that did not brake, and the great gas truck had come roaring down upon it and sent it whirling in the air to roll over in the ditch.

He felt again that thrill of horror as he looked down into the crumpled little car and saw that white unconscious face of the girl, certain that she must be dead. The thrill of relief when he found she was still alive; his overpowering pity for her when she turned that desperate look upon him and told him her mother was dying and she must go for the medicine.

As he looked back upon it all he could not remember a single thought of wonder over what Stephanie thought about his absence or what Meredith was doing. By the light of day neither seemed to matter.

He had been close to vital matters. He had been watching and waiting all night while a battle between life and death went on, and for the time being at least life had been victorious. As he thought it over now, he wouldn't have missed that experience for all the dinners, no, nor for all the Stephanies in the world. The night seemed to have been a sort of eye-opener which had made a number of things plain to him. For one thing he had seen life from another side, the side of suffering and unselfishness, sorrow and pain, and bravery. Beside it, even granting that Camilla and her little unconscious mother had not been interesting in themselves, his life of play, courting emotions of various sorts, seemed the merest trifling. Child's play, that was all.

Oh, he would come back to it, he knew. One smile from Stephanie would lure him as it always did, these last two years, one frown would twist itself in his soul like a sword, and he would be under the same tyranny as before. Only for this one time matters had been overruled and taken out of his hands, and he had been a part of another world. Just now he wasn't anxious to get back to Stephanie. What she thought and felt did not seem so much to concern him as what he was going to be able to do about Camilla's poor little crumpled car.

He experienced a distinct satisfaction in the thought that whatever harm had been done by his absence last night was done already and beyond his power, and that a few more hours could not make any difference. For once he had been saved from bowing to Stephanie's outrageous whims and fancies. For once he would see what would happen now that he had defied her. If she turned from him forever, well, it was not his fault, and there would be some peace at least in knowing that the tortuous problem was settled and over with. If he had to suffer afterwards—well he would have had to suffer one way or the other eventually he supposed. At least he felt more self-respect this morning than he would have felt if he had gone to Stephanie's dinner in company with Myles Meredith.

Now that he had taken this step, unbeknownst to himself, now that the white orchids were in the safe-keeping of another girl, a girl with clear true eyes, a girl who was not out to play the game that most of womankind were playing, he might as well let things alone for a while, keep away from Stephanie and just see what would come. He certainly would never have a better opportunity to test her. And if she wasn't true at heart—well, he didn't want her, did he? Even in spite of her glamour and her beauty, in spite of her poise and her smart dressing, and her ability to thrill and amuse?

In the small watches of the night, while the son of one of the comparatively few multi-millionaires who had not lost their millions in the depression, had sat in a shabby Morris chair listening to the quiet movements of the nurse and the doctor in the sick room, and to the soft breathing of the exhausted girl in the front room, he had thought out a plan of action. It was one of the things that had kept him from thinking long of Stephanie and Meredith and his wasted white orchids.

It gradually became plain to his mind that this other girl, Camilla, would never let him fix up that car for her and pay for it himself. He realized that this plain little house with its shabby air of gentility had a pride of its own, and he began to suspect that that pride had even more self-respect and genuine honesty in it than even the vaunted pride of the House of Wainwright.

And yet on the other hand, he saw with a new insight, gained from the experiences of the evening, that life for Camilla without that staunch little car was going to be a hundred percent harder in the future than it had been in the past. And he knew by the dark circles under her tired eyes, by the whiteness of her face, and by the slenderness of her graceful body that it had been hard enough in the past without the deprivation of that little old friendly car that always got up and went on after every hard knock. He determined that that car must get up even this time and go on. Yes, if he had to learn how and repair it himself!

He didn't know how all this was to be accomplished, but he first determined that it should be, and then worked it out in his mind. The truck driver with the broken leg must be made to help, not by money perhaps, though it might take money to coerce him, but he must be made to own the truth, that the accident had been his fault.

So when morning came he hunted up his traffic policeman and had an interview. Then he went to the hospital where the drunken truck driver with the broken leg had been taken.

The truck driver proved amenable to reason as expressed in dollars, and later Jeffrey sought the office of the Company that employed him, and discovered there a powerful acquaintance well disposed toward the family of Wainwright. A few words with his lawyer, a magic little paper for Camilla to sign, and the matter was arranged. He had been prepared to shoulder the thing himself if necessary, only he had a strong feeling that it would be rather hard to put it over without making the keen-eyed girl suspicious, and he was sure she would never let him pay for having her car repaired. She would extract the knowledge of the exact sum from him somehow and pay it back through the years. So he was greatly relieved that the Company had shouldered a goodly share of the expense, and done it graciously, and he would not have to resort to deception. It was much the easier way, and he was a young man who preferred to be honest, all things being equal.

So he drove to the garage where he had ordered Camilla's car to be taken and had a long talk with the mechanic. It took a good deal of persuading, and a good deal of assurance to make that honest mechanic admit that that little old battered crumpled car could be renewed bit by bit in its entirety, using the one fender that remained intact, parts of the tired old engine, and the cushions,—yes, the worn old cushions that would make it look like its old self again,—yet supplying new parts enough to give it renewed youth. Yes, the mechanic finally admitted, it would be possible, if one had unlimited money to spend, and were fool enough to spend it that way. But he openly declared that no one would be fool enough for that.

Jeffrey Wainwright finally convinced the mechanic that he was that one and only fool in the world who was fool enough to want that little dead car brought to life and made to look like itself again, except for the "touching up" which an innocent driver would feel was absolutely necessary for a car that had been in a smash-up.

The mechanic in wonder finally folded away a bill of such denomination that he patted his pocket with awe to make sure it was real, and agreed to go at the repairs that very afternoon.

"And now," said Jeffrey Wainwright to himself, "that's that, and I'd better get a bite to eat and then go back and tell her."

Of course he could have telephoned, but somehow it seemed a trivial matter about which to cause the blatant ringing of that noisy little telephone so near the sick room, and anyway he had not stayed all night in the anxious household without being eager to learn if all was going as well as when he left.

So he took a quick lunch at an unfamiliar counter, not in the least like the places where his fastidious soul delighted to dine, and drove back to the shabby brick house on Vesey Street.

Camilla was in the kitchen making broth, and there was a flush on her cheeks and a light of hope in her eyes.

"She's better!" she greeted Jeffrey Wainwright as he came softly in like an old friend without waiting to knock, just tried the door and tiptoed in till he found her.

"Oh, that's good!" he said laying a hand each side of her two that she had clasped in her eagerness, and looking into her sweet tired eyes. For just an instant he felt as if he were going to lean over and kiss her eager trembling lips, and then suddenly he knew he mustn't. Knew quite well that would spoil it all, this lovely impersonal friendship that had only existed a day. Knew also that there were other things as well as her attitude toward such a thing that should restrain him, and took his hands down gently from hers, deciding he was a bit lightheaded from staying up all night.

"Yes, the doctor says it is wonderful. He says she reacted marvellously to that medicine that we brought. He says if she had been without it much longer he couldn't have answered for the consequences. And oh, if it hadn't been for you I would never have been able to get it here in time! I shall never get done thanking you!"

His glance melted into her own eager one and he felt a warm glow about his heart. He couldn't at the time recall that he had ever before in his life done anything that was worth such thanks. It was good! Better than all the banter of his frivolous playtime world.

Then presently he told her about the car, and watched a soft pink flush of relief steal up into her cheeks, and a glow of contentment into her eyes.

"Oh, God has been very good to me!" she breathed softly. "I have been wondering all day how I was going to get along without that poor little old car. I never would have been able to pay even for a very little repair. And I'm quite sure there must have been a lot to do on it. As I remember it lying down there in the ditch it seems to me now that it must have needed a lot. I've been remembering what that policeman said about it and trying to make up my mind that I would have to get along without it. You must have waved a magic wand! And to think it's going to be repaired without cost! It seems too good to be true!"

The glow in her eyes fully repaid Wainwright for all the trouble he had taken that morning. He hung around and tried to find something else he might do to help, but there seemed to be little left except to mail a letter for the nurse. Yet still he stayed. He watched Camilla arrange the tray daintily for her mother, the broth in a thin old china cup. He found it hard to tear himself away. Somehow this little shabby house had come to have a deep and vital interest for him, just because he had been passing through a crisis with its inmates. He waited in the kitchen while Camilla took the tray to her mother, ventured shyly to steal a glance through the crack of the door at Camilla in the dimness of the sick room sitting on a low stool beside the bed feeding the invalid. He noticed the soft hair fallen over her forehead, the delicate outline of feature, caught a glimpse of the face upon the pillow framed in white hair, saw a feeble smile on the sick woman's lips, and felt his heartstrings pull with a new kind of joy as if somehow she belonged to him. He wondered vaguely if that was the kind of joy a doctor felt when he was able to pull a patient out of the jaws of death. He wasn't a doctor and he had had but a very slight hand in the recovery of this woman, yet he felt a distinct sense of triumph that she was better, a distinct joy in sympathy with her sweet daughter.

He knew in the back of his mind of course, that this was only a temporary contact; that this little shabby house was entirely out of his world, and he would presently pass back to his own environment. But just for the time he was deeply intrigued, and his heart was touched. The interests and hopes and desires of these people, this mother and daughter, had become his own interests. Passing interests seldom went so deep with him.

So he lingered and watched the glow in the girl's happy face when she came tiptoeing back to the kitchen with her tray and reported that Mother took all the broth, and seemed to like it, and that she had dropped to sleep again.

When he finally tore himself away he promised that he would return that night about the time the doctor usually arrived and be on hand to run any possible errands, and see what report the doctor gave of his patient. He drove home happily, thinking about a basket of fruit that he would take with him when he went back, planning what it should contain.

At home there was a note on his desk in his valet's handwriting. Miss Varrell had called him three times during his absence, and the telephone was ringing madly even as he read the note. This was doubtless Stephanie again. With a frown he took down the receiver and answered. Now there would be a long argument and he hated arguments. Stephanie was not attractive when she was angry.

CHAPTER IV

ABOUT THAT TIME, DOWN IN THE BARBER SHOP OF ONE OF the more exclusive hotels of the city, Myles Meredith, in the hands of his own special attendant whom he always demanded when he was in the city, was being polished off for the day and gathering items of news especially interesting to him. Jean knew his man, and always kept choice bits of gossip for his ears, and produced them tactfully at the right moment. He was a man who made it his business to know all about his customers, and produce what they wanted in the most casual and conservative manner.

Jean had skillfully succeeded in discovering where his customer had been dining the evening before, had made his little joke about the lateness of the morning hour in connection with the revelries of last night, and then, just as if it were an after-thought and not a carefully thought-out plan he remarked:

"Monsieur Jeffrey Wainwright did not dine with Monsieur and the Mademoiselle Stephanie Varrell last evening."

Meredith gave him a quick furtive glance.

"And what makes you say that, Jean?" he asked suspiciously. Meredith accepted all confidences and gave none. Jean understood his man perfectly.

"Oh, I just happened to see him halting under a traffic light, headed out of the city with a very attractive lady by his side."

Meredith gave the man another keen glance and his voice took on a shade of interest—not too much interest.

"A lady?" said Meredith. "Who was it? Not the platinum star from the Lyric last night?"

"No, no!" said Jean selecting a bottle from his array of beautifiers and giving it a professional shake. "No, no, quite different to little Madame Shirley. It was a—what shall I say?—more patrician face. Veri delicate. Veri lovely. Veri aristocratic!" Jean's tone waxed eloquent. "Monsieur Wainwright seemed most interested, the brief glimpse I got. I wondered! He was always so—what shall I say—devoted to Mademoiselle Varrell. But all things change, n'est-ce pas? But—I wonder—!"

"Yes, all things change, Jean, including fair ladies. Isn't that true Jean?" said Meredith with a sinister gleam in his half-closed eyes. "What other news have you, Jean?"

A few minutes later Meredith betook himself to a telephone booth and called up his hostess of the night before.

"That you, Stef! Morning, Baby! How about taking lunch with me this noon? What's that? Where? Oh, your choice this time. And by the way, I happened on some news of your missing guest last night. He wasn't eating his heart out as you fondly supposed. His technique is rather sudden it appears. He attached a most attractive lady I understand and went off in her company, instead of coming to your party. Now will you believe what I tell you next time?"

Back in the shabby old Chrystie house happiness was returning fast. Although Camilla had had to ask time off from her job and knew she was being docked on her salary for every day she took, although the nurse's salary was mounting up minute by minute and Camilla didn't see how she was ever going to pay it, and the coal in the cellar was almost gone and last month's bill not paid yet, and the tiny bank account was all but overdrawn, she felt a song in her heart. For was not her mother growing better moment by moment? And her car was as by miracle being repaired without charge! Oh, there were many things to be thankful for.

There were a few bruises from her accident last night that were developing, but they were trifles, just enough to make her realize how she had been saved from death, or crippling, which might have been worse than death. So her heart sang softly as she went about the little apartment putting everything in as lovely order as it was possible to do with an invalid and a trained nurse to be considered.

When, at the earnest command of the nurse, she finally lay down in the late afternoon to rest, her mind dwelt on the kind friend who had been sent to help her out in her trouble and she breathed a little thankful prayer for him too, and began to try to think of ways she might show him her gratitude.

The great white orchids were in a lovely crystal bowl now, a relic of the prosperous past, and filled the little front room with their distinctive grandeur and loveliness, and Camilla gave a thought of wonder to the one for whom they had been originally intended. Was she a girl he loved? Or a woman he honored? His mother, perhaps?

No, it would not have been his mother. He distinctly said the occasion for the flowers had passed and he didn't know what to do with them. Mothers were always there, if they were there at all. If his mother was away he would have sent them from the florist's. No, these flowers had been for a girl, they must have been for a girl and he had been going to take them to her, take her out somewhere perhaps, or maybe just call upon her.

Camilla worked it all out carefully in her mind and looking at the stately flowers her intuition warned her that she must not let her thoughts get fastened upon this interesting stranger for he surely must belong to someone else, in a world that was not hers.

Yet those lovely weird white blossoms haunted her thoughts and tormented her conscience so that she finally got up softly so the nurse would not be disturbed from her nap and moved them into her mother's room where she could see them if she wakened. They were her orchids anyway.

Then she went back to her couch and resolutely put out of her mind all thought of the stranger. He was a dream. She must not think about him.

It was the next morning while Camilla was carefully feeding to her mother mouthfuls of orange juice that her eyes suddenly fastened upon the orchids.

"Camilla!" she said with a startled note in her feeble voice. "Where did those come from? You—didn't—*buy* them—did you?"

"Oh, no," said Camilla trying to hide her confusion with a low laugh. Fool that she was! Why hadn't she known her mother would question her about them and how was she to explain without alarming her? The whole story of the accident, and her wild evening ride were wrapped up in the innocent presence of those flowers. White orchids did not bloom on every corner around that shabby little brick house, and of course her mother would be keen enough to think it all out and wonder why! Camilla's mother was a great one to scent alarm.

"Oh, no, I didn't buy them," laughed Camilla, draining the last drop of orange juice from the glass into the spoon. "Imagine me getting reckless enough to spend money on white orchids, of all flowers, this season of the year. No, Mother dear, they were sent to you."

"Sent—to—*me!*" said the mother in wonder. "Who—would—who that I know, *could?*" She turned large troubled eyes on her daughter. It was not easy to put anything over on even a sick mother of Camilla.

Camilla had been thinking fast.

"Yes," she said cheerily, "but you *don't* know him.

That's the fun of it. Not yet, that is. Maybe he'll come around again some day though and you can thank him. He is the man who went after the medicine the doctor needed the night you were sick. His name is Wainwright."

"Is he—one of the men—in—your office?"

"Oh, no!" said Camilla with relief. "I don't really know much about him myself, but he's very nice and kind. He brought the flowers in from his car after he had been on an errand for the doctor and said perhaps you could enjoy them when you began to get better."

Mrs. Chrystie's face relaxed into a smile.

"How kind!—A stranger!" she said and turned and looked at the lovely flowers.

Then when Camilla leaned over to kiss her forehead she smiled again and said:

"Dear—child! I've—always—wanted things like that—for you!"

Camilla's answer was another kiss and she hurried out of the room. She didn't want her mother to see her face. She would ask more questions perhaps that would be hard to answer, and the daugher felt she would rather wait until her mother was really strong again before she was interrogated about the strange young man who had taken her to a lonely suburb, and gone with her into an empty house. All that would be quite against her mother's code for a respectable girl, and of course her mother would not understand how very sick she had been, and what the necessity was.

But the very next day Wainwright arrived in the late afternoon with a luscious basket of fruit.

Mrs. Chrystie was decidedly better and feeling quite bright. Her ear was keen and she asked the nurse if that was the young man who had sent her the orchids and the nurse replied that it was.

"I want—to see him!" she demanded with a gleam of real interest in her eyes.

"I'm afraid it will tire you," said the nurse hesitantly.

"Oh, no, I won't talk except to thank him. He—needn't stay—a minute!"

So the nurse stepped into the hall where Camilla was talking to Wainwright in low tones, and announced that the invalid wanted to see him for just a second.

Wainwright eagerly followed her into the sick room,

Camilla in trepidation lingering in the doorway, afraid for what he might say.

But she needn't have worried. Wainwright knew his way around the world exceedingly well. He gave her one of his pleasant grins, said a few graceful phrases, declared he was coming to see her again when she was well enough to talk longer, and took himself away. He seemed to have a fine inner sense that if he lingered around in the kitchen with Camilla, now that her mother was alive to the world again, it might excite her wonder and perhaps make trouble for Camilla.

Camilla watched him wistfully as he took his leave. What a fine kindly friendly person he was! What would it be to have a real friend like him! In spite of the sentinels of caution she had set about her heart to watch her every thought, his brief call had left a warm happy feeling.

He called up the next day to say that he was going to be away for a few days and he wanted to ask how Mrs. Chrystie was before he left.

"Mother has invited some friends to our place up in the mountains and she seems to think I've got to go and help her out," he explained. "I'm not especially keen on it, though the winter sports are always interesting, but I guess it's got to be done. Mother sort of depends on me to look after things."

Camilla thanked him for calling and felt a glow of pleasure that he had cared to inquire for her mother, reflecting how few of the young men she knew would have taken the trouble, when they had so many other delightful interests, to call up and find out about an elderly woman who was practically a stranger. But she discovered that the world seemed lonelier when she had hung up the receiver, just because she knew he could not be expected to run in any more.

"Yes," she told herself, standing by the tiny kitchen window and looking out on the neighbor's ash cans where shabby little sparrows fluttered noisily about trying to find a peck or two of crumbs among the trash. "Yes, you're a fool! Just like other girls! Just because a man has been kind for a few days you let yourself get interested in him! Just because he has an engaging smile. He doesn't care a pin for you beyond a passing interest, and it wouldn't do you a smitch of good if he did, because he is not of your world. You know that and yet you let yourself miss him. Well, it's a good thing he's gone, if you've got to be a fool!"

Nevertheless. when the nurse went out a few days later and brought in the evening paper, Camilla's eye caught at once among the illustrations on the last page, a large picture of a glorified log cabin flanked by stately pines, looking out over a snowy hillside, where young people in smart sports attire were enjoying themselves, some on snow shoes, some on skis, and some skating about the glittering frozen lake in the distance. The caption beneath the picture stated that the Wainwrights were giving a house party at "The Antlers," their winter estate, and described the various sports available to their guests. Her heart gave a little lurch and her eyes grew wistful as she studied the picture. What fun it would be to be included in such a party! That was his world! He belonged there! Playtime and leisure, and plenty of money to carry out whatever whim came into his head. His kindness to her and her mother had only been the carrying out of a very lovely one of his whims of course, and she certainly had no need to quarrel with that. What might not have happened to her mother and herself if he had not been there and been disposed to help?

There was a figure in the centre foreground that suddenly she knew was himself as she studied it. It was something about the pose of his tall splendid body, the heavy lock of dark hair that hung over his fine forehead, or was it his smile that flashed out even from those tiny graven lines, that identified him?

He was bending at the back of a long sled, as if to kneel behind a load of girls and young men already seated on the sled at the top of the hill. One hand was on the shoulder of the girl just ahead of him and she was smiling as if at something he had said.

Camilla's heart gave another lurch, this time of envy. Oh to be a girl on that sled, about to glide down that long white hill, that even a newspaper cut gave hint of its smooth glittering whiteness, and the gaiety in the very atmosphere of the shining day. He was going down that hill behind that other laughing girl, and instinctively she knew the girl must feel safe and happy because he was there looking after her.

Suddenly Camilla straightened up away from the paper,

gave it a quick decided fold that hid the picture, and snapped out into the kitchen to prepare her mother's broth. Fool! Here she was mooning again over other people's happiness! It was in another world he walked, and God had given her a way to walk of her own. If He had chosen quiet ways of service and hard work instead of continual gaiety and playtime what need had she to complain? He had also given her a faith that upheld her, and a hope that she would not surrender for all the world had to offer. And had He not given her back her precious mother from the edge of the grave? God knew best. Whatever He gave was right!

She smiled a tender little smile and then she went about the kitchen singing:

"God's way is the best way,
    Tho' I may not see
Why sorrows and trials
    Oft gather 'round me;

"He ever is seeking
    My gold to refine,
So humbly I trust Him,
    My Saviour divine.

"God's way is the best way,
    God's way is the right way,
I'll trust in Him alway,
    He knoweth the best."

The invalid in the other room heard her and a smile of content grew softly on her lips, peace on her brow.

The nurse hovering about the patient said, as she patted the pillows into comfortable billows:

"You've got a wonderful daughter, Mrs. Chrystie."

And the mother with another smile answered:

"Haven't I?"

"Yes, there's many a girl would be fretting over the everyday ills, but she's taken worry like a soldier." The nurse had reserves in her tone. She did not say that she knew how much personal deprivation Camilla had taken, that she might provide the better for her mother. A nurse grows wise to see the inner workings of a family where she is employed and learns not to seem to see everything.

The next day Camilla went back to her job in the office. It was the nurse who planned it.

"There's no reason why you shouldn't go back," she said to Camilla. "I haven't another case for two weeks, and unless an emergency comes in I really haven't any cause to go back to my boarding place. I'd just love to stay here with your mother without any pay until I'm called. She's lovely and I'd like to be near her. And there really isn't much to be done for her any more. In another day or two she'll be going around as usual. All you want is somebody here to just watch her a little and see that she doesn't overdo. So if you want to board me for being here with her till I have to go I'd really like to do it. It's kind of a stupid place where I board, and I'm sometimes lonesome. Besides, if I'm here I shan't have to pay my board."

Camilla compromised on half-salary to be paid in small installments, as she could, and went thankfully back to her job in the office.

When Jeffrey Wainwright got back to the city he called almost immediately and was disappointed to find that Camilla was not at home.

"She's gone back to her job," explained Miss York, as if he would understand what a cause of thanksgiving that would be.

Wainwright looked perplexed.

"Job?" he said vaguely, and then instantly recovered himself, remembering that to this nurse he was an old friend of Camilla's who presumably knew all about her affairs. "Oh, yes, *job*," he repeated, "of course, she would be expected to, wouldn't she? I hadn't realized that her mother was well enough for her to leave yet."

"Oh, she had to," the nurse explained, "or she would have lost it of course, and in these times jobs aren't so easy to replace you know."

He didn't know. He had read about that in the papers of course, but he didn't really *know*, and he stared at her with his nice troubled eyes and floundered about in his thoughts like one who was beyond his depth.

"But Mrs. Chrystie is better," went on Miss York, "much, much better. She doesn't really need me any more.

I'm just staying here for company till I'm called to my next case. Wouldn't you like to come in and see her? She spoke about you just this morning and wondered if you would ever come to see her again. She did appreciate those orchids so much that you sent her, and she said she never really half thanked you."

So Wainwright went in and met Camilla's mother, clothed now in a simple little gray house dress, silvery like her hair, and quite in her right mind. She was sitting by the window in the Morris chair where Wainwright had once spent the night, darning a tan silk stocking with delicate little stitches, and she welcomed him graciously, and with as much poise as his own mother might have welcomed one of her own set.

So he sat down and talked with her, feeling at home with her at once, she looked so much like a mature Camilla. And Camilla's mother sweetly and keenly proceeded to find out all about him without letting him know that she was doing so.

He followed her lead, telling her all about the winter sports and the hunting on the estate. He had brought with him a present of some venison which he had shot himself, and this made a good opening for the conversation. So when Camilla came in a few minutes earlier than usual and the cross examination was over, Camilla's mother had a fairly good picture in her mind of the snow clad hills, the frozen lake, and the whole round of winter sports in which he had been indulging. She had too a fairly good idea of the log palace with its huge stone fireplaces, its rustic galleries, its great living room furnished with lavish simplicity, and its almost unlimited capacity for entertaining guests. With her own uncanny perception she had visualized Mrs. Wainwright loftily presiding over the gay throng she had gathered under her wide-spreading roof. A cold, hard, tyrannical, self-centred woman she judged her, just from the few sentences about her that had come from the lips of her son. She had even discovered the name of the great fashionable church with which the house of Wainwright had a vague affiliation, and she had almost as good an idea of Jeffrey Wainwright's birth and breeding and the influences which had surrounded him during his childhood as if it had been carefully indexed and catalogued for her.

Camilla came in all rosy and brisk from the crisp outside air. A few snow flakes were falling outside and some had lingered on her little brown hat, and had melted on her cheeks and taken away the pallor that he remembered before he went away.

She had let herself in with her latch key and came upon them before they were aware. She stood still in astonishment, and with a quick leap of her unconquered heart, and saw him talking with her mother. Saw the wonderful smile she remembered so vividly and which she had tried so hard to forget during the past two weeks. Saw the nice curves of it around his pleasant mouth, the flash of his perfect teeth, the light in his eyes as he became aware of her presence. Something leaped within her that she could not control, a gladness and a thrill that frightened her, it was so adverse to her own careful self-control. This was his charm, the charm of the world. This was the kind of man that made one breathlessly happy just to have him here. And this was dangerous, dangerous to a girl who was a fool like herself, whose heart would make more of the occurrence than it had any right to make.

There was that in the touch of his hand, too, that took all her practical good sense away, and she had to steady herself to make herself quietly withdraw her hand in a reasonable time.

"I'm glad to see you again!" he said and stood holding her hand until she withdrew it, looking down into her eyes.

She had to think hard to re-vision that pictured scene on the snowy hillside with the girl on the sled looking adoringly up into his eyes, to make her turn her own away. This was doubtless just his way, the way he spoke and looked at all girls, and he was just calling on a girl he had befriended to see if all was well with her. He was not of her world. She must keep remembering that.

There was a cool clear little edge on her voice as she responded, mindful of his exceeding kindness to a stranger in the street, yet not presuming in the least upon the friendliness he had given so lavishly afterwards.

She sat down a bit formally with a pleasant smile on her face and tried to look as impersonal as a cucumber, and all the while her heart was thumping in the most jubilant way, and crying out till she thought he would hear her, "He has come back! He has come back!"

"You fool!" said her practical sensible self, "they always come back until they are tired of it, don't they? And anyway, even if he has come back, he does not belong to my world!"

But what was this he was saying?

"I wonder if I may take you out tomorrow evening?" he was asking. "You can spare her for a few hours, now, can't you, Mrs. Chrystie?" He gave Camilla's mother a vivid look.

"Oh, that's kind of you," Camilla heard her own voice replying as her jubilant heart slunk low, "but I couldn't possibly be spared. You see Miss York is going away—"

"Not until day after tomorrow!" broke in the diplomatic nurse who had been delightedly hovering in the offing. "You can go just as well as not, Miss Chrystie. It will do you good. You've been so tied down here and in the office you need a bit of change."

"But—I may have to work late at the office tomorrow night," said Camilla in a frightened tone, turning appealing eyes to her mother. "I really don't think I ought to promise. And I'm quite all right. I'm fine now that Mother is improving so fast."

"But it won't hurt you to have a change," said the young man studying her face with a puzzled expression. Had he been mistaken? Didn't she really *want* to go with him? "I could pick you up at your office if you have to work late you know, and then we'd go somewhere and have some dinner, and—well, I'm not just sure yet. I haven't been back long enough in the city to look up the attractions." He smiled with that clear, admiring, speculative look. He thought how different she was from Stephanie Varrell when she declined an invitation. And then it struck him that in some ways she resembled Stephanie. Somehow he didn't like the thought and he didn't quite know why. He realized too that the idea would make Stephanie tremendously angry.

But Camilla was looking up with troubled eyes now.

"I really don't think I should go," she said and turned toward her mother as if to seek an excuse there.

"She means," explained her mother gently, "that she hasn't any festive garments for going out in the evening."

Camilla's cheeks were rosy red now, but she faced the young man bravely and tried to smile. It was as good an excuse as any, she thought, although it hadn't occurred to her yet. Her mind had been filled with a deeper matter altogether.

Wainwright studied her with a dawning understanding in his eyes.

"She looks very nice now," he said with a satisfied grin. "What's the matter with what you are wearing now? Plenty of people wear street clothes in the evening."

Camilla looked down at herself and considered. Then she looked up.

"You couldn't possibly think I look all right this way," she grinned back a challenge. "I've seen you in evening dress, you remember, and I'm positive you know better."

His eyes sobered.

"No, really," he said gravely, "I like you the way you are. It's not clothes I want to take out, it's you." There was something in the way he looked at her, reverently almost, that made her catch her breath and took all excuses away. She felt all her resolutions slipping and turned her troubled eyes toward her mother again.

But her mother was smiling.

"Well, if Mr. Wainwright doesn't mind your being a bit shabby, why don't you go, dear? I think you should. I'd like to have you have a little relaxation after the hard time you've been through. Yes, go, Camilla! It will please me."

After that there seemed nothing more that Camilla could say, except to thank the young man, all the time aware of the flutter of joy in her heart.

"Well, just for this one time," she told herself. "But don't count on it. He's not your kind and you'll probably find it out tomorrow night so don't *dare* be glad!"

"That's great!" said Wainwright. "Then shall I call for you at the office? What time? Or do you have to come home first? I could stop for you any time you say and bring you home, and then wait for you till you were ready?"

"Oh, no," said Camilla hastily, "I wouldn't know just when I would be through. At least—well it might happen I would be early you know. I'd better just come home as usual. I'll do my best not to be late."

"Very well, then, shall we say half past seven, or would eight be better?" and Camilla perceived that his ideas of dinner hours were different from her own, also. Eight o'clock for dinner! Somehow the whole occasion frightened her.

When he was gone her mother watched her silently as she went about putting her hat and coat away, watched her with puzzled eyes. She felt her mother's eyes upon her now and then while they were eating dinner, the simple little dinner that Miss York had prepared.

CHAPTER V

AFTERWARD WHEN THE DISHES WERE WASHED AND PUT AWAY and Miss York had gone out for a brisk evening walk, Camilla came in to the living room where her mother sat.

"Why didn't you want to go, Camilla?" she asked. "Was it just because of clothes?"

"Partly," said Camilla evasively.

"What was the other part, dear?"

Camilla was quite still a minute and then she said slowly:

"I'm not just sure, Mother."

Her mother considered that for a little and then asked:

"How long have you known Mr. Wainwright, dear?"

Camilla was standing by the ugly little painted iron mantel leaning her head over, looking down into the fire on the hearth. The flickering flames rested and shimmered over her gold hair and showed the big soft waves as it swept about her shapely young head. Her voice was hesitant and almost shamed as she spoke.

"Not long, Mother. Only since the night you were sick."

"Is he a friend of the doctor's? Did the doctor introduce him?"

"No, Mother. Nobody introduced him. At least—he introduced himself."

"You mean, Camilla, that he is someone down at your office?"

"No, Mother. He is no one that I ever knew before. He

was just a stranger who came to help me the night you were so sick, when the doctor had to send me to his house for medicine in a hurry—there was no one else to go— and—my car—wouldn't work—at least it got—it had— something—the matter with it—," Camilla was talking fast now, trying to cover her confusion, trying to make her story unalarming, feeling her way along word by word. "It wouldn't *go!*" she added, "and I didn't know what in the world to do! The doctor had told me that every minute counted, and—this man—Mr. Wainwright was right behind me and saw I was—in difficulty—and he got out and offered to take me to where I was going in his car."

Camilla drew a breath of relief and looked up to see her mother's startled face.

"You mean," said her mother after a pause, thoughtfully, "that you got into a stranger's car, that you rode out to a suburb with a man you had never met before?"

"I had to, Mother," said Camilla feeling again the desperation that had been hers the night of the accident. "You don't understand! It meant your life, Mother! I couldn't wait to find somebody I had been introduced to."

Her mother was silent, pondering.

"Of course," she said quietly, "I understand there are times when one does not stand on ceremony. Go on, Camilla, what was the rest?"

"He took me to the doctor's and we got the medicine and came back, and then he went and got Miss York, and after that he stayed all night and helped the doctor, went errands for him. He was—wonderful, Mother! He is a gentleman!"

"I can see that, Camilla," said her mother thoughtfully. "But why then do you not want to go to dinner with him, since he really seems to want you?"

Camilla was still a long time, then she lifted her golden head and looked straight at her mother and said stormily:

"Because, Mother, he doesn't belong to my world. He— wears gardenias on his lapel, and has house parties at an estate, and—well—he is—different."

"You mean he belongs to the world?" asked her mother. "You mean you would not have the same ideas and beliefs and standards, Camilla?"

"Yes," said the girl a bit sadly, "that's it."

After another long pause her mother asked:

"Do you dislike him, Camilla? Because if you do of course it's not too late to ask him to excuse you."

"Oh, no!" said Camilla rosily. "Oh, no, Mother, I don't dislike him."

"Then, child, surely one dinner in his company is not going to harm you. There is always a chance that you may have been sent to witness you know."

Camilla was very silent, looking into the fire for a long time, wondering what it would be like to try to witness of Jesus Christ before a young man of the world.

"Mother, I'm not sure I could," she faltered at last. "I wouldn't know how to talk to a man of the world, I'm sure."

"Witnessing is not always given by words, dear."

"I know," said Camilla with a sigh, "but I think it's more likely this is some kind of a testing of me, rather than a chance to witness."

"It might be both, you know, dear."

Camilla thought about that too, and her mother watched her tenderly, and finally said in a brisker tone:

"Now, dear, let's think about the clothes question and have that out of the way. You'll need a new hat and some shoes. You know those are the really important things about a costume. You can likely find them cheap this time of year, and your black crepe will be quite all right if you have the right accessories. I'm glad your coat is black. Black is always good-looking, and the lines of both your dress and coat are good. They are well cut. You'll be able to get out and buy the hat and shoes at your lunch hour, won't you?"

"Not *possibly!*" said Camilla whirling around with decision. "There isn't a cent to spare for finery, or even for necessity just now. I'll go as I am or I'll not go at all. If I have to mortgage the future to buy a new hat and shoes for this occasion, nothing doing!"

"You mustn't talk that way, darling child. A little hat would probably be very cheap at this time of year, and you ought to have shoes."

"Any price would not be cheap for me just now when you need so many things to help you get your strength. Positively, I will not spend a cent! But don't worry. Aren't there some pieces of black transparent velvet somewhere? Up in that drawer in the storeroom? I thought so. I'll make a ducky little velvet affair and put my rhinestone pin on it. Just you wait! It won't take long, just a twist here, and a fold there and it'll be done. And as for shoes, Mother dear, a smudge of ink on that worn spot in the toe and the old black satin slippers will be all right. I'll shine up the silver buckles too, and look as brave as any lady present."

Camilla ran upstairs for the velvet and her mother brushed away a tear and sighed "Dear child!" under her breath, and then sat and looked into the fire and wondered whether she was doing right to let her precious child go out even for one evening with a total stranger, no matter how harmless he looked.

Camilla was back very soon, the square of supple velvet in her hand, and the two little shabby satin shoes with their tarnished silver buckles tucked under her arm. Her face was interested and eager.

"I found it, Mother dear," she chirruped, "and there's plenty."

So she set to work with pins and scissors, standing before the long mirror and draping the velvet about her head, and presently had evolved a charming little hat so like a distinctive imported one she had seen in a shop window that one could scarcely have told them apart. Set on her golden hair, the bright little pin glittering perkily over the right eye, the effect was most becoming. Her mother was both satisfied and delighted. Then Camilla set to work at the shoes, inked the shabby places, and polished up the buckles.

By the time Miss York came back from her walk the problem of Camilla's attire for the next evening was fairly solved.

"Put them all on, Camilla," commanded her mother, "and let Miss York get the effect. She goes around a good deal among stylish people. She'll know if there is anything wrong about you."

So Camilla donned her plain black silk crepe that she had bought at a bargain, and already, in a stress, worn several times to the office when her other dress was being cleaned or mended. She put on her rejuvenated satin slippers, and the saucy little black velvet hat, and stood up to be surveyed.

Miss York looked her over carefully and pronounced everything perfect.

"I can't see a thing wrong with you," she said with satisfaction, letting her eyes rest in admiration on the lovely golden head crowned with the chic little hat. "You wear your clothes so well, Camilla, that's half of it of course. It isn't every girl with expensive clothes who can wear them so well. You have a fine form, and that dress has really good lines. As for the hat it is delightful. You couldn't have a prettier one. All you need is a string of beads to finish you off. Haven't you got some?"

"Why, yes, your pearls, Camilla. Get them. They're only cheap ones of course, but they have a really good color," said her mother.

"I'm sorry, Mother, but they need restringing. I broke them the last time I wore them, and I just haven't had time since to restring them."

"I'll do it in the morning!" said Miss York briskly. "I'll have lots of time. I can run out to the Utility Shop around the corner and get a bead needle and thread and they will be all ready for you when you come back to dress. Now, what coat are you going to wear?"

Camilla drew a deep breath of determination and set her lips firmly.

"Just my black every day one," she said with a proud little tilt of her chin. "Lucky thing it's black. It will go with the rest of the things, and perhaps won't be noticed. I never liked it very well, but it will have to pass muster. It's clean and it fits well, and the silver fox collar is rather good yet. I might comb it out a little."

"Put it on!" ordered her mother.

Camilla put it on and surveyed herself in the long mirror. She really looked very stylish and pretty.

"It's very good!" said the nurse. "I was going to offer you mine, but I'm larger than you and it wouldn't fit you so well. You look very smart all in black!"

"Yes, Camilla, you look all right!" said her mother in a pleased tone.

Suddenly they came to their senses and realized that it was getting late. They hustled the invalid off to bed summarily, and Camilla hung up her dress and laid the little hat in the bureau drawer with a comfortable feeling that she was as ready for tomorrow night's festivity as she could be under the circumstances. When she finally lay down for the night on her couch in the front room she was too excited and pleased to reproach herself with any questions of whether she ought to be going with Wainwright or not. It was settled now that she was going and too late to bring the matter up again. It might be the one and only time she would ever go anywhere with him, probably would be, but she was going this one time and going to enjoy it as much as possible. She might never see him again, perhaps, but she was going to have this one evening. She sent up a prayer that she might keep her witness true, and stand her testing, if either was in question.

All the next day Camilla worked with a subdued excitement upon her. Not since her father died, and their lovely home and practically all their money had gone through the failure of his partner, and they had moved to this strange city, had Camilla been out for the evening with a young man. She could not but be thrilled by the thought, though she worked hard and left no duty undone.

Twice in the elevator that day she met the elderly typist with gray bobbed hair and too youthful lipstick, who worked down the hall.

"What's the matter with you today, Miss Chrystie?" she asked the second time they met. "You look as if you'd made your fortune overnight. I never saw your cheeks look so pink. Is it a new kind of rouge?"

But Camilla only laughed gaily.

"I am happy, Miss Townsend. My mother is so much better than she was!"

"Humph!" said Miss Townsend jealously, still eyeing her with suspicion. She had neither beauty nor youth nor living mother sick or well. She doubted if that was sufficient reason for such a look of radiance and such a lilt in a voice.

All day the mother thought about her child, thrilling at the simple pleasure in store for her, and yet praying for her often silently when she was alone, wondering if she had done right to encourage her going. Oh, God keep her! He is such an attractive looking man! Don't let any sorrow come to her through this! If I have made a mistake, overrule it, undo it, prevent it, dear Lord, for Thy name's sake!

Miss York was as eager over the hastily assembled costume as was Camilla's mother. As soon as the few dishes were out of the way and Mrs. Chrystie dressed for the day, she hurried out to the little Utility Shop around the corner for the bead needle and cord. She came back with more than a cord. She had bought a pair of soft white gloves.

"I looked through her things and saw she hadn't any white ones," she apologized as she displayed them to the pleased mother, "so I bought these for her. I wanted to have some part in this. I hope they fit. She told me the other night she wore sixes."

"Yes, that's her number," said the mother. "She'll be so pleased."

"She's a dear girl!" said Miss York by and by after she had finished stringing the beads. "One just loves to do things for her!"

"She is a dear child!" agreed the mother with a smile.

"And Mr. Wainwright seems so nice," Miss York rambled on. "I liked him the minute I saw him."

Then after a pause, "Are they engaged?"

"Oh, no!" said Camilla's mother in quick alarm. "He's a comparatively new friend, in fact almost a stranger."

"Well, I didn't know. He seemed so careful of her that first night I came, and then the white orchids and all. I sort of hoped they were. He seems so dependable. I like a girl like your daughter to get the right man. It's such a gamble, getting husbands you know. I've often been glad I hadn't any. Going about the way I do I see a lot of course."

"Yes, you must," said Mrs. Chrystie reservedly. "There are a good many sad things in the world for a nurse to see, aren't there?"

"I should say there are!" said Miss York with emphasis. "The more I go about and see, the more I'm glad I'm free and single. Still, when it comes to a pretty girl like Camilla I'd sort of like to see her get a good man to take care of her. She's so sweet and kind and tries so hard to take care of everybody, that the world is apt to take advantage of her. And then Mr. Wainwright is so good-looking!"

"Looks are not always dependable," said Mrs. Chrystie with gravity.

"That's so, they aren't," said Miss York, "I learned that lesson under sad circumstances when I was a good deal younger than I am today. Now, Mrs. Chrystie, will you have your beef tea? It's almost twelve o'clock?"

So the day sped by and Camilla arrived at home half an hour ahead of schedule, her cheeks glowing and her eyes bright with excitement.

"There is a box here from the florist's for you," said Miss York appearing in the dining-room door, carrying a chubby square white box.

"Flowers!" gasped Camilla, casting a half frightened glance toward her smiling mother.

"Yes, isn't that nice, dear! Open them quick. I want to see if they'll go with your costume!"

Camilla gave a little excited laugh.

"Almost anything would do that, wouldn't it? Weeds, even!" she giggled nervously.

Then she undid the string, took off the cover, folding back the wax paper.

She was so still that her mother looked at her anxiously and saw that she was actually pale.

"Mother!" she said lifting her dark eyes big with wonder. "Mother! They're white orchids!"

"How lovely!" said her mother with satisfaction in her voice.

"But—Mother—what—what shall I do with them?"

"Why wear them, of course," said her mother.

"Why of course you'll wear them, Camilla," said the nurse. "He expects you to wear them."

"But—wear white orchids—*Me* wear white orchids, just to go out to dinner? And with those old clothes! Oh, Mother, isn't it funny?" And Camilla suddenly sat down in a chair with the box on her lap and laughed hysterically.

"No," said her mother, "it isn't a bit funny. It's very lovely. The flowers will just give the touch you needed. White orchids, two dollar pearls, and new white gloves. Your dress is only the background. You are going to look very nice!" There was deep satisfaction in the mother's tone.

But Camilla suddenly sobered down.

"Gloves!" she said. "I forgot all about gloves. I haven't any that are fit to wear!"

"No, but Miss York didn't forget them," said her mother with a pleased twinkle in her eye. "Just go look on my bed where Miss York has spread all your things out and see what she bought for you."

Camilla put her orchids down on the couch and flew into her mother's bedroom.

"Oh, Miss York, you *dear!*" she came flying back with the gloves in her hand and flung her arms about the pleased nurse's neck, giving her a hug and kiss on her embarrassed red cheek. "You shouldn't have done it of course, but I'm so pleased!" she said again. "Such lovely soft gloves!"

"Look! She's put down her wonderful flowers to rave over my poor little gloves!" said Miss York, rubbing the mist out of her eyes.

And then Camilla flew back to her orchids and stood in awe before them, her cheeks rosy again.

"But come!" said her mother presently, "you mustn't spend so much time mooning over your things. This isn't Christmas. You're going out to dinner, child, and the time is flying."

"But I'm having such a good time now," said Camilla, "I don't really need to go out to dinner."

Laughing she went away to get ready, and her mother hung over the lovely strange flowers that seemed so almost human, and prayed again, "Oh, God, keep my child! Let no harm come to her through this venture."

Camilla looked very lovely when she was ready. The cheap little black crepe dress was really very well cut for a "bargain" garment. The long-suffering satin shoes looked quite respectable now with their beautiful bright buckles. The pearls shone as lustrous around the slender white neck as if they had been real, and the sheen of the burnished gold hair was wonderful under the smart little velvet cap.

She fitted on her new gloves proudly, and Miss York stood in the doorway watching eagerly, as pleased as if she really belonged to this sweet girl.

"And now your orchids!" she said.

"Oh, must I really wear them?" said Camilla standing over them with that look of awe on her face again. "It seems almost like presumption to wear things like that. As if I should put on a diamond tiara! Or an ermine robe!"

"Nonsense, child!" smiled her mother. "They are God's flowers. They don't belong exclusively to the social world, even if society has taken them up as about the finest thing in flowers. God made them!"

"Of course!" said Camilla lifting them up with that look of awe still in her eyes. "But knowing how the world rates them I am afraid I'm going to be terribly self-conscious."

"How silly!" laughed Mrs. Chrystie indulgently. "You didn't steal them. Wear them gladly. They are yours. You have a right to them."

"You look like a million dollars!" said Miss York as she helped Camilla to fasten the beautiful corsage in place.

"That's what I'm afraid of," said Camilla with a little nervous laugh, "million-dollar orchids and a five-and-ten costume!"

"It's not like that at all, child," said her mother quickly. "You really look very lovely, and quiet and refined in the bargain. I am perfectly satisfied with your outfit."

"Then it must be all right, precious Mother," said Camilla stooping to kiss her forehead and hide a sudden feeling of tears.

"It couldn't be better!" said Miss York wistfully, watching the look of love between mother and daughter.

"But what would it all be without gloves?" laughed Camilla suddenly giving the nurse another kiss.

And just then the doorbell rang.

CHAPTER VI

LATE THAT AFTERNOON STEPHANIE VARRELL HAD CALLED UP Jeffrey Wainwright's private telephone. She had been calling all day more or less, ever since she had read the morning papers that came up on her breakfast tray, but this time she got him.

Her eyes were narrowed and speculative as she settled back in an easy chair with a triumphant look on her face and prepared to talk with him. She was dressed most becomingly. She had been ready all the afternoon for him to call on her, and he had not come. There was a hint of alarm, too, in her manner, though it did not manifest itself in her voice, which was honey-sweet, as she recognized his.

"Oh, Jeff!" she said in soft tones, "it is really you at last! I read in the paper this morning that you were back from your hunting trip and I've cancelled two delightful engagements and been looking for you to call."

"Oh, hullo, Stephanie!" said Wainwright. "How are

you? Yes, I got back yesterday afternoon but I've been busy all day. Meant to look you up sometime pretty soon you know. How have you been?"

"Oh, fine!" said Stephanie with an angry toss of her chin, "haven't had time to miss you at all, but now that you're home you can take me out tonight and we'll have a good old talk. I've plenty to tell you!"

"Sorry," said Wainwright, "not tonight. I have another engagement tonight and I can't make it tomorrow morning either. I've promised Dad to go over some important papers with him and can't tell how long it may take."

"Oh!" said Stephanie coldly her chin going up again, her eyes smoldering. An engagement! With whom? A date with his dad! That sounded improbable. Was he still sore about Myles Meredith? He'd need some disciplining perhaps.

"Well, what a pity!" she drawled as if it mattered very little. "I can't say tomorrow morning or afternoon either for the matter of that. Every minute is taken. Nothing I can change!—And—tomorrow evening—I have a partial dinner engagement."

She waited for him to suggest her calling it off, but he answered quite casually and pleasantly, "Sorry. Well, I'll be seeing you soon!"

"Oh, very well!" said Stephanie in honey-sweet tones, her eyes snapping dull gold fire, as she hung up the receiver.

Wainwright waited a moment, hesitated with his hand on the instrument to call her back, then laughed and hung up.

"A little longer wait won't do her any harm!" he said thoughtfully. "I've got to get my bearings before I go back to her!"

Then Stephanie arose, slammed down the instrument on its stand, put on her war paint and set herself in battle array.

Stephanie had unusual eyes. Her hair was rather lighter than Camilla's, lighter gold and more unnatural, but her eyes were a peculiar red-gold where Camilla's were dark brown flecked with golden lights like a topaz. Wainwright had always thought of Stephanie's eyes as like a jacinth stone, because of their almost orange lights that could soften and lure and thrill with a look. Yet when she was angry they contracted to very pinpoints and then their orange became dull gold in color and not good to see.

Wainwright was thinking about those eyes now as he hung up the receiver. He knew the siren was angry now, knew it by sharp experience in the past, knew it by the very honey-sweetness of her voice, knew just exactly how those jacinth eyes were looking, with gold fire playing through them, and suddenly he remembered another pair of eyes, framed about by golden hair, eyes whose deep brown depths were the very essence of truth, whose golden lights reflected clearness of vision, unselfishness of living.

He stood there for a full minute with that telephone in his hand thinking about those two pairs of beautiful eyes, startled at his own thoughts. Was it possible that he had always been afraid of something in Stephanie's eyes, those eyes that had first attracted him to her? Was that why he had never yet actually been at peace about sharing his life with her?

And tonight he was going out with the other girl. Just a plain little girl he had picked up in the dark by accident. What was he doing anyway? Well, perhaps tonight would tell him. He had seen her heretofore only under the extremity of her mother's illness. She had seemed lovely. Even after an absence of two weeks she had stirred him. Could it be that it was her likeness to Stephanie that interested him? Could it be that she reminded him of the girl he thought he loved? He must go carefully. He must not confuse two personalities. Life was a strange mix-up. Two girls who had some of the same charm, might yet be very different.

When Wainwright entered the little Chrystie living room and saw Camilla ready waiting for him wearing his flowers he paused in amazement wondering if his eyes had not misinformed him. To his eyes, she was garbed as smartly as any girl in his own circle of friends. The effect was charming, and even the watchful mother and nurse with jealous eyes fixed on his face, were satisfied with the distinct admiration they found in his expression.

"She has a truly distinguished air about her!" thought Wainwright as he smiled upon her.

"You're looking wonderful tonight!" was what he said in low admiring tones, that pleased, while it frightened a trifle the watchful mother.

He helped her into the car with deference just as he might have helped that girl on the sled in the newspaper. And now that she was started out into the night, with Wainwright still looking at her with that deep admiring glance, which she felt even in the dark little street, she was just a bit apprehensive.

She was going out of her world into his, just the edge of it probably, but she wondered why she had consented.

Then he spoke.

"I thought you said you had nothing to wear," he reproached.

"It's still true," said Camilla laughing, "I haven't a new thing on except the gloves, and they were a present from Miss York. This is the very same dress and coat I wore yesterday to the office, and the hat I made out of a piece of black velvet I had. It's your wonderful flowers that have glorified my old garments. White orchids would glorify anything."

"On you, perhaps!" He spoke in low reverent tones. He was filled with admiration. "Did I understand you to say that you *made* your hat?"

"Yes," said Camilla humbly. Somehow she wanted him to know the worst about her as she entered his world for a brief glimpse. She wanted no illusions.

"But—I didn't know that—ordinary—that is to say— girls could make hats. Not hats like that. It looks to me quite charming."

"Almost anybody can make things if they *have* to," said Camilla. "I saw one in a shop window the other day and admired it, and when I found this velvet I just twisted it up like the other one as nearly as I could remember. I'm glad you like it."

"I certainly do!" he said fervently. "You must be very clever."

"Oh, no!" laughed Camilla. "It's just that I've usually had to contrive things or go without them. You can't think how wonderful it is to me to be wearing real orchids. I never dreamed of having any, and it seems to me almost as if I had stolen into some other girl's place."

Wainwright looked at her startled and remembered how Stephanie had commanded him to bring her white orchids. He had never taken Stephanie white orchids. Somehow they didn't seem to belong to her. But on this girl the white orchids seemed regal. Even with what she called her shabby garments.

He answered her slowly, after a pause.

"No," he said, deliberately, "you haven't. I never gave any other girl white orchids. I almost did once, but—I'm glad I didn't!"

She caught her breath over that and wondered with a throb in her throat just what he meant by it. His saying it had thrilled her, it seemed so very beautiful and sincere. But she must remember that she was out in the world for only this one evening.

She couldn't think what to answer to that and they rode along in silence for a long time, but it didn't matter. He didn't seem to mind. It was as if they had known one another for a long, long time, almost as if they had grown up together, and understood each what the other was thinking. She couldn't understand why that should be. And it was a pity, because he was not of her world. She was sure he was not, and she must not forget it. She kept reminding herself over and over all the evening, saying it like a charm that she must repeat to keep her safe.

When the lights of the more crowded part of the city came into view it seemed like Fairyland. She had been out very little in that part of the city at night and had not realized how beautiful it was, the millions of multi-colored lights flashing on and off like many Christmases massed into one. It seemed as if this display was something Wainwright had ordered for her especial delight, though of course she knew better. But she would never forget it. It would be always associated with her going out with him for the first time, and with the orchids, and that feeling she had of being well dressed, and having his approval. It put her very much at her ease.

Yet she was a bit frightened again when they stopped before an imposing place that she recognized as one of the haunts of the rich and favored. Yesterday evening at this time she would have protested, have begged him to take her to some quieter place for dinner, but the orchids and his admiration had given her a confidence and she found herself entering the spacious dining room with only a little quickening of her natural heartbeats.

A person in uniform had taken his car away, uniformed servants bowed deferentially, and gave her looks of approval as she entered on Wainwright's arm. Long mirrors were everywhere she looked and they reflected a girl with gold hair in a fetching velvet hat, a girl she did not recognize at first as herself. Well, if that was the way she looked to his world, all right, she could hide behind that other girl for the evening, and just have a good time. It wasn't her plain little self at all, but if he was satisfied she needn't worry. And she certainly did look, at least in the distance, as well as most of the people she saw. Of course there were some with low-backed dresses, and ermine capes, and glittering things in their hair, but there were plenty too in street garb as he had said. It made her feel quite comfortable, and ready to enjoy her outing.

As they passed among the tables here and there people spoke to him, and cast courteous inquiring glances at her. The headwaiter was leading them to a far quiet table as if they were especially invited, expected guests. He had arranged about that beforehand of course. It was all so strange, just for herself! Yet she rather enjoyed the whole thing, this masquerading harmlessly as a girl she was not, and never could be. Just a costume and an escort and there she was.

Wainwright even paused beside one table where an elderly opulent couple sat, an old man with white wavy hair, and florid complexion, and a stunning woman in black velvet and diamonds, and introduced her:

"Aunt Fan, Uncle Warren, I want you to know my friend, Miss Chrystie. Mr. and Mrs. Warren Wainwright, Camilla!"

There it was again! He had called her by her first name, as easily as if he had always done it. And these were his rich relatives, and they would wonder what poor little church mouse he had found and befriended. But because of those orchids, and the quite composed glimpse she caught of herself in a far mirror, she found herself smiling and speaking quite easily to the imposing couple. And they were very cordial to her. But of course they were only looking at his orchids, and didn't realize how really plain and insignificant she was.

"You have an inferiority complex!" she told herself. "You have it badly. Stop it! You are God's child and it doesn't matter what anybody thinks!"

But that little old inferiority complex attended her nevertheless, slinking in to be on hand whenever she lost sight of real values, and other-worldliness.

So Camilla sat down at a table lovely with linen and lace and silver and crystal and flowers, and looked about her on the vast gorgeous room, took in the quiet air of refinement and beauty, the softly shaded candles, the flowers, the perfume, the soft tinkling of a fountain somewhere beyond a bower, and then the wonderful stringed music that broke upon her senses like soothing balm on a tired heart, and she felt as if she had almost reached heaven.

Wainwright carried her through the intricacies of ordering with the skill of a connoisseur, and then sat back quietly with a pleased smile, his eyes meeting hers with a sweet intimacy that thrilled her.

"I'm glad Aunt Fan and Uncle Warren were here. They're grand old sports. I was proud to have them meet you," he said happily.

Camilla felt a glow of pleasure. He was not ashamed of her then. And of course a young man took different girls out to dinner. There was nothing so very personal in being taken out to dinner, she must remember that. She was just one of his friends, at least for tonight.

"And now, Camilla," he said watching the lovely expression of her eyes as she lifted them to his, "don't you think it is about time you began calling me Jeffrey? I've been calling you by your first name right along, and you slide around impersonally without calling me anything."

Camilla answered him with a level gaze, smiling a little, thinking rapidly. Was this going to take her too far? Nonsense! She could be sensible and friendly with him as well as with the boys who had grown up with her at home. God's standards did not include primness.

"After a man has slept in your own hall in an old Morris chair," she giggled to herself, "and carried down an army cot and a down comforter in his shirt sleeves, it is really absurd to stand on ceremony with him." And then she said steadily, with a friendly smile,

"All right, Jeffrey, if you like."

The waiter came back then and handed Wainwright a menu card, saying something to him in an unintelligible tone. Wainwright looked at the card, and looked up at Camilla.

"We didn't order anything to drink," he said. "What wines will you have? Champagne—?"

Bang! Down came something hard and icy into her heart, knocking her faint and dizzy. He drank then. Of course! All fashionable society drank. One read of it on every hand, but she hadn't thought of that as one of the questions she would have to meet tonight. Somehow she hadn't connected it with Jeffrey Wainwright!

Camilla came from a long line of Prohibition ancestors, reaching away back before the Civil War time. Her principles were ingrained in her very nature, and here suddenly was a terrible reminder of the wide gulf that was fixed between her world and his.

Even while she heard her own voice clear and quiet saying "No wine, thank you!" she felt her heart sinking down, down, and down, and her very lips grew white.

She knew he wouldn't understand her feeling. She didn't intend he should ever know how she was feeling, but she suddenly knew in her own heart that in spite of all her careful warnings of herself, here she was thinking so much of this dear bright handsome fellow across from her, that it was like a knife in her heart to know of this gulf between herself and him. And it wasn't as if it was anything that could be bridged over either, like ill-manners, or poor taste in clothes, or lack of culture. It was something that had to do with moral standards, and it wouldn't be right for her to change, and it wasn't in the least likely that he ever would.

She heard him quietly dismissing the thought.

"No wine, waiter." Just as if it had been butter or soup he was talking about. He did not question her decision nor seem surprised. He did not order any for himself. He was a perfect gentleman. He just went on quietly talking as if nothing at all cataclysmic had happened. She was so thankful for that.

And yet he must have seen her sudden quietness. Could he guess how she felt?

He did not offer her cigarettes. She was glad of that. She noticed now that many women all about them were smoking. Yet he did not smoke himself. She wondered if that was just his politeness? He surely was not different from his world. And this was his world. She could never have realized it so definitely if she had not come here with him tonight.

He studied her quietly, with pleasant eyes, talked easily of music, books, and lovely things that she knew and enjoyed, and presently her color came back, and a portion of her pleasure, but the light was gone from her eyes and he missed it. He was trying to understand just what had happened.

But he did not talk about it. He put her at ease again. He began telling her about different people in the room, who and what they were. There was a famous broker from Wall Street. Across at the next table was a great oil magnate. That woman with the Titian hair and emeralds was a noted actress. Her companion was a famous artist. Just across the room were three authors. Those three women down the room to the right were daughters of multi-millionaires whose names were known all over the world.

Camilla studied them all and grew more and more silent, troubled, almost. The gulf between her and her handsome courteous playmate was widening minute by minute. When she went out of this room and went home with him it would be the end, a sort of sweet dream that turned into a nightmare. And she cared! Oh, shame! Camilla cared so much! And it wasn't his fault. He had been perfectly nice and friendly and impersonal. Oh, he hadn't an idea what he was doing to her little trembling unsophisticated self. And the worst of it was she had had plenty of warning in her own soul.

Oh, she would get over it by-and-by of course. She had to. But now, tonight it hurt so! If she only could have had this one whole evening unspoiled. But of course it had to be this way or she would have gone on getting deeper all the time into an acquaintance that did not, should not belong to her life.

They were waiting for the dessert now, and she had grown very silent. She saw the great room in a blur. She watched the figures of men and women dancing a little way down the room where there was a clearer space. The women were beautifully gowned. Most of them had no backs to their dresses. They sparkled with jewels, though many dancers were just in street costume like her own. Her eyes followed them, scarcely seeing them, quiet, troubled.

He thought how very lovely she was, and tried to break the spell of quietness that had come over her, to find out what were her thoughts, her lovely thoughts behind his flowers that she wore so well. It was then he asked her if she would like to dance.

"No, thank you," she said and seemed to shrink as she lifted her honest eyes to his. "No, I don't dance. Oh, I oughtn't to have come here!" There was almost a cry in her tone although it was very low. No one else could have heard it.

"You see," she tried to explain, "I don't belong—to your world! I ought to have stayed in my own. I knew it. It is not just a difference in clothes, nor only a difference between rich and poor. It is that we belong to different worlds."

"That isn't so!" he said earnestly. "Anyone can see at a glance that you are to the manor born. The way you walk, your tone of voice, the way you carry yourself, like an empress. There is grace in every movement, refinement in everything you do and say. I will not admit that we are of different worlds."

Camilla looked at him thoughtfully.

"I'll admit," she said slowly, "that my people were educated, refined, used to having cultured friends and lovely things about them, but it isn't just a matter of that. Yes, I was well born even as the world reckons, but it's more than that. It's a matter of standards." She hesitated and her golden lashes went low upon her flushed cheeks, "It's a matter of beliefs—and of literally different worlds. You see—I've been born again!"

He stared at her for an instant in a kind of consternation. He did not know what she meant. He wanted to understand but what she said conveyed nothing to him. Born again!

Just then occurred a digression over by the door. Some new people were coming in, a bit noisily for the formality of the stately place, and all eyes were turning toward the door. The music had died away at the end of a lovely number, and there was a sudden silence, that brought every eye around to see what was happening.

Camilla too, out of her confusion of confession turned her eyes to the door, and Jeffrey Wainwright looked also, and gave a startled exclamation, a very low one, but audible enough for Camilla to hear.

Among the little knot of new arrivals at the doorway,

two people stood out. A dark frowning young man with an arrogant manner and an imperious glance, and a girl with gold hair and jacinth eyes. A girl in black velvet, cut high in the front and low in the back, a gorgeous string of great pearls about her neck. She had just taken off a marvelous ermine cape that reached to the floor and handed it to her escort, and there she stood staring over the room with hurrying piercing eyes, looking for someone. She was wearing orchids too, but they were green ones, strange weird wraiths like gnomes of flowers, and Camilla watched her, startled.

The man who was with her was searching the room too, with unhappy restless eyes.

"Behold! Your double!" said Myles Meredith to Stephanie. "Where did he rake her up?"

Stephanie turned her head in the direction he was looking and beheld. Her jacinth eyes became stormy, her red mouth, painted to ghastliness, grew sardonic.

"Come!" she said, "we will go there!" and she pointed to a table just vacated, quite near to where Jeffrey Wainwright and Camilla sat. And suddenly Camilla knew that this was the worst moment of all.

They came straight on, those two, with their eyes on her escort, and Camilla giving him a quick fleeting look, saw that he had regained his poise, and his quiet glance.

"Hello, Jeff!" said Stephanie, nodding to Wainwright carelessly. She turned her head slowly toward Camilla and gave her a stare of contempt, then swept on giving Wainwright no chance to make the introduction he had intended.

Wainwright followed her with an astonished glance and then turned deliberately away. Camilla could see that he was deeply annoyed, but he did not glance again at those other two.

"It's just as well," he said in a low tone to Camilla, "I shouldn't care to introduce that man to anyone. Shall we go, Camilla?"

Camilla arose and managed somehow to get herself out of that place. She was somewhat reassured by the visions of herself in those many mirrors all about. They startled her, they looked so much like the other girl. She could feel the other girl's eyes upon her as she went. She could feel the fire and the hate in her glance, yet she knew she maintained her own poise. She owed that to her escort.

"And now," said Wainwright when they were out of it all and waiting for the car, "what shall we do next? Would you like to hear some more music, or would you enjoy a good ice-hockey game at the Arena? We'll be in plenty of time for the second game, and there are some exhibition skaters there tonight."

"Oh!" said Camilla, breathless, "oughtn't we to go home? Isn't it very late?"

"No, it's early yet. Aren't you having a good time, Camilla? You aren't tired yet, are you?"

He looked down at her with his charming smile, and Camilla looked up with another. She couldn't help it. There was something in his smile that melted down all her fortifications.

"No, I'm not tired," said Camilla, struggling to find words that were true. "It's been—wonderful!"

"Well, suppose we go to the Arena and get something entirely different, just to freshen us up a bit."

All the way to the Arena he talked brightly of interesting things. It wasn't far. He did not touch on what they had been saying when the digression occurred. Camilla was grateful to him for that. Somehow she did not want to go back to it. She had a feeling it was a closed incident.

All through the hockey game and through the solo skating which came between the rounds of the game, he kept her interested and happy. The joy of the first part of the evening had returned, to a certain extent. It was not quite the same, it was a more subdued joy, like the sweetness of a pleasant farewell, but she was grateful for it. It was going to be a pleasant ending to a wonderful experience. She was glad not to have had it end when they left the restaurant after that other girl came in.

Camilla loved the skating and the hockey game. It filled her with a new interest, and during intermissions Jeffrey was telling her about the winter sports up at their estate in the mountains. He said he would like to take her there sometime, he knew she would enjoy it. Camilla smiled back at him just as if she were not sure she would never get there, and said she was sure she would.

At last the evening was over and he took her home, his gracious lovely manner just the same, his attractiveness and strength and the flash of his smile, even the way his voice said "Camilla," were all hers just as they had been when they started early in the evening. Just as if Camilla didn't know in her heart that this was the end.

And he hadn't yet referred once to what she had said.

Then, just as Camilla gave him her key to let him unlock the door for her, he took both of her hands in his and pressed them gently.

"Camilla," he said, "you're a great friend, and I'm glad I've found you, and some day pretty soon when we can get time and a quiet place without too many people around, I want to talk more about what you were saying when we were interrupted."

And right there on her own doorstep, with all the little sordid shabby brick houses up and down the street asleep, and not a soul in sight either way, he suddenly laid his lips on her trembling ones and kissed her.

"Good night, little girl!"

He unlocked the door for her and swung it softly open, for they had agreed to be quiet lest they waken her mother, and Camilla said a faltering little frightened good night, and slipped inside the door, closing it softly behind her.

He was gone. She could hear his car driving away! And his kiss was burning on her lips!

Oh, Camilla! Camilla! What had she done? Let him kiss her and said never a word. Yes, and yielded her lips to his!

It was sweet, but it must be the end! Absolutely the end!

CHAPTER VII

CAMILLA LOCKED THE DOOR SILENTLY AND STOLE INTO THE front room, stepping out of her satin slippers at once so that she should not disturb her mother and the nurse, although if she had only known it, both of them were wide awake and had been for the last hour awaiting her coming. But each for the sake of the other lay quite still. The mother could not sleep because she had gone in imagination through every detail of the evening with her beloved child, but she had lain almost without stirring because she did not want the nurse to scold her and give her hot milk or a tablet to make her sleep. She was enjoying every minute of this outing for the daughter who had so little to take her out of the round of hard work.

The nurse had gone to bed early and lain very quiet for her patient's sake, but she too had been renewing her youth, full of excitement over the beautiful young girl, and the man who had not only unusual attraction, but wealth and charm besides. It seemed like a real romance to Eleanor York, and she lay there planning it out as if it had been a storybook she was reading.

So the two left at home were by no means asleep when Camilla came in and went about her preparations for bed with as few movements as possible.

Perhaps it would have been better for all three if Camilla had frankly wakened them and gushed a little bit about her evening. Certainly it would have taken her own mind from the things which disturbed her.

But she slid into her couch that stood waiting for her, with its covers carefully turned back, flung the covers over her with one movement and lay rigid, her conscience already beginning to grill her with the details of the evening, hauling out and displaying before her every disturbing element, until she felt like writhing.

Beginning with that kiss, that sweet, burning kiss that lingered hauntingly upon her lips, her mind travelled backward over each moment she had been away, sensing the preciousness of it all, even while she rejected it as something she must not have for her own.

Then back again from the moment she had left her home, down through each little thing; how clearly it was impressed upon her mind. Wainwright's smile, the way his eyes had searched hers when he asked a question, the way their thoughts had seemed to travel together, the way they understood one another, his easy grace as he helped her out of the car and led her to the table, his pleasant compliments. Were they genuine, or did he say those things to every girl? She could not believe they were not genuine, not just for herself alone.

Ah! But there was that other girl! That girl with the jeweled gold hair and the mocking red lips, who had called him "Jeff" and stared at her so insolently! The iron went deep into her soul as she thought of her! And there were all the other things that made up his world, the wine, and the dance, and all the gay frivolity that constituted the difference between his world and hers, the great gulf fixed that might not be crossed, the gulf between Life and Death, light and darkness, unalterable and eternal. That he would ever accept the Life she possessed seemed as improbable as that a camel should go through the eye of a needle.

Yet how gentle he had been with her on the way home. Almost as if he understood that something had been a shock to her. Of course he had laid it to the way the other girl had acted, he wouldn't have understood the other even if she tried to tell him. It was a spiritual thing and had to be spiritually discerned.

Yet humanly he had a wonderfully fine understanding and sympathy. She felt that instinctively, and she warmed to the remembrance of his manner toward her on the way home, and then—that kiss! If anyone had told her earlier in the day that she would have allowed a young man to kiss her, unrebuked, a strange young man at that, one to whom she had never really been even introduced, she would have been angry indeed. Yet as the memory of that kiss came back to her she could not seem to be indignant. It had not been given flippantly, nor grossly. It had been reverent. Utterly so. It had not even seemed a liberty. And yet if some other girl had tried to explain such a thing away she would have curled a lip of scorn at her. No, according to her own confessed standards it was wrong, and yet, when she thought of it, in spite of all her theories and beliefs, even in spite of facts, she felt as if that kiss had been a sort of benediction, a tribute laid at the feet of her womanhood. It had been so reverent, so gentle. There had been nothing wanton about it.

Was this the thing they called falling in love, and was she after all her careful teaching, after her most heartfelt convictions, to lose her head and become engulfed in a love affair with a man who did not belong to her world? No,

no, no! A thousand times no! This must be the end. She
would tell him so. She must make him understand!

But perhaps he too felt that this was the end. Perhaps
that had been the real meaning of that kiss, a kind of
wistful sorrowful farewell. For he must see that she was
not of his class, no matter how much he might say or think
about her being to the manor born. He could see she was
unsophisticated. He must understand that there could be
nothing more between them than the friendliness which
had been that first night when he went out of his way to
help her in distress.

Beating this over and over in her mind she sank at last
to sleep, with the hope that somehow the tangle would
unravel, and all would yet be simple and normal with her
as it always had been. But in the night there came a dream
which carried on all the joy of her evening and none of the
fears, and when she awoke in the morning it was with a
tender memory of his lips upon hers that made her glad in
her secret heart that she had had that one beautiful moment when he had said good night to her. It would be
something to remember all through the years if love came
never nearer to her than it had last night. It would be a
way to be sure what love might be between two souls who
were rightly mated.

But it was late when she awoke and she could see the
eagerness in the eyes of the two who had so willingly
helped her to be ready last night. She knew that somehow
she must give them their meed of joy in her outing, for
they had done all in their power to make her happy. This
might be the end of things for her, but they deserved their
bit of description, their glimpse of the excitement and
beauty of it all.

So while she dressed, and hurriedly ate a few bites to
satisfy their anxiety for her, she gave vivid word pictures
of her evening, omitting all that had troubled her, and
omitting that precious kiss at the end. She gave them a
fair sense of her own excitement and joy in the scene, she
even managed a few bright funny descriptions of people
she had seen, and she described Wainwright's uncle and
aunt gravely and briefly, made plain their cordiality and
friendliness, till she found Miss York's eyes fixed on her
in eager speculation, and her mother's eyes filled with
mingled pride and anxiety.

So Camilla made much of the gorgeousness of the famous restaurant, spoke of how stylish she felt with her new gloves, and thanked Miss York for putting her orchids in water on the table where she could see them while she ate. But she utterly refused to wear them to the office.

"No," she said decidedly. "They don't belong down there, and I don't wish to give false impressions."

Then with a good-bye to Miss York who was to leave that afternoon, and an earnest invitation for her to come back and visit them whenever she could, she kissed her mother and was gone.

She felt as she walked to the nearest car line that she had suddenly grown a great deal older since last evening. It was a relief too, to be away from the dear kind eyes that loved her and searched her face so keenly.

Nevertheless, as she went her way into another part of the city and threaded through traffic from one car line to another, and then to a bus, she found she was hugging to herself every pleasant thing that had happened last night, every look and tone and smile and kindly word. Wainwright had told her that her car would be ready now in a couple of days, and she realized what a wonderful thing he had done for her in looking after the repairs on that. She was sure if it had been left to her own engineering she would never have had that little old car again. But now he had assured her it would be as good as new. And to think he had arranged it for her so that she would not have to pay a cent! Well, that was something to let her heart sing about anyway, even if she must not let herself think about the young man.

And she mustn't! She had got to conquer this thing! She looked into the pleasant sunny morning and drew a deep breath, forcing a smile, and decided that she was just going to be happy and not worry about anything. Think of her mother who was well again! Able to help clear off the table that morning! Think how her car would soon be repaired which would carry her so much more quickly, yes, and cheaply too, to her office! Think that she had a job to go to, and with careful economy a prospect of paying both nurse and doctor before long! Think that there were orchids still at home—! No, she must not think about those darling orchids! They would inevitably lead to other thoughts which must be taboo for her, or she would presently find herself in deep waters like any other silly girl!

Yet when she finally arrived at her office, just in time, and went to hang up her coat and hat, she found her heart singing, singing, singing! Why? Silly heart that would sing in spite of depression and thoughts she must not think!

That night her mother asked a lot of questions, and she answered them gaily, glibly. She had been schooling herself all day and did very well, even under those keen loving eyes.

"And what did you think of the young man, Camilla, after spending a whole evening in his company?" asked the mother at last, watching the sweet transparent face of the girl.

"Oh, just what I thought of him before!" answered Camilla with a trifling little laugh. "Charming, of course! Mother, it does make a difference to be brought up with lovely things about you. I'm sure it does. He is so much more gracious and courteous than most of the men in the office for instance! But then, of course, he belongs to a different world."

Camilla caught up the tray full of dishes and hurried back into the kitchen, feeling that she had done very well under inspection.

When she came back for the rest her mother went on:

"You still feel that, do you, Camilla?" There was just the hint of a little sigh at the end of the words and the girl caught it. She was sensitive to her mother's very thoughts.

"Oh, yes," she laughed lightly again, "I knew that at once when I first met him. But—" she paused for some casual ending to her sentence, "it is nice to know him. It is broadening, don't you think, Mother, to have at least one really cultured friend outside the family?"

Her mother smiled at the glib way she spoke of him, so formally as if he were some kind of a specimen. She knew she had not got down to the heart of the matter yet, but she was wise enough to say nothing more about it.

"I suppose it is," she agreed with a smile. "Well, child, dear, don't lose your heart to him!" but she said it with the least hint of another sigh. It would be nice to have a friend for Camilla like that one who was fine and right in every way, a real true man—if he was all that! She dreaded the thought that she might be called away from earth some day soon, and Camilla be left alone. She knew she had been very near the borderland in her last illness.

But Camilla, even while she was finishing the dishes, and putting back into place the articles of furniture and bedding that had been changed about to accommodate the nurse during her mother's illness, found her heart on the alert for a step at the door, a tap on the old iron knocker; caught herself looking wistfully toward the telephone for a ring that did not come. He had said when he parted from her that he would be seeing her soon. Yet the first night and the second night passed with no sign from him, not even a phone call, and then indeed her heart began to sink. She hated herself for the feeling, but it was there, a sorrow that he had not come. A deep-seated conviction that he would not come. That it had really been the end!

But when she reached home the third evening and opened the front door a subtle fragrance greeted her at the very threshold, the perfume of hothouse roses! Her heart leaped up with hope. Was it hope or joy? She didn't stop to analyze it. She went at once to the source of that fragrance, the great bowl of golden roses on the little mahogany stand in the front room, like a bee to the honey, and buried her face in their sweetness.

Glad, glad, glad! Yes, it was joy! Pure joy!

Her mother came in a moment later, a knife and spoon in her hand and a smudge of flour on her cheek.

"Too bad you couldn't have got home early tonight," she said with a lilt in her voice. "He's been gone only about ten minutes. He stayed as late as he dared. He had to catch a train! But he's left a note for you."

"A note?"

Camilla accepted it as if it had been gold and treasures. She dropped down just where she was without taking off her hat or coat and read it, a glow on her cheeks and a tumult in her heart. Her mother watched her furtively from the hall, lingering with a wistful smile upon her face, trying to read the heart of her girl through the flush on her cheek and the glint in her eyes.

"Dear Camilla;

"I'm so sorry to have missed you. I've been hungering for a long talk ever since I left you, but I had to help Dad with some important business, and now Mother's had a

bad case of bronchitis and has been ordered South at once.
Dad can't get away yet so Mother has commandeered me.
I hope to return in a few days, but can't be sure how soon.
Meantime keep in mind what we were talking about, and
don't forget me.

Yours,

Jeff.

Your car will be back tomorrow sometime."

Camilla sat still studying that note, trying to subdue the
surge of happiness that went over her, trying to act casual,
trying to feel casual. Now just what was there in that note
to make her feel so glad, so light and relieved? It was a
perfectly commonplace note, wasn't it? Anybody might
have written it to anyone else? And yet all the heaviness of
the past three days was lifted. Why? Well, he hadn't
forgotten her, and she had fully persuaded herself that he
had, and at least to him this wasn't the end—not yet. That
in itself was a song of thanksgiving. For since she had made
up her mind that it was the end there seemed to be many
reasons why she wanted to see him again. For one thing,
she wanted to be sure that he did not think less of her
because she had allowed that sweet quiet kiss. She wanted
to look into his face and read what he had meant by it.
Not that she was at all in doubt about the impossibility of
any further growth of their friendship, but that she wanted
to read fineness and cleanness of purpose in his face, and
always be able to think well of him when she remembered
him.

Presently she looked up and caught a glimpse of her
mother's questioning face, and her own broke into a smile.

"Did he come in, Mother?"

"Yes, and waited three-quarters of an hour. We had a
nice talk together. He has great charm."

"Yes," said Camilla dreamily going over to the roses and
burying her face in their sweetness again, closing her eyes
while she drew in a long delicious breath. "Yes, he has
charm. I suppose all people of the world have charm,
haven't they, Mother? I haven't met so many of them you
know."

"No!" said the mother sharply. "Not all of them. In fact
I have known many who had none. Their money and posi-

tion seemed to have made them hard and sharp and disagreeable. Is—the—letter—about your car?" Mrs. Chrystie hesitated, her eyes on the paper held close in her daughter's hand. Was her precious girl in danger? If she could only see that folded note she might be able to read between the lines.

Camilla opened her note again and read it over, the color coming softly into her cheeks. Then with a lingering smile she suddenly held it out to her mother.

"It's nothing, Mother," she said with her most casual air. "Read it if you like! Just a friendly apology because he couldn't come down yesterday or day before as he promised, to—tell me about the car."

Her mother gave her a steady look, then read the note slowly, while Camilla hurried about singing a soft little excited song, trying to seem disinterested.

But her mother came straight to the point.

"What had you been talking about, Camilla, that he wants you to keep in mind?"

"Oh," said Camilla airily, her cheeks growing a trifle redder, "just,—why—as nearly as I can remember, something about being to the manor born!"

Her mother looked at her thoughtfully for a moment.

"Oh!" she said, and handed the note back.

They were very happy that night eating supper together, the first supper the mother had cooked, for Miss York had made up several dishes that would last for a day or two until the invalid was used to being quite on her own again.

"Everything tastes so good, Mother!" said Camilla looking up with happy eyes.

Somehow it seemed as if she had had a reprieve. She didn't have to keep her conscience constantly awatch over her thoughts. He was away at least for a few days, and she might get rested and think it over at her leisure. And just for this evening at least she meant to enjoy home and Mother.

But her mother brought the roses and set them in the middle of the table as they sat down, and there they were in their beauty to remind of the giver.

They had a cheery meal and a happy time putting the kitchen in order, and the mother wisely said no more about the young man. But after the lights were out she did much praying. It was a situation that she did not feel herself able to judge aright, so she prayed for guidance that her girl might not be tempted into anything that would bring her sorrow.

It was the next day that the little old reconstructed car came shining home in a new coat of paint and looking as if it were brand new throughout. And when the wondering girl started its engine it purred as silkily as if it were finer than it had been originally.

A few days later life settled down into the old routine. The roses had faded, and Camilla was becoming accustomed to the newness of her old car. The accident and all that had followed it had been softened into the semblance of a dream, and save that she could not look at her mother without continually giving thanks for her renewed strength, all things seemed as they were before her mother's illness. Even Wainwright had become for the time being only a dream-hero who had appeared to relive her necessity and vanished into oblivion, and she was able to forget him hours together, and sometimes to go to sleep without recalling his farewell. She congratulated herself that she had come back to sanity.

She did not see a taxi containing a handsome dark foreign-looking man following her little car home one night. She noticed him no more than anyone else in traffic. She did not notice the same man hovering in her street the next morning when she left for the office, nor notice another taxi following her to her parking place, and the same man trailing her to the office door. She was wholly unconscious of it all, and settled to her work as usual that winter morning, thankful that she had a warm woollen dress that was respectable without having to buy a new one before the doctor and nurse were paid. She looked down at herself proudly and smoothed the skirt, noticed how well the blouse looked in spite of home cleaning and blocking, and then she settled down at her desk and to work, steadily refusing to let her mind even hint at the thought that time was going on and Wainwright might be coming home soon. It wasn't a thought she had a right to think, and she wasn't going to allow it. She was proud of herself for having conquered her foolish interest in a passing stranger.

CHAPTER VIII

It happened just after her employer had come through from his private office and gone down in the elevator for his lunch hour. Marietta Pratt, the other girl who occupied the desk opposite Camilla's, had gone to lunch also. Camilla had chosen to let her go first today, because of some letters she wanted to finish for the afternoon mail. She was trying to have them ready for Mr. Whitlock to sign when he came back from lunch.

She was working away like a whirlwind, her mind intent on what she was doing, her fingers flying over the typewriter keys with a skill and rapidity beautiful to watch. She had a feeling that she could work better when the other girl was gone, because she was a fidgeter, and a fusser, always coming over interrupting to ask a question.

Suddenly as Camilla worked she became aware of the presence of someone in the room, and looking up startled she saw a girl standing in the open door, her hand still upon its knob, looking at her with scorn and anger. A girl with gold hair, ghastly red lips in a chalk-white face, and eyes that seemed to be strange evil red-gold stones, yet stones that could pulsate and flame with a kind of hidden fire.

Camilla even as a child had always been strangely calm in a time of crisis, so now, even as she took in the identity of this other girl, and realized that she had come to wreak some kind of vengeance upon herself, the startled look went out of her eyes, and her face became a well controlled mask filled only with a polite business inquiry. Her hands had half dropped, poised over the keyboard of her machine, and her expression showed no sign of recognition. The intruder was nothing more to her apparently than any other stranger who might have chanced to come to the office on business.

She looked up and waited an instant as if expecting the

visitor to speak, but the other girl only stared at her speculatively, appraisingly, still scornfully, with white fury in her gaze.

Camilla lifted her lovely chin a trifle, with a pride she had received by inheritance, and let her eyes coolly appraise the visitor. Then she spoke in a tone as of one in authority.

"Did you wish to see Mr. Whitlock?" she asked, and her voice bespoke all the generations of cultured, educated people who had been her forebears. "He has gone out to lunch. He will not be back until half past two."

The beauty stared indignantly.

"No, I didn't come to see Mr. Whitlock nor anybody else but you!" she said haughtily, "and you needn't think you can hide behind anyone. I came here to talk to you, and I mean to do it."

"Why, certainly," said Camilla courteously, whirling around from her typewriter and facing the stranger. "Won't you sit down? I'm sure I don't know why I should wish to hide from you."

"Well, you probably will before I get done with you," said Stephanie Varrell vehemently, "and you needn't put on that sanctimonious look either. I've had a hard enough time finding you, and you needn't think I'll let you off easily, either. I've had to employ three men and a taxi two days to locate you, but I did it! I've come to tell you where to get off, and you probably know what that means. If you don't heed what I'm going to tell you I'll find ways to put you out of the running somehow."

Camilla found herself growing very angry indeed, and her ancestral courage rose as the other girl grew more and more insolent. She was a trifle white about her lips, and her eyes grew dark and unsmiling, but otherwise there was no change in her appearance.

"Wouldn't it be a good thing if you were to explain what this is all about?" she asked quietly.

"Oh, you're terribly innocent, aren't you? You don't need any explanation. I know your kind. A girl of your type doesn't pick up the son of a millionaire and make him take her to the place where I saw you last week with Jeff Wainwright without knowing just what it's all about."

Camilla was thankful that she was not a blushing girl. She could fairly well depend upon herself to grow perhaps whiter in an emergency, but not red, and now though her heart gave a sudden lurch and seemed to turn right over in her angry young breast, she kept her poise and looked steadily in the eye of the other girl, who had taken out a gold cigarette case, lighted a cigarette, and was puffing it furiously at her foe.

"I don't understand you," said Camilla coolly. "It is quite a common circumstance, isn't it, for a girl to go out to dinner with a friend?"

"Friend?" sneered the other girl. "You call him a friend do you? That's preposterous! I wonder what he would say if he could hear you? A man doesn't make a friend out of every girl he plays around with! And don't fancy he'll ever marry you. He's not the marrying kind. And besides all that a man like that doesn't seek a wife in the laboring class. You are not of his class. You are just a low-down working girl!"

Stephanie's voice was like the hiss of a serpent.

Camilla was very angry indeed now. She wanted to rise and strike this insolent girl in the face. She wanted to scream and cry out at the insults that were being flung at her. She knew that both tears and hysterical laughter were hovering very near the surface, and she was holding her emotions back by the mere force of her will. She hoped her voice did not tremble as she answered calmly.

"I really hadn't considered marrying him!" She took a deep breath, to steady herself. "You see," she went on, "you are quite right about our not being of the same class. But you are mistaken about my being so terribly low born. It so happens that though I am working at present I really belong to royalty, and you know perhaps that it is not permitted that royalty should marry outside of royalty."

There was just a little ring of triumph in the clear voice as Camilla gathered strength with her words. There was also a light in her eyes that somehow startled her visitor and made her pause in her angry torrent of insolence. Camilla was certain of herself, and did not seem at all quelled by the taunts that had been flung at her. Camilla had a poise that the other girl had never known.

Stephanie Varrell surveyed her contemptuously, amazed that this mere fragment of the working classes should dare to stand out against her and smile in a superior way and answer back. Royalty! Could it be that there was some mistake?

"Royalty!" she sneered, looking her over from the tips of her shabby little brown shoes to the top of her perfectly groomed golden head. Camilla was always exquisitely dainty, even in her working hours. She had lovely hands most carefully cared for. Her nails were not stained red, nor allowed to grow long and pointed like claws. They were artistically lovely hands fascinating to watch. Camilla was neat and trim and stylish, too, even in the little brown knit dress, the work of her mother's hands, that had served a long term of wear, and still had time ahead. Camilla was a lady, and the other girl could not help seeing it. Just for the moment she was baffled. She looked as an angry bull might have looked when persented with a bunch of clover instead of the red rag he had been charging.

"Royalty? Are you then a foreigner?" As if that accounted for it.

"Yes," said Camilla with a bell-like quality in her voice. "Yes, I am a foreigner. I don't belong here." She sounded as if she were proud of the fact.

"Oh," said Stephanie, "one of those little defunct nations, I suppose, that you find it hard to locate on the map?"

"Oh, no," said Camilla lightly, "none of those. You won't find it on your map. My citizenship is in heaven. And now, don't you think we've said about enough? I really can't spare any more time to talk. I have work to do," with a glance at the clock, "and I must get back to it at once. You will excuse me, I'm sure," and she swung her chair around to her typewriter and began to make her fingers fly rapidly over the keys, blindly writing whatever came into her head.

Stephanie Varrell stared at her for an instant incredulously, then she said in a shocked tone:

"You must be crazy!"

But Camilla did not answer. She went right on writing, the click of her typewriter keys filling the silence eloquently.

Stephanie Varrell watched her, her face gradually hardening into anger again.

"You think you're very smart, don't you?" she mocked. "But all the same you'll find out that it's dangerous to interfere with what belongs to me. Jeff Wainwright is mine, and I'm not going to have other girls playing around with him! Understand? If you happen to transgress again you'll find yourself out of a job quicker than you can think. I happen to know Mr. Whitlock well, and I have ways of making people do what I say. You'll find that out too, if you choose to ignore this warning, royalty or no royalty!"

The high shrill voice ceased and Stephanie Varrell walked out of the office and slammed the door viciously. But Camilla kept on making her fingers fly over those keys blindly until she heard the elevator stop, its door open and shut, and move on down. Then she rose and flew to the dark little cloak room where she kept her wraps, and burying her face in the sleeve of her old black coat burst into tears, sobbing as if her heart would break. They were almost silent tears however, for she did not know what minute the other stenographer would come back, and very soon she was able to control herself. That was a hard thing about being a working girl, she hadn't leisure even to weep!

Yet afterwards she knew it was better so, for if she had cried long her mother would have noticed it when she went home. Mothers always saw through everything. But Mother mustn't know about this. It would kill Mother to know that anybody had dared talk to her that way.

She hurried to the wash room and dashed cold water over her eyes, and by the time Marietta Pratt returned she seemed to be her sweet self again, perhaps a little dewy about the eyes, but all right otherwise. She was ready to leave as the other girl came in, and gave even her sharp eyes little chance to inspect her fellow worker. But Camilla as she walked down the hall to the elevator had a feeling that she was leaving a conversation behind in that room that would somehow get across to Marietta. How terrible it would be if conversations had a way of making themselves perpetuated and audible to others. It almost seemed as if she ought to have opened the windows and let some of those dreadful words out. She shivered as she stepped into the elevator and the elevator boy grinned at her sympathetically and said, "Cold day!" Camilla gave him a wan smile through lips that were stiff with the shock of what she had just passed through. She was thankful that her recent caller's words were not rolling down the big stone corridors of the building in audible form for the world to hear!

It seemed to her as she walked out into the bright winter day as if the very sunshine hurt her and the keen air went through her. Humiliation was upon her the like of which she had never dreamed that any well-meaning person could suffer! To have been dragged down into such a mortifying situation! To have been forced to listen to such charges! To have been the target of such insolence, such implications!

She walked down the street and past the restaurant where she usually took her lunch without even noticing it. She was not hungry. She only wanted to get out away somewhere and try to get her bearings once more. She wanted to get calm. But as she walked her mind fairly seethed with indignation. Everything that other girl had said came back again and shouted itself at her until it seemed to her the passers-by must hear, and every step of the way she was thinking of something keen she might have said in answer. Her cheeks were burning red and her eyes were flashing with a great light, but it was not a light of humility. It was a light of pride and anger.

Presently she found herself in a small park where a few chilly sparrows hopped noisily about. She sat down on a wind-swept bench and tried to keep warm. It seemed as if her limbs were too tired to bear her farther. And then she felt the tears stinging into her eyes again. This would not do. She must not cry here where passers-by could see her. Somebody would presently be offering help. She sat up straight and stared into the distance, and it was just then she remembered the haven of her soul and began to pray.

"Oh God! Oh, God!" but when she tried to go on she found it was in words somewhat similar to the imprecatory psalms. Ah! Was there something wrong in her own heart? Surely this terrible experience which had come upon her was not in any way her fault! Or was it! Was there some lingering doubt in her mind about her own conduct? No, not really. She had not sought that young man. He had come out of the darkness to help her. He had insisted on staying by her and helping. He had come back of his own accord, without invitation. He had sent her flowers. There wasn't anything she could have done about it without being rude and ungrateful. Of course she didn't have to go to that dinner with him, but her mother had approved, Miss York had thought it was wonderful, a chance for her to have a little innocent relaxation. No, it was something more than that that was troubling her. It was that kiss that she had allowed, nay in which she knew she had participated. Just the yielding of her lips, just the answering sweetness to his, a kiss that had seemed so reverent. Yet now she so loathed herself for having allowed it, and having cherished it in her memory afterward. The man was likely engaged to this terrible girl, and yet he went around kissing other girls!

That other girl was beautiful. If she was his why didn't he stay with her? Oh, it was a sickening world, all topsy turvy. You couldn't trust anybody but God and your own mother. And perhaps even Mother had been wrong in thinking it was right for her to go to dinner with a stranger. And yet he hadn't seemed like a stranger. Oh, what should she do? How was she ever to look herself in the face again, how endure the thought of that session with that awful girl? How ever respect herself again?

Well, it was what came of trying to go with people of the world. It was all right so long as he was just helping her out of trouble, being kind and nice, but she ought to have made it stop at that. She knew what he was of course. It was well enough to excuse herself by saying she mustn't misjudge a stranger. That was only an excuse. His very dress and manner marked him of another world than hers, and she knew in her heart, even if her mother didn't know, that he was not in her class. Well, she had her lesson now. Never would she forget the humiliation through which she had passed.

She put her head down on her hand and closed her eyes and tried to pray, but she found so much indignation in her heart that the prayer was choked.

She began to think over what she had said. She was glad at least that she had claimed her heavenly citizenship, her kinship to the royal family of God. And yet, she began to wonder whether even that had pleased God. She had done it in pride and anger, not for His glory. She remembered the words: "But God forbid that I should glory, save in the cross of our Lord Jesus Christ, by whom the world is crucified unto me, and I unto the world."

She hadn't been crucified to the world while she was getting off those smart sentences about belonging to royalty. She had been trying to show off, to say something that would startle that insolent girl. If she had been entirely crucified to the world, dead with Christ, and in this death-union with Him entering into His risen life, His resurrection power, mere words could not have hurt.

And now indeed a crimson color of shame rolled into her cheeks. Now she was honestly facing facts. She had boasted of her heavenly citizenship just as the world might boast. She had not boasted of the so great salvation that had come to her life. She had said nothing of the fact that she had been a sinner saved by an infinitely loving Saviour. She hadn't boasted of the cross of her Lord Jesus Christ which had put her into the royal family. She had boasted in an earthly way and tried to make that girl think she was great in the earthly sense.

The wind grew suddenly sharp and cut through her thin coat, making her shiver. The sunshine faded to drab, and the day seemed overcast. There were even worse things than having a girl of the world class her with common flirts and women of the street. It was worse in the eyes of God, yes, and in her own eyes now that she realized it, to have swaggered and boasted of her heavenly lineage as if it were some inherent good in herself that gave her the right to claim such glorious kinship with the Most High.

That was the bitterest hour that Camilla had ever passed, sitting there looking into her own heart and seeing no superiority in it whatever. Robbed of her own spiritual conceit, robbed of her budding joy in her friendship with a man whom she had of course idealized,—she saw that too now,—robbed of a certain family pride which had helped her out many and many a time when the going was hard and rough, she was just plain shamed Camilla Chrystie with nothing to boast about at all, save that the Lord Jesus Christ had shed His precious blood on Calvary to redeem her.

Suddenly she was recalled to the fact that it was freezing and that the deep-toned bell of the great clock on the City Hall was striking two o'clock, and she was due back at the office at one-thirty! The letters, the important letters were not finished!

She arose hastily and walked on feet that were numb with cold and excitement, almost ran back to her office, and arrived breathless.

"Well, I'll say you had plenty lunch!" said Marietta Pratt shifting her gum to the other side of her jaw and inspecting

Camilla's chilly anxious face. "Wha d'ya do? Have a heavy date?"

"No," said Camilla sharply, "I,—it was something—I had to do. I—didn't have any lunch at all. I thought I'd get back sooner. You didn't by any chance get your letters finished, did you? I wanted to get them all off by three. Hasn't Mr. Whitlock come back yet?"

Marietta who had improved the time in the absence of Camilla and the chief by reading a library book full of murder thrills and mystery, furtively slid the volume under some papers in her desk drawer and whirled about to her typewriter.

"Naw, he hain't come in yet. He phoned ta say he'd be late. Some conference he's got on. Naw, I didn't get my letters all done yet. I'm workin' on 'em now. I didn't know there was any hurry. Say, why'n't you go on out an' get some lunch now? He won't be back fer awhile, an' I'll tell him you're comin' right back."

"Thanks, no," said Camilla wearily, "I've got to get this work done and off," and she sat down at her typewriter and her fingers fairly flew. It was good to get to work again, good not to have to think, just to do the mechanical routine work, and forget her humiliation. She ignored the gone feeling in her stomach, the dizziness in her head. She wrote like a mad machine running away from its driver.

Along toward four o'clock Marietta paused in her own machinations, gave a languid chew or two to her gum while she surveyed her companion, and then said commiseratingly:

"You don't look sa good! You better go out 'n get a good strong cup a coffee! That'll set ya up. It don't do ta go 'thout meals, not 's hard 's you work!"

"Oh, I'm all right," said Camilla briskly, "I've just got a little headache that's all."

" 'F I was you I'd go home. I would. Like as not Mr. Whitlock'll never come back this afternoon 'tall. He'd never know. I won't tell."

Marietta did want to find out who did the murder in her book and if Camilla went home there would be nothing to stop her reading. But Camilla only shook her head and smiled vaguely.

"No," she said, "I've got to finish my work. I'm quite all

right." And she wrote on faster than ever, and poor Marietta was forced to work too.

As a matter of fact Camilla stayed at the office later than usual that night, for Mr. Whitlock came rushing in a little before five with two very important letters he wanted answered that night and Camilla had to take dictation for another half hour and then wait to type the letters and mail them.

But Camilla was glad. She had an excuse to give her mother for her great weariness. Mother always noticed when there was anything the matter.

So at last Camilla's long day was done and she was free to take her car from the parking space and go home. She wended her way carefully through traffic, reminded sharply of that other night not so long ago when she had started on that wild trip for the doctor and had met with disaster and found a friend. Suddenly a kind of faintness swept over her. She must not count him as a friend any more. She would never think of him as a friend without remembering the words of that disgusting girl. Those words had swept away from her in one brief instant all the pleasant comfort of his friendship. It reared a wall of unknown possibilities. It made him out a creature of whims and fancies whom it was not safe to trust.

Not that she had expected to continue the comradeship any more, now that the incident was past, not that she had ever counted on anything more than friendship, but to have to feel that any thought venturing in his direction must be forbidden seemed like snatching away a pleasant perfume, a lovely flower. It placed all that she thought she had on a sordid basis.

Her face flamed in the dark as she thought of it again, and then she knew by the imminence of tears that she positively must not think of this or she would be sure to cry as soon as she reached home and then Mother would be distressed, and she could not tell Mother. Mother would be shocked and horrified. Mother would feel that her very respectability had been assailed, her family insulted, her young maidenhood outraged. Mother was that way. She belonged to the age where those things mattered so much. If Mother had been a man and a southerner she would have considered the experience of the morning reasonable grounds to send a challenge to her assailant. Quiveringly she smiled a sad little smile over the folly and futility of pride. Dimly her vigil in the park had showed her deeper things than mere pride.

And back of it all was that kiss! The kiss that she had wanted to feel was a holy thing, a thing not of the flesh, but a spiritual thing, yet that in the light of present events would probably not prove to be so if it were brought out into the open. Camilla did not mean that it should be brought out into the open. Between herself and God she would ask forgiveness for her part in it, for her leniency with it, her pitiful eagerness and thrill over it. Then she would put it away as a thing that was dead. A thing that had had no right to be, and ask God to blot it out of her life. But never would she bring it out to the light of day and examine it. If it were real it was too precious to be handled lightly. Since it could not be, why suffer any more? She had learned her lesson, which was probably the reason it all had happened.

CHAPTER IX

CAMILLA PUT HER CAR IN THE SHABBY LITTLE GARAGE AND went in as briskly and casually as possible.

"Sorry I had to be late," she said, as she saw the anxious look on her mother's face. "I should have telephoned, but I kept thinking I would get away in a few minutes, and I didn't realize the time."

"Oh, my dear!" said the gentle voice, "have you had to work so late? That's inhuman! Couldn't you have promised to come down a little earlier in the morning and do the extra work? You look so tired!"

"No, it had to get off in the night mail. Yes, I am a little tired," Camilla pressed her hand to her temples, "and I've got one of those miserable mean old headaches in my eyes. But don't worry. I'll be all right when I get some dinner and a good night's rest. You know this doesn't happen often, Mother dear!" and she gathered her frail little mother into her arms hungrily and kissed her soft warm cheeks. She had her mother anyway. She mustn't worry about other things. What did anything else matter when Mother was well again?

She summoned a fairly bright smile and sat down. She did not see how she was going to eat a mouthful, but yet she had to for Mother's sake. And then everything was so good that presently she found herself enjoying every mouthful.

"It's all so good, so delicious!" she said like a child who had been lost somewhere in a barren waste and had just got home where it was safe and comfortable. The day behind her seemed so wild and the way so hard.

"I'm glad I didn't make potpie after all," said her mother contentedly, watching her eat. "I was going to make potpie first because you like it so much, but I changed to biscuits instead. I thought maybe you'd be late and the potpie won't wait you know. It has to be eaten right out of the pot or it falls and is heavy as lead."

"These biscuits are wonderful!" murmured the girl happily, thinking that perhaps after all the day had been but a bad dream, and life was going to be liveable again. She and her mother together were enough to be happy without others.

But later when everything was in order in the kitchen, the table set for breakfast, the light out, Mother asleep and Camilla in her bed in the front room, then came the memories in a wild flock like so many cormorants and sat about her on the dim shapes of the chairs and tables and other furniture in the dark room. They shouted out tauntings and arrogance to her until she felt that she would scream aloud presently and her mother would be sure to hear and demand to know the whole story. She thought she would never get to sleep. The night was going and the morning would come and she would be unfit to go to the office. Oh, what should she do?

But sleep did come after all, and she awoke startled to find the new day full of sunshine, and her troubles not quite as heavy upon her as the night before. At least she was able to look forward to going back to the office without quite so much dread. The young woman with the gold hair would not likely haunt her steps the rest of her days.

And since Wainwright was in Florida it wasn't reasonable to suppose that the girl would make her any more trouble, at least until his return.

So she went back to her office with her mind intent on her work, determined to keep so busy that she would have no opportunity to think any more about the matter. It was an incident of the past and that was all. Probably the young man would have forgotten all about her by the time he came back.

So she tried to cheer herself into contentment and forget the things that troubled her.

But now something new loomed on her stormy horizon. Mr. Whitlock, usually so quiet and courteous, so staid and dignified, came into the office with a frown on his face.

"I am looking for a letter," he said after he had searched through his desk and looked carefully over the letters in the letter tray. "It should have come in yesterday afternoon. Miss Chrystie, are you sure you did not see it? It was from Cleveland. The firm you wrote to last week, you remember? They promised me an answer not later than yesterday. Are you *quite sure* nothing came? You put all the mail in my usual letter tray? You are *sure?*"

He looked at Camilla with almost an accusatory gleam in his eyes. It was evident that he was greatly excited.

Camilla told him she was sure the letter had not come. She got up from her work and went over to help him hunt, although she was positive no such letter had arrived. He kept insisting that it must surely be there somewhere, perhaps had fallen into an open drawer, or the waste basket.

At last he turned toward Marietta who had been placidly polishing her typewriter and told her in no very uncertain terms that she was wasting her time, and that she should have been at her typing long ago. He spoke more sharply than either of the girls had ever heard him speak before.

He sat down at his desk and wrote out several telegrams for Camilla to send off. Then he had a couple of stormy conversations over the telephone, and finally, in going over to the rack where his hat and overcoat hung, his anxious eyes still searching for the letter which he was sure must have come and been carelessly mislaid, he spied Marietta's ubiquitous novel sticking out of the lower drawer of her desk.

"What's that?" he snapped sharply.

"It's—just a book," said Marietta with a frightened look in her eyes. "Just a liberry book."

"What's it doing here in the office?" he asked sharply, eyeing the girl, who drooped under his gaze and dropped her eyelashes over her startled eyes.

"Is that what you're doing while you're supposed to be working for me? Is that why my work doesn't get done on time? You are reading novels between times? Your mind is on some mystery story or other instead of on your work?"

"Oh, no, sir!" Marietta hastened to explain glibly. "I just brought it along to leave at the liberry on my way home. It's just—a—book—my stepmother borrowed!"

He looked the girl keenly in the eyes.

"Don't try to lie to me!" he said dryly. "Pick up that book and take it in the cloak room, and don't bring any more novels into this office!"

Then he went out, slamming the door hard behind him.

"What's eatin' the poor egg?" said Marietta as the man went out. She looked suspiciously toward Camilla as if she ought to be able to explain the mystery. But Camilla went right on working.

"He's the crankiest old thing I ever saw," finished Marietta with an ugly frown. "He told me yesterday morning before you came in that he didn't know as he'd want me after this month was over. He wasn't sure but he was going to make an entire change in the office force. Did he say anything to you?"

"No," said Camilla trying to keep her voice from trembling, "he has scarcely spoken to me for a week. Something must have gone exceedingly wrong in his affairs."

"I'll say!" said the girl shortly, and then most unexpectedly she banged her head down on her machine and began to cry with great shaking sobs.

Camilla looked at her an instant in consternation and then she summoned voice to speak.

"Don't feel bad, Marietta," she said. "Maybe he's only got indigestion."

"Indigestion nothing!" gurgled out Marietta. "He means it! I'm sure he does. He's got something on his mind. I been knowing it fer sometime. He's made me do every last thing over twice for three whole days. And I've just—b-b-be-gun—ta—buy a fur-r-r coat!"

"Oh, well, I wouldn't worry," said Camilla with a secret qualm for herself. "There will be other jobs."

"Not ef yer turned off. Not in these days!" said Marietta firmly, sitting up and mopping her wet eyes and getting out her lip stick and tiny mirror to repair damages in her facial landscape. "I heard when I came here he was kinda queer, but he was so nice at first I thought they had the wrong dope, but now I guess they were right. Anyhow, I don't know what I'll do. I'm buyin' it on installments."

"Well," said Camilla trying to smile for the other girl's sake, "there's always something that can be done."

"Mebbe fer you, but not fer me," said the other girl dejectedly. "You're lucky! You c'n always get by. You work hard and know your job. And besides all that you're a good-looker. Good-lookers always get by."

"Oh, no!" said Camilla sorrowfully. "Sometimes they get into worse trouble than the others. But Marietta, looks don't have anything to do with it. If you do your work well you'll be sure to get a position. If he turns us both away we'll go out together and hunt a double job. How about it?"

Marietta looked up in amazement.

"You mean that? Say! You're great! I really believe you'd do it. I knew the minute I laid eyes on you you were different from the common run. I couldn't make out what made it, till I sighted you readin' that little Testament the other day, and then I knew. You're a Christian, aren't you? A real one, I mean, not just a bread-and-butter one, nor a whited-sepulchre kind. Well, I'm real pleased you said that, even if you don't ever have to do it, and I don't expect you will. You're too good lookin' ta get the go-by! He'll never let you go, even ef he didn't like your work, which he does. But I'm pleased ta know there is one girl in these days that's an out an' out Christian."

Camilla was thoughtful a long time after that. Of course this might be the beginning of the end, and she must be prepared for it; but there was something that touched her in this girl's speech, and presently she said:

"Marietta, aren't you a Christian?"

Marietta laughed.

"Not me!" she said derisively. "I'm a devil! You oughtta see me at home. I live with my stepmother and she's some hot shot. She dresses up like all good night and goes out ta parties and plays bridge and never gets me a thing. I wouldn't stay with her a day ef it wasn't fer my kid stepbrother. He's a cripple, an' I can't bear ta leave him alone with her. She never loved him much, an' after he was hurt and his back began to grow crooked, seems as though she just hates the sight of him. I gotta stick by an' bring a little fun inta his life, ur I'd been gone from home long ago."

"Oh, Marietta!" said Camilla with instant sympathy. "Isn't that too bad! I wish I could do something to help. But—doesn't your father care for him?"

"He's dead!" said Marietta sadly. "Yes, he liked Ted, and useta hold him in his lap an' bring him toys and nice things ta eat when he could get by with it, but my stepmother she didn't like it much. She just hates *me!* She'd send me flyin' now ef it weren't that I take Ted out Sundays and leave her free ta go. She's flighty ya know. She wasn't more'n five years older 'n I when Dad married her. He told me that was the mistake of his life. He thought she'd be good comp'ny fer me. Good-night! 'zif I'd want her comp'ny! Why, I ain't had a decent good time, ner no pretty cloes since my own mother died, an' I can't scarcely remember that! Not until I got this job. An' now ef I lose it I don't know what I'll do. I'm 'fraid she'll go an' put Ted in a Home ur somethng, an' that'll kill him poor kid!"

Marietta was sobbing again and Camilla's heart was deeply touched. After all there were deeper trials than her own. She might lose her job but she still had her dear mother, and God would somehow provide for them. He always had.

So she laid aside her own fears and tried to comfort Marietta. And on her way home she was planning how she might invite Marietta out to see her some week-end, perhaps let her bring the little boy along and give him a really happy time.

She told her mother about Marietta that evening while they were eating their dinner, and Mrs. Chrystie was interested and sympathetic as always with anybody in distress, and ready to plan to give the little cripple boy a good time.

"I'll make some cookies tomorrow, Camilla," she said, "and I'll make some in funny shapes, a dog and a cat and a man, with currants for eyes, the way I used to for you when you were little. Children always like them. I saw the old cutters the other day when I was looking on the top shelf for a pan I needed. I'll make a little bag full for him and you can take them to his sister. And can't you find one of your old books that you can lend him or give him?"

"Why, yes," said Camilla brightly, and went hunting up in the attic for old books and toys. She got so interested in getting the things together that she forgot her own troubles for a while. Not once during the evening did she think of Wainwright or the girl with the jacinth eyes, and even her fears for her job were only dim forebodings now and then hovering on the margin of her mind.

But on the way down to the office next morning she remembered what Marietta had said, and felt again that dread for herself. What if she should lose her job now, while they were still in debt, and Mother by no means out from under the doctor's care? Oh, what could she do? Where could she go for another job? Now in these times when jobs were almost impossible to find?

Then she remembered that God knew all about it. He had her life planned out for her. He knew her walking and nothing was hid from Him. She had been reading that verse in her Bible that very morning. He had planned everything in her life from the foundation of the world and she need not be afraid. There would be a way out of this, the very way that He had planned!

Mr. Whitlock was in the office when Camilla arrived. He gave her a curt nod in answer to her good morning, and went on with his writing. Camilla as she went to the cloak room to put away her things felt her heart sinking. This day was going to be like yesterday, or more so. Any moment now she might be blamed for something, any moment she might be dismissed!

Marietta looked frightened when she came in, and hid the paper package she was carrying under her arm. But Mr. Whitlock did not even look up nor notice her entrance. He was very intent on his own affairs. Marietta hung up her things and hurriedly went to work.

Mr. Whitlock stayed at his desk until the mail came, and then with a set grim look on his face went out. Marietta worked more steadily than usual, and Camilla saw no book about. She did a fair amount of work and seemed anxious to let Camilla know how much she had accomplished, though she did not interrupt her as much as usual.

At noon Camilla produced the book and a few simple puzzles she had found in the attic and asked Marietta if she thought Ted would like them, and Marietta was overjoyed. Sh also told her about the cookies her mother was making for him and actual tears came to the homely girl's eyes.

"Say, now, isn't that wonderful!" she exclaimed. "My, how lucky you are to have a mother like that! My, if I had a mother I'd do just everything she said! Say, I guess that's one thing that makes you different from other girls, isn't it, having a mother like that? My! I'd like ta see her sometime! But she wouldn't approve of me! Me, I'm a devil! That's what my stepmother calls me!"

Camilla wanted to say something kind and comforting to the girl who seemed so forlorn and lonely, but just then they heard Mr. Whitlock's quick impatient steps coming down the hall and Marietta scuttled into the cloak room with the things Camilla had given her, hid them, and was back working away at her machine with unusual celerity when he finally reached the door and entered.

CHAPTER X

FOR THE REST OF THAT WEEK MATTERS AT THE OFFICE WERE exceedingly strained. Mr. Whitlock came and went, scarcely looking at either of his stenographers, saying nothing except what was absolutely necessary, smiling not at all, and each day found Camilla's hopes going down lower than the day before. It seemed to her as if she should scream if this kept up much longer. Then one morning the letter from Cleveland came and things relaxed a little. There was obvious relief in Mr. Whitlock's face as he read it, and his tone was more like his old self, gracious, courteous, reserved, as he dictated the answer. Camilla thought she understood partly what had been troubling him, and she drew a free breath and took heart of hope.

Marietta, child of emotion, on the other hand, unbound

from the leash of fear once more, lapsed into her novel on the slightest pretext. Not the same novel by this time of course, but another of like thrilling interest, and at once her rate of production dropped again. Marietta bounced up from her temporary grinding industry as gaily as a bird let loose, and tried to be chummy and friendly with her dignified employer, just to reassure herself that the strain was all over.

But Camilla could not so soon forget her anxiety, and she redoubled her efforts to be letter-perfect in every way in her work.

Yet as things grew brighter again at the office, and her fears began to drop away, her thoughts went back to dreaming again, and she could not keep Wainwright out of her mind. Would she never get this thing conquered, or was it just that she had been under so much strain that her thoughts sought naturally the only little incident in her monotonous life that had given a bit of a thrill?

Then she would recall bit by bit the incident of Stephanie Varrell's visit, and her hateful insinuations, until her pride would rise and put the whole matter out of mind.

Sometimes it seemed to her that she just must tell her mother everything. There was no one but her mother who could help to take the sting out of the whole affair and make her see things sanely, and be able to laugh at it all, rather than to brood over it.

But still she could not bring herself to put it upon her mother, for in spite of all she would say, and the way she would smile over it and say it was not worth worrying over, she knew it would be a mortification to her mother that the girl had dared to come to her that way.

And also, perhaps Camilla hesitated just because she didn't want her mother to lose her beautiful faith in Wainwright. She wanted her to go on admiring him, as she could not admire him perhaps if she knew of his friendship for such a girl as Miss Varrell—if she knew of the kiss that he had given her own daughter!

So Camilla closed her lips on the whole affair and did her best to close her heart and her mind to it also.

She was just congratulating herself that she had put it all behind her and had not thought of it for one whole day, when Marietta Pratt came to her one morning with a page from the society news of the night before.

"Say," she said with a grin, "whatcha putting over on us? Have you got a double or do ya take a plane an' fly down ta Palm Beach week-ends, ur what? Mebbe it's only week-ends, but here ya are as plain as day."

She spread the page across Camilla's desk, and there, occupying the larger portion of the upper half of the sheet, was a full length picture of the golden-haired beauty who had visited her in that office but a short week before! And by her side, tall, easy, grinning his own adorable way, stood Jeffrey Wainwright! They were attired in bathing suits, the lady's white and most abbreviated. Camilla did not need to read the names below, for the eyes of Jeffrey Wainwright looked gaily into hers with his own friendly confidence, and gave her heart a terrible thrust. She knew the girl also, immediately, in spite of the fact that the expression on her face was far from being the same one she had worn the last time she saw her.

The caption below, though Camilla tried not to read it, went deep into her consciousness and undid all the careful control of a week. "Two Who are Often Seen Together on the Beach" it said, "Millionaire's son and Noted Beauty." "Jeffrey Judson Wainwright, son of Robert Wainwright of the famous Wainwright Consolidated Corporation, seen on the beach in America's greatest winter playground, with Stephanie Varrell, former stage star and divorced wife of Harold Varrell of California. Rumor has it that the two are engaged, though there is a famous foreign actor who seems to be second in the running if one may judge by appearances."

Camilla turned sharply away after getting the first line, but Marietta read it aloud, rolling each syllable like a sweet morsel under her tongue, and kept on reading it after Mr. Whitlock entered.

"Look, Mr. Whitlock," she called out familiarly, holding up the picture, nothing daunted by his entrance, "isn't that fer all the world like Camilla Chrystie? I'd swear it was her if I didn't know she'd been here all week."

Mr. Whitlock, with his habitual gravity, looked down at the picture and then cast a quick look at Camilla, seeming to take in her delicacy and loveliness for the first time.

"Why, yes, it does resemble Miss Chrystie," he said, and Camilla saw him glance over the paragraph below the picture. But she took good care to be hard at work when he glanced up at her again. She was glad that he made no further comment.

The day went forward busily like other days and no more was said about the picture, but Camilla was strangely shaken. Somehow she could not put the thought of it away. Here was all her work to be done over again. It seemed she hadn't forgotten the charming stranger at all nor the girl who carried venom under her tongue. She had to be seeing them all day running around in bathing suits together. She had to see that nice straight grin on his fine features, and the possessive cocksure smile in the other girl's eyes as she looked up at him in the picture. How it all made her anger rise, and she felt more than ever her own helplessness. How she began to wish she had never seen either of them! How she loathed herself!

She stayed late in the office that afternoon after the others had gone. Somehow her work had lagged and she had not accomplished all that she knew she ought. It was better now that her employer and Marietta were gone.

She was still working away at her typewriter when Mr. Whitlock returned and unlocked his desk to find some papers he needed. When he had locked it again he lingered and hesitated, looking toward her.

"You needn't finish those letters tonight," he said graciously. "There is no great haste. If they get off by eleven tomorrow they will be in plenty of time."

Camilla looked up surprised at his kindliness. He was a man of few words.

"Thank you," she said with a weary little smile, "I'm on 'the last one. And tomorrow's work will be coming on. I'd rather finish each day in itself whenever possible."

"You're very faithful," he said gravely. "Suppose when you are done we go out and get some dinner together."

Camilla looked up surprised.

"Thank you," she said gratefully, "but I couldn't. My mother hasn't been very well you know, and I don't leave her alone evenings yet if I can help it."

"I see," said the man pleasantly, noticing the delicacy of her features, the golden sheen of her hair where the light over her desk fell full upon it. "You shouldn't of course. Some other time perhaps."

He said no more and Camilla went on with her work.

When she had finished her last letter she closed her desk

for the night, put on her wraps, and paused just an instant beside her employer's desk to say a deferential good night.

He looked up and said good night and suddenly his face broke into a smile. It occurred to her that she had never before seen him smile, except gravely when there were strangers in the office. It made his face most attractive. The smile lighted up his eyes. He had nice eyes. Who was it they made her think of? Someone she liked?

She was puzzling over it as she went out and down the hall, while she stood waiting for the elevator. Nice eyes! And his voice had been kind and friendly! The echo of his good night seemed to follow her and be even yet ringing quietly in the marble hall. And here she had been worrying for a whole week lest she might be going to lose her job! It comforted her that he had gone out of his way to be nice to her, asking her to go out to dinner with him. It made her position more assured in these uncertain times. And of course he was a friend of the Barrons in her home town. It was only decent that he should show her a little friendliness after the letter of introduction Mr. Barron had written for her. Well, he had nice eyes whoever it was that he looked like when he smiled!

Then suddenly she knew. Jeffrey Wainwright! Was she always to be thinking of him every minute? How ridiculous! Mr. Whitlock didn't resemble him in the least of course, and something in her inmost soul resented the idea that she had thought so for a minute. Well, she must be going crazy to have such an obsession about Wainwright. She must snap out of it at once. It was a good thing that he had gone away when he had. A good thing that she was busy and could put him out of her mind!

Then she reverted pleasantly to Mr. Whitlock's invitation and his kindly smile. Well, here at least was something nice she could tell her mother. Mother would appreciate a thing like that and she would never have an idea how fearful she had been all the week lest she might lose her job.

But when she reached home that night she found her mother in quite a flutter over a crate of luscious oranges and grapefruit that had arrived that afternoon with Jeffrey Wainwright's card enclosed, and Camilla was so filled with mingled delight and dismay that she forgot all about Whitlock's invitation. For a few minutes her heart got beyond all bounds and exulted. He hadn't forgotten them after all!

She went about putting away her wraps and then came and looked at the wonderful golden spheres, so much more beautiful than any they could buy in the north, and her eyes shone and her cheeks glowed with more than the glow of the crisp air of the evening through which she had been driving.

"And he sent them to *me*," said her mother shyly smiling. "Wasn't it lovely of him? Did you notice the marking? Though of course they were really meant for you."

"Not a bit of it!" said Camilla with her chin up in a moment. "There was no reason whatever for him to send anything to me. It was just beautiful of him to send them to you. And I certainly am glad he had such good sense. You know you are really the one he admires. He sent his first orchids to you. But how did you get the crate open?"

She watched her mother's eager face as she answered and was glad, glad, even though this was going to upset again all her fine self-discipline of the past week.

"Why, I made the drayman open it for me and gave him ten cents extra. And, Camilla, there were some real live orange blossoms wrapped in wet gray moss stuck down among them. Go look at them. I put some of them on the table. Aren't they wonderful! Smell them. I remember that fragrance. Your father took me down to Florida once when we were first married and we boarded for a whole week across the road from an orange grove. It's such a spicy odor. There is nothing else like it. I can remember how I felt about it. I used to lie in the hammock on the porch and listen to the mocking birds singing and the whispering winds in those great tall pines, and smell those orange blossoms, and think that heaven must be almost like that. It didn't seem as if there could be anything better in this world anyway."

Camilla, to hide the tears that insisted upon stinging into her eyes, bent her tired young head and kissed her mother.

"You're a dear poet!" she said breathlessly. "Yes the fragrance is wonderful indeed. Some day when I get rich I'll take you down there again, and we'll spend a whole winter smelling them. Now, I must wash my hands and face. They are just filthy!" and she slipped away to the bathroom to stop those tired tears, and get some color into her face before her mother should have leisure to inspect her.

"He meant them for you, of course," said her mother as they sat down to the table where the nice little supper was set out so invitingly.

"Oh, no!" said Camilla quickly. "Mother you must get that idea completely out of your head. Please, Mother, that young man has no more idea of doing anything for me than the president of these United States has. You don't realize who he is. I've been seeing his name in the papers. Mother, he's the son of the head of that great Wainwright corporation that we hear so much about. He's rich as Croesus and is only tossing some golden guilders to a little beggar girl whom he picked up by the way when she was in trouble. It was nice of him to remember you. He must be unusual to remember even a dear sick lady like my precious mother, even a lady who resembles a very costly cameo. Mother, don't get notions in your head. He's just being *nice*, and I'll say that was *very* nice. And nicer still that he sent them to you instead of to me, for now I won't be put to the trouble of writing him a letter of thanks. *You'll* have to do it, and I'm *glad!*"

"Well," said the mother eagerly, "I'll do it! Of course I'll do it. I'll love to do it! I think he's wonderful and I'll tell him so. He may be rich and he may be playing, but he doesn't forget kindnesses and that's a great thing in this busy world."

"Oh, yes," said Camilla with worldly wisdom, as if she were the elder, "only Mother dear, don't get notions about him, for you'll only have to get over them if you do. We likely shan't see him again. He doesn't belong to our world."

Her mother gave her a quick keen look.

"It is all God's world, Camilla," said her mother softly.

"Yes, but we're not all God's children," said Camilla, almost wearily, "only in the sense that God made us. You taught me that yourself, Mother. You said we were not God's children till we were born again."

"How do you know he is not born again, child?" said the mother after a thoughtful pause.

"I'm sure he's not," said Camilla with a deep breath. Oh, must she be probed this way forever? "That is I'm pretty sure," she added, "He didn't speak the shibboleth."

"We can pray for him," said the mother softly.

"Yes, we can pray," sighed the girl, as if just now she had very little faith to pray for a man like that, "but—we aren't in his class. But, anyhow, these oranges are great, aren't they? And wouldn't it be nice to send half a dozen to Miss York?"

"Send her a dozen," said the mother eagerly, and forgot to probe farther.

And then Miss York herself came walking in.

"Just for a glimpse of you two," she said wistfully. "Somehow you seem more like home folks than anybody I've met since Mother died."

They had a nice cheery little talk, and a good laugh over some of the funny things that happened in the new household where Miss York was nursing, and Camilla forgot her troubles for the time, until they were at work packing the basket of fruit for the nurse to take with her.

"Put a spray of orange blossoms in," called the mother from the other room.

"No, no, don't waste orange blossoms on me!" said Nurse York stooping over to smell them. "I'm out of the running for orange blossoms at my age. All omens have failed on me. Keep them all for Camilla. They belong to her. I always said it wasn't but a step from orchids to orange blossoms, and it looks as if it had proved right again."

Then suddenly weary Camilla flushed crimson.

"Don't! Please!" she said sharply and hurried out to the kitchen to get a few more oranges, and hide her tortured face.

She was back again in a minute though trying to laugh it off.

"You're all wrong," she explained with an elaborate smile on her face. "The orange blossoms and the oranges were sent to Mother, not me, and perhaps you'll recall that the most of the orchids were Mother's."

"Oh, yeah?" said Miss York with a very good imitation of a small boy with his tongue in his cheek.

"Well, you can laugh," said Camilla seriously, "but really you are all wrong and you'll just have to put aside all your silly romantic notions for I have it on very good authority that the young man you are talking about is as good as engaged to another girl."

Camilla brought out the words clearly as if she were reading a lesson to her own soul. Her mother eyed her keenly, but Miss York only said, "Is that so!" mockingly, as though she had inside information and were enjoying her own thoughts.

Camilla went and got her purse and paid the nurse her monthly stipend that had been agreed upon between them. She did it with satisfaction. Come what would her debts were that much smaller anyway.

Camilla did not expect to sleep much that night. She had intended to take out her troubles when her mother was asleep and look them over carefully and pray about them, but when morning came she found that instead she had fallen asleep almost the minute her head touched the pillow, and with only the briefest kind of a prayer though she was so much in need of one.

CHAPTER XI

Mr. Whitlock was in the office when Camilla got there the next morning. He looked up with his pleasant new smile of greeting and Camilla went happily to her desk and began to get ready for the day's work.

Suddenly her employer spoke in a pleasant friendly tone:

"How about going to lunch with me this noon, Miss Chrystie?" he asked. "There's a matter about the office that I would like to talk over with you. Some changes that I'm thinking of making to which I would like to get your reaction. I thought we might find a quiet place where we could talk it over while we eat?"

His manner was gravely quiet, though there was still that friendly light in his eyes and Camilla could not help feeling pleased, although she had no special desire to go out to lunch with Mr. Whitlock. Still, this was more or less a matter of her job she supposed and of course she would go. She probably ought to be pleased that he thought it worth while to consult her about the office. At least it would keep her thoughts from other things.

"Thank you," she said, "I shall be glad to go."

It suddenly occurred to her that this would be something more she could tell her mother, and that she had been so full of interest in the oranges that she had forgotten last night to say anything of the day's happenings.

"Very well," said Whitlock, "I'll arrange to be here at the office for you at one o'clock."

And just then Marietta came in.

Whitlock sat still at his desk writing for several minutes more, while Marietta was taking off her wraps in a leisurely way. Her scare was a thing of the past and she had fully recovered her spirits. The door of the cloak room was open wide and she was watching Mr. Whitlock, wondering if he were in a good mood, and if she dared to ask for the afternoon off so she could take Ted to the movies.

But just as she was about to come out to her desk she saw Mr. Whitlock rise with an envelope in his hand and step over to her desk. He laid it down beside her machine, and immediately took his hat and coat and went out of the room.

With a dart of sudden fear in her eyes she went out and snatched up the envelope which she saw was addressed to herself. She tore it open frantically, and read with growing horror in her face.

Camilla was writing away at top speed, trying to get a lot done before she went out to lunch, in case she should be detained beyond her usual time. She didn't want to have to stay late again that night for she knew her mother would be uneasy having her late two nights in succession. But there was something so weird and heartbroken in the sound that Marietta gave forth that Camilla had to turn around and see what was the matter.

There stood Marietta with the letter in her hand, consternation in her homely stubby young face, and a check lying at her feet.

"I'm fired!" she cried in a tone something between a wail and a squeak. "I'm *fired!* And I promised last night to take Ted to the circus! And now I can't even pay for my fur coat!"

Camilla couldn't help but smile over the order in which

her woes had culminated in her primitive mind, the circus and the moment would always come before other considerations with Marietta.

"I'm fired! Can you beat it?" asserted Marietta, as if it were something almost beyond her comprehension.

"Oh, Marietta!" cried Camilla sympathetically, "not *really?*" and suddenly Camilla took in the full possibilities which might involve herself also. Her heart began to sink. And here she had been pluming herself over the fact that she was invited out to lunch with her employer to be consulted about office affairs, and was therefore immune to this danger! How did she know but this would be his polite way of breaking the news to her, a little less abrupt than the method he had used with Marietta because she had been introduced by an old friend and was from the home town? That was probably it! He was taking her out and explaining to her why he had to make changes in his office force! Consternation spread over her face also, but she managed a tender look of commiseration for Marietta.

"Oh, Marietta, I'm so sorry!" she said as she saw the big tears begin to rain down the poor girl's face.

"You aren't fired too, are ya?" Marietta paused in her grief to enquire sobbingly, " 'Cause if you are I'm gonta tell him what I think of him. You aren't, are ya?"

"Not yet," said Camilla bravely trying to manage a wan smile, "but I'll probably come next. But anyway, I'll do all I can to help you get another job, whether I'm dismissed or not."

"Say—you're—all—r-r-right!" sobbed Marietta. "I'll—always—re-member—you—saying that! But—maybe you won't get fired. Mebbe he means ta make you do all your work and mine too!" she blubbered noisily. "He's mebbe cutting down on expenses like everybody else, an' he's keeping you 'cause you're the most ef-f-f-ficient! Oh, I know you are!—I—never was m-m-much—g-g-good!"

"Don't talk that way, Marietta. I'm sure if you would just put your mind to it you could be as efficient as anybody."

"Oh, I know," said Marietta hopelessly, "that's what they told me the last place I worked. But some days I just *can't!* Life is so awful dull, just working! I havta have some excitement! I can't help thinkin' of other things besides just work. If I didn't I'd *die!* I haven't got dates and fellas like other girls! I'm not good looking like you are. Nobody cares a hang about me!"

"Oh, don't say that, Marietta!" cried Camilla pitifully. "I'm sure little Ted is fond of you."

"Oh, yes, poor kid!" said Marietta hopelessly, "but what's he? And he wouldn't care a hang either if he had another soul in the world to turn to. He wouldn't look at me if his good-looking mother paid any attention to him!"

"Oh yes, he would," consoled Camilla, "children aren't like that, they respond with love when love comes to them, I'm sure, and you've given him love. He must love you."

"Oh, well, he's the only one anyhow. There isn't another soul in the wide world cares about me."

"Yes," said Camilla softly, thoughtfully, "there is another One who cares a great deal! He cares so much that He came down here to die for you. He loves you more than even an own mother could love!"

Marietta stared at her.

"Whaddya mean?" she asked getting out her handkerchief to mop up her face.

"I mean the Lord Jesus Christ. Marietta, He really loves you and takes account of every single thing in your life."

Marietta's expression was incredulity, and a deep gloom settled down over her homely face.

"Then what does He let me lose my job for, if He loves me so much? Why did He let that happen," she asked belligerently. "Naw, you can't make me believe that bunk! Look at all the rotten times I've had. If He cares why would He let all that come to me?"

"Perhaps to make you listen to Him," said Camilla thoughtfully.

Marietta turned to her fellow worker her swollen tear-stained face on which the cheap make-up was badly streaked, and stared.

"Listen to Him? What in time can you mean?"

Camilla spoke eagerly.

"You know God speaks to every one of us. He wants to make us hear His voice, and sometimes when everything is going beautifully and we're having a good time, we just won't listen. We never even think of Him! I think very likely that is often why He has to take everything away from us for awhile, so we can hear His voice in our hearts."

Marietta looked at her in bewilderment.

"But what would He want of us?"

"He wants us to love Him! He wants our companionship and love!"

Marietta shook her head.

"Not me!" she said decidedly. "He wouldn't want me! Nobody wants me. I'm not good-looking, and I'm not good. I'm a devil, I tell ya, a little devil! Why, Camilla Chrystie, I'm a *sinner!*"

"Yes," said Camilla sweetly, "but we're all that, and Jesus said He came not to call the righteous but sinners to repentance."

"Aw! Sinner nothing. Everybody ain't the same kind of a sinner. You don't know what I mean by sin! Why I've lied, and I've stolen—I stole some money off my stepmother once ta get a box of candy fer little Ted when she had slapped him! And I've hated! I've hated her so hard I could have killed her ef I'd had a chance, yes and been glad of it! Oh, you don't know what a sinner I've been! He wouldn't want me except ta punish me, and I 'spose that's what He's doing now."

"But you don't understand, Marietta, single sins don't make us sinners, they only *prove* we're sinners. We sin *because* we're sinners. There is only one sin anyway that can keep you from God and that is unbelief, refusing God's Son as your Saviour."

Marietta was silent, almost thoughtful for a long minute, staring at Camilla.

"I'd believe all righty ef He'd just give me back my job!"

Camilla shook her head.

"We can't make conditions with God. We've got to take His conditions. He says belief must come first, belief accepts salvation. Why, if you know somebody loves you you're not afraid to trust them to do their best for you. And God's best for you may be a great deal better than anything you have dreamed of for yourself."

Marietta looked uncertainly at Camilla and slowly sat down in her chair, staring off into space sorrowfully.

"I can't see it," she said shaking her head hopelessly.

"You don't have to see it," said Camilla. "You just have to trust Him and let Him prove it to you."

Camilla leaned over and picked up the check from the floor, laying it in Marietta's lap. Marietta looked down at it with a long quivering sigh.

"He's paid me for the whole month," she said sadly, fingering the check. "I 'spose that's the last money I'll get the feel of for many a day! He says I can leave tamorra morning ef I want! But Gosh! What'll I do?"

Bang went her head down on her typewriter again and she began to cry afresh.

Camilla went over and patted her rough crimped head gently. She felt very pitiful toward her. She almost forgot that she herself might be presently in the same predicament.

"Come, dear," she said suddenly stooping over and smoothing Marietta's stiff locks away from her hot forehead, "let's get back to work. This won't make things any better. We've got to finish up this day's work honorably whatever comes!"

"Not me!" said Marietta looking up with flashing eyes. "I'll not do another stroke for the old snake!"

"Oh, yes, you will, Marietta. You'd only be justifying his dismissal if you do that. Come, let's get to work and see which will finish first."

Suddenly Camilla followed an impulse and stooping over kissed Marietta's hot forehead gently.

Marietta started back.

"What did you do that for," she asked fixing Camilla with her dark hunted eyes.

"Why, I guess because I loved you and felt sorry for you," said Camilla with sudden surprise at herself.

"You couldn't!" said Marietta. "That's impossible for you to love me! Why should you love me?"

"Why, I guess it's because you are dear to my Lord Jesus," said Camilla, taking knowledge of her heart and realizing that she was speaking the truth. This unattractive girl had suddenly become surprisingly dear to her. "Whatever is dear to my Lord is dear to me!"

Marietta considered that a moment, then she said, speaking slowly, with a kind of awe in her voice:

"Well, if you really mean that, and you want me to, then

I guess I've gotta do what you said. But I don't know's I know how ta do it."

"You just tell Him so!" said Camilla with a sudden joy in her heart that drove out all her fears and perplexities and put her in touch with another world.

"You mean pray?" asked Marietta embarrassedly. "Right here? Now?"

Camilla nodded.

Down went Marietta's head on her machine again, and there was silence. Then in a moment more she lifted her face with a kind of shamed look on it, and yet a deep relief.

"I did!" she said almost sheepishly, as if she were playing a child's game.

"Good!" said Camilla, "and I prayed too! Now, let's get to work and make up for lost time!"

For a couple of hours the two machines clattered away without interruption, and Camilla knew by the sound that Marietta was really doing her best. Then suddenly they heard Mr. Whitlock's steps coming down the hall, and for an instant both girls held their breath and fell to trembling. Then Camilla realized that her strength was in her Lord and she must go on working. He would take care of whatever was to come.

But Mr. Whitlock gave no sign that he had noticed them. He took his mail and read it, and then called Camilla to take dictation.

Camilla was glad to notice that Marietta did not stop for even the lifting of an eyelash, but went steadily on with her work. She gave her a furtive glance once while Mr. Whitlock was looking in his drawer for a paper he wanted enclosed in a certain letter, and saw that Marietta's eyes were still red and her face badly streaked with make-up that had been much smeared during her weeping, but she was evidently set to do her best for that one morning at least.

It was exactly twelve o'clock when Mr. Whitlock finished dictation, closed his desk and said briskly:

"That will be all this morning, Miss Chrystie!"

Then he swung his chair about toward Marietta's corner.

"You might go to lunch now, Miss Pratt," he said in his usual curt office voice, "Miss Chrystie will have some copy ready for you by the time you return. I'd like you to do one hundred individual copies using the addresses in this list. Miss Chrystie will go to lunch as soon as she has the copy ready for you, and if she hasn't returned when you get here you'll find full directions on your desk. I want this work done, finished, by four o'clock sharp!"

"Yessir!" said Marietta meekly, casting a frightened glance at Camilla. She got her hat and coat and hurried out. Camilla wondered if perhaps she would not bother to return?

Whitlock gathered up some papers and went out without any further word, and Camilla wondered if he had already forgotten about taking her to lunch? However, it was only twelve. But his brusque manner to Marietta made her uneasy.

She snapped a new sheet of paper into her machine and went on with her work, trying to keep her mind from worrying about the coming interview. Praying for strength to bear whatever it should be. Praying too for poor ignorant Marietta.

She had scarcely finished the copy for Marietta when the door swung open and Mr. Whitlock entered, gave a quick glance about the room, then came over to her desk and there was that friendly smile again, that disturbing smile that seemed more intimate with her than he really was. That smile that reminded her of another man who didn't resemble him in the least, and yet who could smile deep down into her soul. Oh, was she always to be tormented by this vision, and just because of an unfortunate kiss? She must somehow manage to get rid of this obsession and see nothing but Mr. Whitlock in that smile, and not another's eyes smiling through his. Besides, this was business, and might prove pretty important business at that. She must put her mind upon it. Perhaps it would mean promotion, a larger salary, if she conducted this interview wisely, or it might mean losing her job if she did not. She was pretty well convinced however that it meant the latter.

"Are you ready?" he asked in his friendly tone, so different from the one he had used all the morning that Camilla smiled in relief.

"Yes, just a moment till I arrange these papers for Marietta," she answered.

He held the door open for her deferentially, and again she was struck with a memory of Wainwright. Were all cultured men alike in the way they attended a lady, the way they held open a door? That was it of course. She was remembering how Wainwright had done everything. Till Wainwright came it had been so long since she had been attended anywhere by a gentleman that she had forgotten the feel of it and now she was just remembering how nice it was to be taken care of. That was all. It wasn't Wainwright she was remembering, it was culture, and good times, and all that belonged to just ordinary social intercourse. She had been too much apart from people, too much filled with her own problems, and now just this little bit of social life, going out to lunch with her employer for a business talk to save time, was getting entirely out of perspective. Well, she must snap out of this. She might be going out to get her dismissal of course, and if so she must have her wits about her and take it with her head up.

CHAPTER XII

Jeffrey Wainwright was writing a letter.

The room where he sat looked out on a sunlit sea, and the breeze that came in the window and wafted the delicate curtains was laden with the mingled perfume of many flowers. On a tray at his hand a cooling drink frostily invited him, and a great dish of tropical fruit stood on a table not far away.

Down below beyond the terraces of the hotel there were fountains playing and tall palm trees waved their graceful fingers above tesselated walks and tiled pools. Off in the distance one could see the bathing beach already dotted with eager bathers, some lying like porpoises well browned in the gleaming sand. Farther on were the tennis courts where a couple of world-renowned champions were to play a match game that afternoon, and farther inland some of the best of fairways awaited his attention. Cars shot here and there on the hard smooth roads, gay voices called to one another, bright garments attracted the eye, birds sang unearthly sweet carols, slow gulls floated lazily over a summer sea, hovered and floated again, little ships like toys lay in the harbor, or floated afar on the blue,—whether sea or sky who could say?—and gay youth awaited and grew impatient, yet Jeffrey Wainwright sat in his room writing a letter to Camilla, Camilla who was driving away on her typewriter at mad speed trying to forget him and suffering as only a girl can suffer who sees all the things she wants one by one drifting away from her.

A liveried servant with a silver tray tapped at the door and delivered a note and a telegram, and waited deferentially for the young man to read them. He tore open the telegram, read the message, "Can't possibly get down there this month. You'll have to carry on a little longer. Dad." Then he took up the note, glanced at its unintelligible scrawled summons. He knew it was a summons without reading its particular form, and threw it carelessly down on the table.

"That's all right, Tyler," he said to the waiting servant. "No answer."

"Excuse me, Mister Wainwright," said the boy, "Miss Varrell said I was not to come down without an answer."

"All right, Tyler," he said with a frown, "then tell her I can't come at present. Tell her not to wait for me. Tell her to go on without me."

The servant left and Wainwright went back to his letter. "Dear Camilla," he wrote, and paused to look distantly at the sea and conjure up the vision of Camilla. And every time he almost got the sight of her off there against the blue, she turned into Stephanie, with her jacinth eyes, imperious smile, and red, red lips. Camilla's eyes were deep, deep brown, and her lips were touched with rose as they should be, not painted vivid fleshly red like a bleeding gash. Yet every time he tried to think the vision through and get a flash of Camilla herself, Stephanie came jarring through. It was like trying to sing a sweet new tune that yet had some notes of an old outworn one that would keep coming in and making discord. Why could he not see her face? It was almost as if Camilla were only a figment of his imagination. Yet she had haunted his thoughts until he sat down to write to her, and now she would not seem real to him.

"Dear Camilla," he looked at the words and poised his pen. There were things in his heart that he knew he must not write. Things that were not yet in words, nor even consciously in thoughts, but yet he had to write to her.

He wanted to write and let her know that there was a good reason why he did not come to her, but very likely she had not noticed that he had not. He had no reason to think she would care one way or the other. No reason except that there was something between them, an unspoken something that passed in that kiss he had given her. When he thought of it he had to close his eyes, it seemed so holy to him. It seemed to mark a time in his life, an epoch that could never be forgotten, a something like a pledge from him to her, and yet he did not exactly know what that pledge was, only that it was a pledge and he meant to keep it.

If he closed his eyes from looking at the sea to see her lovely face and her golden hair against the blue, he could feel again the thrill of that kiss, like no kiss he had ever given or received before. It made all other kisses seem common and unclean. This was something quite holy and apart. It was not only a pledge, a tie, between him and the girl to whom he had given it, but it went deeper, it pledged something far beyond, something spiritual that he could not understand. It was as if a door had opened when his lips touched hers, and he had seen into a far and lovely place where things were not all as they were in the rest of this gay sordid earth. Where everything had meaning, and life was a greater thing than most men saw, it reached deeper and farther and had no end.

He understood that there were things for him to learn, though he did not know what they were. They were vaguely associated with words that she had spoken, though he could not always remember the phrases she had used. He only knew there was something she had which he must have.

All that was most vague and sometimes greatly disturbing because he did not know what to do about it. Obviously it was his part to find out, but how? Yet he had to let her know that he had not forgotten.

And sometimes he wondered if the girl understood all this. If that kiss and pledge had meant as much to her as to himself? Or had she long ago forgotten even as other girls forgot? No, she was not like that. She did not have jacinth eyes. He was glad that her eyes were brown and deeply true, and sometime he would have a chance to tell her all about this that was in his soul which he could not express in words. But now, he must write her, nevertheless.

She had said she was not of his world. So much he remembered and it had stricken him with its possibilities. Very well, there was a story like that in mythology. A maiden of the sea and a man who was of the earth? Or was it the other way around? He could not remember. They had somehow come together because they really belonged together, wasn't that it? Had the man plunged into the sea? Or the maiden? Somehow they had found each other. It had meant the death of one to his own environment, but he had gained infinitely! Well, then he would somehow become a part of her world. He would find a way. What was that she had said that night before they were interrupted,—a strange phrase,—be "born again"? Was that it? How would one be born again?

And so he lingered looking at the sea, and holding his pen over the paper, and asking age-old questions of himself that he could not answer any more than the rich young ruler of old who found the price too great.

Yet one thing worked out of that long hour of thought, perhaps deeper thought than he had ever given to any one subject before, and that was that he must find this thing whatever it was that would make him of her world; and not alone for her sake, but for something even deeper, some hitherto unsuspected longing in his own breast that demanded it of him and would not otherwise be satisfied.

Out of the chaos of that lovely hour, and that bright illusive head against the sea with deep sweet eyes, he drew this one clear thought. This thing he sought was not being sought for her, not even for love of her, though he knew he loved her, but was being sought for its own sake, because she had made him see that it was the only thing in the universe worth while. It was better than herself. It was enough in itself even without her, and it was not to be sought just for her sake but for its own sake and for his sake.

When he came to that point, where he was sure of his own heart about that, his pen was free and he could write.

It was only a little commonplace letter that he felt he

had any right to write, but the words came quick and hot from his pen, and his face lighted with a new kind of joy.

"Dear Camilla,

"You can't think how annoyed I am that things have shaped themselves so that I cannot come home and see you. There are questions I must ask you, and things that I would understand, and I cannot find their answer anywhere down here, but I am not free to leave yet, for Dad can't come. And now Mother has taken a notion that I must go on a camping spree with my kid brother, down in the Everglades. The scout-master is a stranger to us, and she can't feel safe unless I go along. It's fishing and hunting and a little exploring perhaps, with a few Indians thrown in, just the thing a kid brother is crazy about, so I've promised to go for a day or two and see that it's all right. Then as soon as I can get away I'm coming north again and I want to see you as soon as I can. I want to understand what you were saying when we parted. Perhaps you'll remember what I mean. Please don't forget.

Your friend,

Jeff."

Jeffrey was humming a gay little tune when he came down in the elevator with his letter. To the girl with the jacinth eyes and the red-gold hair who sat in the opposite reception room with an open unread book in her lap and watched the elevators all the afternoon as a cat might watch for a mouse, he looked most disconcertingly handsome in his white flannels and that strange light in his eyes that so set him apart from other young men—from her! She could not understand that light in his eyes. He did not use to have it. It was a new development and she wanted to find its source.

She saw the letter in his hand, watched his jealously as he went over to the desk and dropped it in the mail box. Then he walked out to the terrace and stood surveying the beach from afar.

But she did not go out to him at once. Instead she stole to a window where she could watch him from behind a curtain, and waited until he turned his footsteps down toward the beach. Then, watching her opportunity, she went over to the desk and dropped a letter into the mail slot in the counter, and slowly, casually walked away. The letter was only an advertisement of a frock shop and had been opened. Suddenly she stopped, opened her book and looked hastily through its leaves, then turned back to the desk.

"Oh, Billy," she said sweetly addressing the clerk behind the desk in her husky drawling tone, "I've made a mistake and dropped an opened letter into the box along with another. Get the box out for me, that's a dear, and let me find it?"

Billy came all smiles to do her bidding. She had known he would. When she spoke in that tone with that kind of a smile all male population everywhere came running.

Billy reached under the counter and pulled out the mail box that stood on a shelf under the counter, setting it up on the top for her inspection.

"It must be right on top," she said peering in speculatively, and sighting Jeffrey Wainwright's handwriting at once just below her own letter.

"There it is!" she caroled, and reached in her hand.

Just then a gruff old gentleman came up and demanded his key.

Billy turned alertly to take it from its hook, and Stephanie skillfully slid her own letter over Jeff's and picked both up at once, holding them firmly together so that they looked like one. She hadn't hoped for such a break as this. She had merely hoped to be able to see to whom that letter was addressed.

"Thanks awfully, Billy. You've saved me a lot of embarrassment," she said with a twinkle, as the good-natured clerk turned back and slid the mail box down into its niche again.

Then slowly, innocently, Stephanie walked away from the desk, laying the letters carefully in her book as she rang for the elevator, and arose to her room with the stolen letter safe in her possession.

Half an hour afterward she appeared on the beach in a becoming bathing suit, and with narrowed eyes called a gay greeting to Jeff as he strolled by, still trying to conjure brown eyes and gold hair against a summer sea.

But the letter that had taken so long to write lay in little flecks of ashes in a jeweled ash tray, and the beautiful young vixen with jacinth eyes sat far into the night watching the curl of those ashes and gloating over them and over the girl who would wait forever for a letter that would not come.

But the jacinth eyes were smoldering with thought, and were not satisfied. There was something behind all this. A casual letter like that and yet something had somehow changed him. She was not sure she wanted him herself exclusively, at least she was not sure she wanted to be his exclusively, but she did not want another girl to have him. What had those two been talking about when he left her? That was what she had to find out. That was what she would find out one day. Without that secret she was powerless to conquer him.

In the early dawn of the tropical morning just as the sun was beginning to tinge the sea with celestial asphodel colors and cause the world to resemble the Holy City let down out of heaven from God, Jeff stole forth from his room clad in a hunting outfit.

He went down to join his kid brother and the campers at a little rendezvous beside the sea beyond the confines of the world where Stephanie Varrell moved. So he disappeared from the life of the great playground, into a queer new playground of his own, seeking something whose name he did not know, and conjuring with the thought of a kiss, and a bright head with eyes of brown.

CHAPTER XIII

CAMILLA WENT OUT OF THE OFFICE AND DOWN THE MARBLE hall in company with her employer, a sudden constriction in her heart. What might not the next hour bring forth? But there was just one thing of which she was resolved. If there was a chance at all she would put in a good word for poor Marietta. She would take her own medicine as well as she could. But she would tell her employer just what a proposition Marietta was up against. If he had a heart at all she would touch it. Perhaps the story of little crippled Ted would reach him. Of course, she knew that Marietta was by no means a model stenographer, but perhaps she would do better if he would take her back and give her another trial. At least she would put in a word for her if it seemed at all practical.

Whitlock put her in his luxurious car and threaded his way gravely through traffic, out to one of the older parts of town where quiet culture still reigned for three or four ancient blocks, and vague quaint footprints of aristocracy were visible in massive stone walls, the flute of a column, the grill of a gate, or a balcony.

Camilla looked about her in surprise. She did not know where she was. She lifted a quick questioning glance to her escort's face.

He was smiling down at her, almost as if she were something he had found and captured, a butterfly or a strange bird, out of the sunshine.

"I'm taking you to a quaint old place that I love," he said in answer to her questioning look. "I felt you would appreciate it. Have you ever been here before?"

"No," she said wonderingly, "where is this?"

"Hampden Row," he answered, pleased at her interest, "and this is the old Warrington Inn. This is where the élite of fifty years ago used to come for their dignified social life. It happens that business in its ebb and flow has left these four blocks here high and dry, just as they used to be. A queer twist of circumstances has kept the march of progress from touching a finger to these fine old buildings. Fortunes have been offered for the land they are built upon, but the unusual phrasing of a will has so far prevented the original estate from being divided, and the absence of an heir, whose heirs in turn cannot be traced, protects them. Meantime, those who are in the secret can enjoy the quaint old-time place and its ways. I thought you might be one of those who could appreciate this."

Camilla was intrigued at once. She had forgot for the time being her troubles and perplexities and gave attention to this quiet oasis in the midst of the whirl and noise of the city traffic.

They entered the old Warrington Inn with its mellowed

oak beams and its great stone fireplace, its quaint interiors and vistas, its spacious air of the dignity of other days, and immediately Camilla felt a quiet peace descend upon her.

"Oh," she said softly to her escort, "how my mother would love this!"

"We'll bring her here sometime!" said Whitlock instantly. "I would enjoy bringing her here!"

"Oh, you must excuse me!" said Camilla with flaming cheeks, "I didn't realize what I was saying. I didn't mean to hint!"

"Of course you didn't!" Whitlock's eyes were wearing that pleasant smile and he looked down into her troubled brown eyes. "I really mean it. I would love to bring her here. How soon will she be able to come?"

"Oh, I don't know," evaded Camilla, "several weeks I'm sure. She hasn't been out yet. You are very kind, but you mustn't trouble yourself. I can bring her around to see it sometime in the spring when she is able to go out. I have my little car you know. And Mother would be terribly distressed at my going around hinting things. I really didn't realize. I was just talking to myself."

"Don't worry!" he laughed. "I'm glad you did. It rather lets me into the group doesn't it? I must do myself the honor of calling upon your mother!"

Camilla looked distressed and rather dismayed.

"I'm afraid you won't feel it much honor," she said, frankly embarrassed, "not when you see the little old grubby house where we live."

"I am quite sure the house is being greatly honored by the people who are condescending to live in it," he said gracefully, and Camilla looked up to see a different Mr. Whitlock from any she had known before. The stiffness and dignity, the brusque manner and sharp glance were gone, and in their place were all the graces of a courteous genial gentleman. Not that he had been discourteous before, but this was a new kind of courtesy. Social courtesy.

He saw to the ordering in the easiest way, suggesting unusual dishes that were in order when the inn was built, delectable old-fashioned things. And then he began to tell the history of the inn, of famous occurrences in its time, of noted men and women who had been its frequenters, incidents, brief stories of this one and that, until Camilla could see them seated at the various tables in their queer old-fashioned garb, and as she ate her delicious meal she felt as if she were in a fairy story. Mr. Whitlock was certainly a fascinating conversationalist. But why was he wasting it all on her, just his secretary?

Suddenly she came to herself and glanced furtively at her watch.

"Oh!" she exclaimed, "Mr. Whitlock! Do you know what time it is? My lunch hour was over long ago!"

"I have been boring you!" he said quickly. "I'm sorry!"

"Oh, no, you haven't bored me at all," said Camilla eagerly. "It was delightful! You made me entirely forget that I am an employee, not a guest, and that we came here to talk business. And you haven't said a word about the business."

His eyes studied her and she could see that he was pleased that she had enjoyed herself.

"But you're not an employee. You're my guest today. And as for the business, that can wait. I was only going to ask you what you thought about Marietta? Is she hopeless or do you think she could be trained? Consider your answer with deliberation, for if she has to be trained the training will largely fall upon you I'm afraid."

"*I* train her? Oh, I wouldn't know how!" said Camilla, "and I don't believe she'd take it from me."

"She would if I told her to," said the man watching the play of lights on the girl's face. "You see it's this way. I've had the offer of a Miss Townsend from the Fortescu office. She's already trained and quite efficient I understand, but— well, I don't like the style of bob she wears for her age."

Camilla couldn't help laughing, and enjoyed the answering twinkle in her employer's eyes. Then she grew more serious. This then was what all this pleasant nooning had meant, he had brought her here to put it up to her whether he should dismiss herself and Marietta and put Miss Townsend in their place. For of course Miss Townsend was an old hand and would be more efficient than both of them put together. Mr. Whitlock had taken this way to soften the dismissal. Her heart sank deep and missed a beat or two, but she tried to summon her courage and self-respect. If she was to pass out of the office this way by all means let it be done bravely!

"You mean," she said trying to steady her voice and look the man coolly in the eye, "that you would take Miss

Townsend in our place? I should think that there was no
question about what would be best *for you*. Miss Townsend
is most efficient, and would certainly be worth both of us
put together."

"Where do you get that 'our place'? You surely don't
think I'm going to let anyone take *your* place, do you?" He
gave her a deep pleasant look as if they had been close
friends a long time, and Camilla's tired heart gave a leap of
relief. Then he didn't mean to dismiss her after all. The
relief was so great that it almost hurt.

But after the pain was gone there was a perplexity in the
back of her mind. A little bewilderment over that look he
had given her, as if perhaps he were looking to her for
more than she realized. But the thought did not come out
in the open in so many words. It simply remained there, a
little uncomfortable impression. Yet when she tried to
analyze it she laughed at herself. Truly she was making
mountains out of mole hills. There could have been nothing but a belated interest in his eyes. His conscience had
probably troubled him that he had not more definitely
looked after her before this, a friend of friends from his
home town, and now he was trying to show her that he
had a real personal interest in her. That was the way with
busy people, they didn't quite realize what impression they
were giving out by their manner and expression. Well, she
was glad and relieved that she was not going to have to hunt
another job in such hard times! But what she said was:

"You're very kind, Mr. Whitlock, and of course that
relieves me a lot. It wouldn't be easy for me to lose my job
just now when Mother has been so ill and there have been
so many extra expenses. Still, I wouldn't want you to feel
that you had to keep me if you could get somebody that
would do your work better. And of course I know it
would easily be possible. I haven't had long experience as
Miss Townsend has."

"Well, I don't want anybody better than you are at
present, so you can forget that," he smiled graciously,
watching the play of expression on Camilla's speaking face.
If she had only known it he was wondering how it was that
he had never noticed before how lovely she was. "But I
was thinking about Marietta. Do you think you could do
anything with her, or shall we let her go? In fact I
practically dismissed her this morning, told her she could

go tomorrow morning if she wanted to hunt another job. Then I began to think it might be better to consult you."

There was something delicately flattering in his tone, but Camilla was thinking of the woebegone Marietta who had been weeping all over her make-up that morning, and it came to her that perhaps after all there might be a way to help her.

"She's having a hard time," said Camilla speculatively, "did you know about her home life?"

"Mercy, no! I don't know a thing about her except that she's the worst I ever tried. She seems to me a mess. I don't know why I question keeping her at all except that I thought I would consult your wishes before I made any definite changes."

"You are very considerate," said Camilla gratefully, "but I think it should be what you need, not what I want. However, personally I'd be very glad if you could see your way clear to keep Marietta. I feel dreadfully sorry for her. She's never had half a chance, if what she tells me is true. She has a flighty young stepmother who hates her, and a little crippled stepbrother whom she adores, and apparently she's the only one who cares for him. I don't know whether I could do anything to help her or not, but I'd be glad to try if you think she wouldn't resent it. I certainly think it is going to be terribly hard for her if she loses her job now."

"You don't say!" said Whitlock thoughtfully. "I never thought of her as having any background at all. Of course I'm not running a philanthropic organization, but if you are willing to give her a few hints I might give her another try. I'll have a talk with her when I go back. But one of the worst things about her is her appearance. I suppose perhaps she can't help that, but she's so untidy, and she chews gum continually, and she tries to be so familiar, even when there are people in the office. It's her idea of being chummy I suppose, but it doesn't make for a good office appearance."

"I see what you mean," said Camilla thoughtfully, not noticing his glances of admiration, "I'll be glad to try at least. I'm sorry for her."

"Well," said Whitlock, "I'll give her a chance of course if you say so. Now, I suppose we ought to go back. I have an appointment with a representative of that Brooklyn firm in half an hour. This has been a real rest to get away from business."

"It's been delightful," said Camilla rousing to her duty. "I've enjoyed the place and the lunch and I've very much enjoyed your conversation. It has peopled this wonderful room with characters, and made me forget all my perplexities."

"I'm sorry you have perplexities," said the man in such a gentle tone that she looked up surprised, and then summoned a proud little smile.

"Oh, they're not as great as they might be," she said lightly, "in fact when I think of Marietta's life I feel I ought not to call them perplexities. It's awfully fine of you to be willing to try her again. I'll do my very best to make her a success."

All the way back to the office Whitlock was his genial pleasant self, nothing of the employer about him, but when he swung open the office door his reserved manner returned upon him.

They heard poor Marietta's typewriter clicking away as they approached the room, and she sat there stolidly working as they stood for the instant in the doorway. Then she looked up with a start, not having heard them coming, and her face was wet with tears. She certainly was not a prepossessing figure as she sat there plodding away at her work, a goodly pile of finished letters lying on the desk beside her. Her face was still streaked with make-up and her hair was uncrimped and sticking out grotesquely about her head. Camilla's heart sank for her as she noted how little like the model secretary she looked.

Whitlock stood there a moment considering her, then he hung up his hat and coat and sat down at his desk watching her.

Camilla went to the cloak-room with her own things and came quietly back to her desk and began to work at some envelopes she was addressing.

"Miss Pratt," said Whitlock in his cold brusque tone, and Marietta jumped and turned toward him sweeping off an avalanche of typed pages with her arm. She stooped in great confusion to pick them up, saying "Yessir?" but her voice was choked with suppressed emotion.

"I've been talking with Miss Chrystie about you," said

Whitlock when Marietta had replaced the papers and turned once more toward him.

"Yessir!" said Marietta in a hopeless tone.

"Miss Chrystie suggests that I give you another chance. Would you like to stay and try it again?"

"Oh—!" said Marietta with a quiver of her lip looking at him as if she could not believe her ears. "Yessir!" she said with a quick little breath almost like a sob.

"Would you be willing to take suggestions and act upon them, Miss Pratt?"

"Oh—*Yessir!*" said Marietta in an excited tone, her syllables fairly tumbling over one another.

"Up to the present time, Miss Pratt," went on Whitlock, his tone brusque and critical, "you have been most unsatisfactory in three ways, I might say in every way. In your work, which has been erratic and slouchy in appearance, and slower than any office should tolerate; in your appearance which is both unattractive and untidy, and in your manner which is often uncouth and bold. If you are willing to try to change in these things I am willing to give you another chance. If you will take Miss Chrystie's suggestions and be more like her, there might be some hope for you."

"Yessir," said Marietta giving him a wild wistful look. Then suddenly dropping her head down on her machine, she sobbed out:

"But I can't never be like her. I haven't got her looks!" and then her stubby shoulders shook with sobs.

Whitlock looked distressed at the effect of his words, but he cleared his throat and tried to speak above her weeping.

"I was not expecting you to perform miracles," he said kindly. "I merely want a neat efficient worker who knows how to act and how to dress and when not to speak. Suppose you talk it over with Miss Chrystie after your work is done and see what you think you can do. Perhaps you'd both like to go into the inner office for a few minutes. I'm expecting a man right now and it won't do to have you weeping all over the place."

Marietta arose precipitately and went into the little back office which was used mostly for the storage of supplies, and Camilla following found her sitting on a pile of typewriter paper shaking with suppressed sobs.

"Come, dear," said Camilla putting her hand hesitantly on the bowed head. "Let's snap out of this. We can't do anything if we give up at the start."

"We!" said Marietta looking up. "It was you made him say this, and I'll never forget it of you. But it isn't any good. He'll never keep me. I can't ever be like you."

"Hush, Marietta, that man has come and he'll hear you. You don't want to finish yourself before we begin do you? Slip quietly into the wash room there and wash your face. Wash it hard and get all that lipstick and rouge off."

"But I haven't any more to put on," said Marietta remorsefully, "I left my vanity at home."

"That's where you'd better keep it then, if you want to please Mr. Whitlock. He doesn't want you to look like an actress. He just wants you neat."

"But I've got an awful sallow complexion," sighed Marietta.

"Well, we'll see what we can do about that later, but you can't make it better by smearing on grease paint. Go wash your face!"

When Marietta came out of the wash room she had a clean subdued look like a little wet hen that had been in the suds much against her will. Her hair was draggled about her face and in wet tags in her neck. Her eyes were swollen badly but the streaks on her cheeks were gone, and her mouth had assumed its normal shape and lost its ghastly cupid's bow.

"I don't see how this is going to help," she wailed, "I look awful."

"Where's your comb, Marietta?" said Camilla.

Marietta produced a small broken affair with several teeth missing.

"Sit down in this chair," ordered Camilla.

Marietta submitted herself to the other girl and Camilla combed the recalcitrant locks till they were fairly smooth. They were not very clean and Camilla shrank from contact with them but she was determined to do her best for Marietta. She couldn't do much with such hair in a few minutes, but she managed to subdue it to neatness at least, and tucked the ends in, using three of her own hair-pins. Such hair would never make a pretty bob, and it did seem almost hopeless.

"You're coming home with me tonight," said Camilla as

she finished her task. "I'm going to show you another way to do your hair if you'll let me."

"Oh, will you?" said Marietta eagerly. "Say! That's wonderful! I never could make my hair look like anything."

"Well, we'll find a way," said Camilla surveying the stubborn locks dubiously. "Now, Marietta, run back to the wash room and wash those spots off the front of your dress. That dress needs cleaning, if you want to come up to Mr. Whitlock's standards."

"Oh, I know," said the girl, "but the sleeve's ripped half way out of the only other good one I have and I didn't have time ta mend it. Neither I didn't have money ta send this ta the cleaner."

"Clean it yourself! That's easy enough. I'll show you some splendid cleaning fluid I have. And then, you know, soap and water will do a whole lot if you just take a little care."

"Oh, my land!" said Marietta aghast. "You'd be an awful trouble to yourself."

"Why, yes certainly, Marietta, if you want to keep your job. You don't know what a difference little things like that make. If you only hadn't started to buy that fur coat! You know you really need a good well-fitting office dress."

"I was gonta get a figured crepe with two flounces going diagonal on the skirt, and puffed elbow sleeves. It has red and white flowers on it and it's only five ninety-eight!" said Marietta eagerly.

"But you know that's not the kind of dress to wear to the office. You need a quiet dark dress, with white collars. Dark blue would be good for you. And you don't want flounces, you need a simple dress and underthings that will make it fit well. You might have to pay more than that. How much have you paid down on your coat?"

"Five dollars," said the girl, "and I'm to pay two-fifty every week. It's coney, white with a big collar! It's swell!"

"But Marietta, you don't need a white fur coat unless you are going to parties and operas. And coney is nothing but rabbit and won't wear a season. Why don't you just drop it, Marietta, and use the money as you get it to buy a few very well cut dresses of good quality, that will give the right appearance for the office. That is really what you care for, isn't it?"

Marietta's eyes got large with disappointment.

"But I like pretty cloes," she said with something like a wail in her voice.

"Yes, of course," said Camilla wisely, "but they must be suitable for the place and time in which you wear them or they are not pretty. You haven't any place to wear a white fur coat, nor dresses with diagonal flounces. And elbow sleeves are not fit for the office, except perhaps in very hot weather in cotton material. You know to wear a cheap party dress to work in is not good taste and does not make a good impression. It sets you down as third-class right away. Mr. Whitlock wants girls in his office who look their part, well-dressed and efficient, not cheap little frowsy girls who don't know any better than to wear dressy frocks to work in."

Marietta stared at her sorrowfully.

"All right," she said at last, "I'll give up the coat, but it was awful pretty and I don't guess I'll ever get another chance for a fur coat. And all that good five dollars gone!"

"Well, you certainly couldn't have kept the coat if you lost your job. And if you keep your job and get to be the right kind of secretary, some day you might be able to buy a squirrel coat, if you need it, who knows?"

"My!" said Marietta. "I never thought of that! You think of a lot of things don't you? I like you an awful lot. I guess I'll try ta do what you say, though I don't know anybody else I'd do it for."

"All right!" smiled Camilla, "then I'll help you all I can! Now come on in the other office and let's get these letters off. It's half past three. We have a half-hour. How many more have you to type?"

"Only ten more. I'd uv had them all done ef you'd been another ten minutes."

"Good work! Are they letter-perfect? Are you sure?"

"Yep, I went over each one as I finished it."

"All right, I'll fold them and stamp them for you while you finish the rest. But say, Marietta, if I were you I wouldn't say 'yep.' It isn't being done by office girls who get on. It doesn't matter with me of course, but it's always best to keep in practice even when it doesn't matter. You don't mind my telling you, do you?"

"Nop— No, I mean," said the girl. "I want ta get right if I can. But say, don't I look awful plain with my hair this way?"

"It's neat at least," said Camilla, "and we'll fix it better tonight. Come, let's hurry!"

Mr. Whitlock did not return that afternoon. Instead he telephoned Camilla, and seemed pleased that the letters had gone out. Marietta was listening. Her eyes shone when she heard his tone of commendation. She drew a sigh of relief as she started away from the office in Camilla's company.

"My, it's nice ta have a girl-friend!" she said with satisfaction, and Camilla's heart stood aghast at the thought. She was wondering how many unpleasant things this helping of Marietta was going to let her in for? Well, she was the Lord's servant. She couldn't refuse an obvious duty like trying to help Marietta keep her job, even if it wasn't going to be the pleasantest thing in the world.

"What'll your mother say, me coming home with you like this?" Marietta asked as Camilla opened the door with her latchkey.

"She'll be glad to see you," said Camilla, thanking her stars that she had such a mother upon whom she could count in emergencies.

"Mother, I've brought Marietta home with me for supper," sang out Camilla as she entered the tiny hall.

"Now isn't that nice!" answered Mother Chrystie at once, appearing in the dining room door. "I'm so glad I decided to make potpie. I thought maybe we'd have company tonight! I'm delighted to meet you, Marietta. Camilla has told me about you. Now get your things off quickly girls. The potpie is all ready to be taken up."

Marietta was shy and embarrassed at the table, but her eyes were shining. She watched the loving looks between mother and daughter hungrily, and once she said: "My, I wish I had a home like this! I never tasted potpie before. My stepmother doesn't know how to cook very well."

She helped with the dishes, and afterward Camilla took her in the bathroom and taught her how to shampoo her hair, and then how to curl it softly and loosely around her face, and how to coax the long stiff locks in her neck into a neat little knot. Camilla hunted up an organdy collar she had made recently, and told her to mend the sleeve of her other dress and wear the new collar next day. Marietta vowed eternal loyalty to her, and declared she'd try to do everything she was told. Mrs. Chrystie gave her a bag of cookies for Ted, and so Marietta went happily home at last wearing her hair in an almost becoming style, and holding the new collar and cookies tenderly.

"Thus endeth the first lesson!" laughed Camilla as she finally shut the door after her guest and sank wearily into a big chair. "Mother, I don't know what you'll think of me but I had to undertake her reformation. She was about to lose her job."

"Dear child!" said her mother understandingly, "but I'm glad you did it, though I can see that it's not going to be all rest and pleasure to you. But it's a heavenly thing to do, and I think the angels watching you love it that you are doing it."

"The angels?"

"Yes," said her mother brightly, "didn't you know we had an audience all the time, we Christians? I was just reading about it this morning how we are made a spectacle for the world and for angels. And it seems that word angels includes bad ones too, demons who are watching the Christians' walk. Yes, I'm glad you did this dear, and if there's any way I can help I will. Poor, homely, lonely girl! But you know, Camilla, she didn't look so bad when you got her hair fixed. She really didn't."

When Camilla, weary with the day, crept into her bed, it came to her suddenly that she hadn't had time to think about Wainwright and Stephanie Varrell all day long. Then just as she was falling to sleep there came that sharp sweet memory of a kiss that seemed like a dream that had never been.

The next few days were interesting for Camilla. Mr. Whitlock was suddenly called to New York on business, and he left with only a few hurried directions and a promise to call her up later and find out what was in the mail. He was gone before Marietta arrived at the office, which was a good thing perhaps, for Marietta had not been quite such a success with the arrangement of her hair as Camilla had hoped, and it had to be done over again. But Camilla fixed her up and began to stimulate her to work and see what she could accomplish while Mr. Whitlock was away, to surprise him.

This was perhaps the very stimulus Marietta needed, for she was still a child in many ways and was greatly intrigued by the idea of surprising and pleasing her employer.

Camilla, moreover, was pleased that he had entrusted her

with his affairs during his absence, and took a pride in having everything move on as if he had been there, and even Marietta caught the spirit, and tried to act brisk and business-like when anyone came in.

She brought no more novels to the office to read. She was too anxious to work every minute and get the pile of typing done that had been assigned to her.

And then Saturday afternoon Camilla took part of her precious half-holiday and went shopping with Marietta, to help her find just the right things. Mr. Whitlock was returning Monday morning and Marietta was determined to get some new clothes before he arrived.

By this time she was getting fairly skillful at managing her unruly hair, and even in her ill-fitting unsuitable clothes she looked much subdued. Camilla hoped that with the purchase of a few much needed garments Mr. Whitlock could not help but see a change even in so short a time. So the shopping expedition was planned and Marietta was almost too excited to work all Saturday morning.

They went to Camilla's house with their packages and Marietta dressed up in her new dress, a trim dark blue with white collar and cuffs. Miss York came in and was introduced and approvingly entered into the scheme of things without having to be told at all what it was all about. And before Marietta left she slipped in her bag a sheet of paper on which was written in the nurse's clear handwriting a few rules for bathing and breathing, exercise and diet, that Miss York told Marietta would greatly improve the complexion she was deploring. Take it altogether Camilla was quite satisfied about her protégé, and it was with much eagerness that she anticipated Monday morning and the return of Mr. Whitlock. She hadn't done anything in a long time that was so interesting as fixing up poor little homely Marietta Pratt. At least, not anything real. She kept telling herself now that her contact with Wainwright had not been real, only a sort of fairy tale, and fairy tales never came true. They were only to dream about. And dreaming like that wasn't at all wholesome, so Camilla entered into the redemption of Marietta Pratt, physical, intellectual and spiritual, with all her heart. She wanted to keep from thinking. She wanted to keep from dreaming.

CHAPTER XIV

JOHN SAXON WAS A FINE EARNEST YOUNG MAN WHO WAS taking a year off from his medical studies to earn some much needed money wherewith to complete his course.

He had been offered the opportunity to take in charge a dozen young boys whose parents or guardians had either no time or inclination to look after them themselves. Two of the boys were not strong enough to stand the northern winters, therefore Florida had been selected as the scene of his activities, and more especially because Florida was a sort of native land to John Saxon and he knew well all its possibilities.

It was to this group of unfortunately wealthy youngsters that young Sam Wainwright had attached himself, and he refused to be separated from them. And when in the well-planned and educative program of John Saxon this young company were to move down into the Everglades for a hiking-camping-fishing-exploring trip Sam Wainwright went into the particular kind of gloom that he knew how to create, until his mother consented that he should accompany them, provided John Saxon would take him on, and would also allow his elder brother to be one of the company.

Having thus gained consent, young Sam became forthwith so angelic for the next two days before the expedition was to leave that he almost overdid the matter, and got his mother to worrying about him lest he was going to die. So after all it was with the greatest difficulty that he finally made his departure.

John Saxon had not cared overmuch for the idea, it is true, of having an elder brother along who would likely be superior and try to interfere, but the extra money that was offered, which would hasten the time when he should be able to go back to the work he was eager to do, made him yield.

The two young men had not seen one another until the morning that they were to start. All the arrangements had been conducted by young Sam, and naturally the two approached one another with a thoroughly developed case of prejudice on either side.

Looked at from the standpoint of an outsider they were not unlike. Both were young and strong and good looking. Perhaps Wainwright had an inch or two of height in his favor, and on the other hand John Saxon had several lines of experience in his fine strong face which were yet to be developed in Jeffrey Wainwright's. Yet they seemed well matched as they met on the beach in the pearly dawn of that tropical winter morning and measured swords with their eyes as they shook hands. "Soft!" Saxon was saying to himself, just because he had never seen a face before with such an easy-going happy smile that at the same time concealed strong character, character that had not been severely tried as yet, but still strong character.

"Tough?" said Jeffrey to himself with a question mark, and somehow was not convinced of that. This man did not quite fit any of the types of men he knew.

There was a certain gravity behind the sparkle in Jeffrey's eyes that John Saxon could not help liking, and Jeffrey on his part was not long in discovering the strength and authority, with a certain grave sweetness in Saxon. So they started on their way bristling with question marks concerning each other.

But in the mind of young Sam there were no question marks. He thought his big brother was the greatest thing that ever happened, and he thought that John Saxon was the next greatest.

The sun shot a crimson rim above the opal sea and tinged the waves with ruddy gold, and strange colors gleamed and leaped in the sparkle of the waves. The sand grew alight with color, and little eager white birds with pink kid feet went hopping here and there along the rim of the waves to catch the sand crabs without wetting their feet. A big white gull sailed out over the waves looking down for fish, and then circled back and settled down on a pile that stood out in the sea a few yards, surveying the strange group with their khaki outfittings and paraphernal-

ia. Strange changing groups this wise bird saw at different
times along this coast since it had been fashionable to
winter in Florida, but it made no difference to him. The sea
was there and did not change, and he wore the same cut of
white feather coat from generation to generation, so why
bother about mere humans?

John Saxon gave Jeffrey a quick firm grasp of the hand
as he looked into his eyes, said "Wainwright!" just to
acknowledge his presence, showed neither joy nor sorrow
over the fact that he was going with them, and Jeffrey was
left to the company of the sea and his own thoughts while
the small army was forming for the line of march. Then
when they were drawn up in line there were a few questions.

"Everybody gone over the list?" All hands were raised.

"Everybody got every article on the list?" All hands
again.

The young captain let his eyes sweep the row, and
acknowledged with a faint shadow of a grin the fact that
Jeffrey had raised his hand both times as if he were one of
the boys. The stranger was perhaps going to be game after
all. Nothing haughty about him so far.

"About face!"

Jeffrey obeyed the order. He was standing at the end of
the line.

"Forward march!"

Jeffrey fell in step with the rest. At least he knew
enough for that.

"By twos, march!"

This brought Jeffrey marching with the youngest boy in
the crowd, one Carlin de Harte by name, and a little devil
by inheritance if he might be judged by his actions.

Carlin was the son of divorced parents and had been
shunted off on others wherever it seemed easiest to bring
him up. He was a recent importation and not yet under
full discipline. The young chief eyed the combination
doubtfully. He had not expected the son of the millionaire
bond king to choose to walk as one of the boys.

But Jeffrey looked down with a friendly wink at Carlin,
and Carlin looked up with sudden respect when he saw
how tall Jeffrey was, and grinned. Suddenly John Saxon
knew that Jeffrey was going to be an asset instead of a
pain in the neck.

The way led at first along the silver-gilt beach of the opening day, and Jeffrey Wainwright drew in deep breaths of the clean sea air and rejoiced in the emptiness of the beach. They had it practically all to themselves except for the kid-footed bird catching crabs, and an old fisherman out in a dory.

When they had got so far from human habitation that they couldn't see anything but sand and sea and palms and pines, and everybody was wondering what came next, John Saxon called a halt and set his young minions to work, gathering sticks, unpacking a hamper, making a fire, setting up a contrivance for cooking. Each boy had his job and knew what was expected of him. They went at it like trained ants hurrying around excitedly.

Jeffrey dropped down upon the sand and watched for a while, surprised at the efficiency of his young brother. But when John Saxon passed he arose and saluted.

"Say, Captain, what's my job?" he asked with a grin.

Saxon measured his height admiringly but answered with a reserved smile:

"Guest, I think," he said, "or maybe, critic, whichever would suit you best." There was still smile enough about John Saxon's lips to keep the remark from being an offense, but Jeffrey watched him sharply.

"Nothing doing," he said quietly. "If that's all the place you've got for me I'm afraid I shall have to walk all the way back alone."

John Saxon took his measure again and relaxed his lips.

"All right, if you really want to work. I thought you just came along to protect your brother."

Jeffrey looked him in the eye.

"I came along because my mother insisted Sam shouldn't come without me, but I'm staying because I like it—and because I like *you!*" he added with a genuine ring to his voice. "If I go back I shall leave my brother in your care and tell my mother there's no cause to worry. But I'm staying on if you let me have a part because I like you and I think it's great!"

John Saxon put out his hand and grasped Jeffrey's in a hearty clasp.

"All right, Brother," he said with a new light in his eyes, "there are two of us! Suppose you open the milk bottles and fill the cups! I was going to do that myself but I've plenty besides, and I'll see to assigning you a regular place when we're on our way again. I think you're going to be a big help. You've already subdued our worst particular little devil. If this keeps up we shall have him a model child before the trip is over."

Jeffrey felt a warm glow about his heart as he watched this other young man with his strong clear-cut features, his crisp brown curly hair and his very blue eyes that had dancing lights in them and yet could look sternly at miscreant charge, or scorn a casual multi-millionaire's son. It all intrigued Jeffrey immensely and he felt the thrill of a new admiration. He was not going to be bored on this expedition. It was going to be interesting.

Stephanie Varrell would have been amazed to see him pouring milk into tin cups and cutting bread, distributing butter, and heaping up the tin plates with the second helping of baked beans and frankfurters. She did not know how he had served his apprenticeship at washing dishes in a tiny apartment kitchen with her rival. She did not even know yet that he had disappeared from the playground where last night she had tried and failed to inveigle him to walk in the moonlight with her. She was having her breakfast in bed about the time of this midmorning repast that was served so many miles away from her, down the beach.

The way led inland later in the day, after a dip in the sea and a romp on the beach, and then a rest on the sand. Inland among the palms, and the taller pines, which now were draped more thickly with the long gray moss. Other, stranger, trees appeared also, and the way grew wild and picturesque. Strange blossoms peered up at them from the ground, strange lovely weird ones peered down from the branches above their heads. Orchids! Those were orchids! Green orchids, with almost human faces!

Jeffrey thought of white orchids, a girl with gold hair and deep brown eyes, and her way of holding aloof in another world.

The way led through dense hammock land, where lovely vines trailed across and barred the way with strong yet gentle hands, and yellow jessamine filled the air with heavenly perfume. More orchids looked down in stranger color combinations, looking more like humans than the first ones, and Jeffrey thought of a girl with dark eyes and wished she were beside him, wondered if it would be at all possible to pack a box with these wonderful orchids and hope to get it to her before they died?

Glimpses of wild creatures they had, of deer, and little beings of the forest. A bright eye, the whisk of a tail, a stirring leaf and they were out of sight. Glimpses of serpents, slithering along their native haunts, great copperheads and rattlers. Once they stopped to take a lesson on serpents, and on what to do in case of being attacked, how to render first aid. A great copperhead lay coiled below them in a little hollow by a log while they were listening, and Jeffrey marvelled at the skill of the young teacher in controlling the harum-scarum boys in order to give them the most out of his teaching. And then, just as if he had been trained for the act the big creature uncoiled his lengths and slid away beneath the undergrowth, and the boys stepped back with eyes large with a new understanding, more ready to meet possible danger, less cocksure of their own little human might pitted against real deadly peril.

Their eyes grew wise and sharp, looking for the signs of enemy life about them, learning to know the names of the growing things they passed. How much the young leader knew, and how well he told it without seeming to be trying to impart knowledge! No wonder his price was large and it was difficult to get opportunity to join his groups.

A stream developed later in the day as they climbed over fallen logs. The stream in time led to a lake, clear, sparkling, like a jewel in the forest, and here canoes awaited them, and they saw their first Indian guide.

Almost in awe they took their places as ordered and sat quiet, full of deep satisfaction, too weary to disobey.

They touched in a little while upon a shore and saw not far away a huge alligator lying dormant, partly out of the water. Story book life was becoming real to those boys.

There were rude accommodations for camping, and a fire was all ready to start near the shore. Two old Indians muttered unintelligible phrases to the young leader, and presently the tired boys were eating a supper of fish from the lake cooked over the fire, bread that they had brought with them, and fruit, oranges that had been sent on ahead.

It was suddenly dark before they had finished, and only the light of the fire to eat by when they got to the oranges. Just as if somebody had touched a button and the light went out, so the sun had dropped down out of sight and left not a vestige of gleam behind. That was Florida.

John Saxon had been collecting pine-knots before this happened, and now he stuck several in the fire till they caught, then set them here and there in buckets of sand.

They washed their tin dishes in lake water, looking furtively toward the place where the alligator had basked, and then sat round the fire while the moon rose, a mammoth moon, from behind the forest across the lake. John Saxon, reclining near one of the pine-knot torches, took a little book from his pocket and read how a man of the Pharisees, one Nicodemus, came to Jesus by night, and asked Him the way of salvation, and He answered, "Except a man be born again, he cannot see the kingdom of God."

Jeffrey Wainwright, wearier than he ever remembered to have been before, yet greatly charmed with this weird strange place of stillness and night, had been watching the scene indifferently. He was thinking that for once this wise magnetic leader had made a great mistake in trying to run in any reading on those tired boys after a day's march and excitement. Studying the strong fine face of the other young man, he fell to wondering how he got that way anyway. He was not listening intently until he heard that phrase, "born again," and suddenly he sat up sharply and began to listen.

On through that simple story he listened, through those matchless words that have reached round the world in every language, and reached down through the ages from God for everybody. "For God so loved the world, that He gave His only begotten Son, that whosoever believeth in Him, should not perish, but have everlasting life. For God sent not His Son into the world to condemn the world; but that the world through Him might be saved."

He listened to the condemnation that comes through refusing the light. Only a few verses, but so impressive, there with that great moon looking down, and the glinting silver of the lake ahead, and the black still darkness of the forest shutting in, where the firelight flickered solemnly, and a far strange bird let forth a weird night cry. He could see that even the weary boys were impressed and liked it all. Their leader had hold enough upon them for that, after a long day's march!

The little book was closed and stuck back in John

Saxon's pocket and John Saxon's voice suddenly started a chorus:

"I know a fount where sins are washed away!
    I know a place where night is turned to day!
Burdens are lifted, blind eyes made to see,
    There's a wonder-working power in the blood of
        Calvary!"

The rich tones died away, and the leader's head bent reverently:

"Lord, we're glad You love us and understand us all. We're glad we can come to You for forgiveness of our sins, for cleansing, for strength by the way, and wisdom. And now tonight we come for rest, for blessing, for protection through the night. We ask it in the name of Jesus Christ our Saviour."

It was very still when the prayer was over, and for an instant no boy stirred. Then John Saxon said in his ordinary voice:

"Now, boys, every man to his cot. Five minutes to get ready and five to get quiet!"

Jeffrey lay on his hard cot that was too short for his length and felt a great peace settle down upon him. Outside the pine-knots sputtered and flared, and the fire flickered, and flamed up when the old Indian watchman fed it with more pine-knots, and the great silver moon shone on, but there was quiet in the camp.

His brother Sam was in the next tent, but in the cot beside him little Carlin de Harte reached out a timid hand and touched Jeff.

"You don't think God would let that alligator get in our tent do you? Nor the old long snake?" he whispered.

Then Jeffrey's hand came out and clasped the lean young claw of the child and held it warmly.

"No, kid, I don't think He would!" said Jeffrey. "You go to sleep now, and I'll help God watch!"

The boy sighed contentedly, and soon his regular breathing told Jeffrey that his fears were over for that night. But Jeffrey lay thinking of the words he had been hearing, and of Camilla and what she had said about being born again. Was this what she had meant, and was it something that came to you, or did you have to go out after it? He would listen and see if he could find out, for this was what he had come questing for. And presently Jeffrey too was sleeping.

CHAPTER XV

BACK AT THE FASHIONABLE RESORT THAT JEFFREY WAIN-wright had left that morning, Stephanie Varrell patrolled the beach in vain, in vain questioned this one and that one if they had seen him that morning. She searched the golf course, the tennis courts, and even the airport, and put the bell boys and desk clerks through a regular inquisition, to discover whether he had left yet, but found out nothing at all about the disappearance of the heir of the house of Wainwright.

At last, when everything else had failed, she approached Jeff's dignified mother, sitting with her knitting on the wide veranda talking quietly with two of her friends. She assumed a honeyed smile and said:

"Pardon me, Mrs. Wainwright, I'm sorry to interrupt, but we've an expedition on for this afternoon and we're anxious to find Jeff. Of course he's included, and we can't seem to place him. Could you give us an idea where to look?"

Mrs. Wainwright looked up when she had finished count-ing her stitches and studied Stephanie up and down, much as Stephanie might have looked at another whom she con-sidered beneath her notice, and then said coldly:

"My son is away today."

"Oh, really?" said Stephanie in well assumed surprise, "he didn't mention any such thing last night when I talked with him. Could you tell me when you expect him back?"

"I couldn't say," said Jeffrey's mother, her voice still colder and more disapproving. "He may be away several days, or even longer. He wasn't sure when he left!"

"Oh!" said Stephanie, a pretty dismay in her voice, but

with a mean gleam in her jacinth eyes. "He—hasn't gone back north yet, has he? Oh, I hope not."

Again Mrs. Wainwright favored her with another cool scrutiny.

"Well—not *yet!*" she admitted with a slight shrug of her shoulders, "but of course, he's liable to be called back almost any time. You'd better not base any of your plans on his movements for he's a very uncertain quantity at present," and she turned with a haughty little laugh addressed to her two friends, as if the unsought interview was now terminated.

Stephanie stood wistfully for a moment posing in the attitude of bewildered disappointment, and then with a narrowing of her jacinth eyes and a slight almost imperceptible shrug of her own pretty shoulders she walked away.

She went to the farthest corner of the hotel piazza she could find, which was on the sea side, and stared out into the sparkling blue for a few minutes, her thoughts growing more intense as her slender brows drew into a deep frown. Then she arose hastily and made her way to the telephone booths, calling up her lawyer in New York.

She had to wait a long time before he could be discovered, but at last she heard his voice, and she spoke peremptorily:

"Mr. Glyndon, I want you to go out and purchase a piece of real estate for me! I want it no matter what it costs, and I want the matter attended to today. I want to get it without fail at once, and you needn't wait to communicate with me and tell me it isn't worth buying at any price, for I know that now. But it's worth *anything to me*, anything I have to pay. I have private reasons for wanting it and I don't care whether it is a good buy or not. Do you get me?"

Mr. Glyndon got her. He had had her before, and knew what to expect unless he did her bidding.

"Where is the property?"

Stephanie gave him the address that had been on Jeff's letter that she had burned in her ash tray.

"And listen, Mr. Glyndon, there are tenants in that house and I want them to vacate immediately. Offer them any kind of a bonus you have to to get out at once. I want the house vacant by the end of the week. See? Even if you have to *move* them."

Mr. Glyndon tried to protest but Stephanie was firm. "It isn't as if it wasn't my own money, Mr. Glyndon," reminded Stephanie, "nor as if I didn't have enough to do what I want with it. Buy it today, please, and telegraph me tonight how you came out. But you've *got* to come out, understand? Good-bye, Mr. Glyndon."

Stephanie left the telephone booth with a gleam of danger to somebody in her jacinth eyes, and donning her most daring bathing suit went down to the beach to captivate some new and interesting admirer in the interim.

When Mr. Whitlock got back to the office Monday morning a new Marietta was already there, her typewriter burnished for action, a large neat pile of finished typing lying in regular order on the end of her desk, and she herself seated at work upon some routine typing that was always on hand to fill in between special work.

She looked up as he entered, and he looked her straight in the face but did not know her. He stood there staring for a second, hesitating, about to ask her what she was doing there, when Camilla came in from the cloak room and handed her a paper.

"There it is, Marietta. I must have dropped it in the closet Saturday."

Then she saw Mr. Whitlock and gave him a pleasant good morning, almost breaking down with laughter at the astonished look on his face. His expression fully repaid her for her hard work in getting Marietta into shape.

He smiled with that nice light in his eyes when he spoke to Camilla, and then he turned back to Marietta.

"Ah, Miss Pratt," he said pleasantly, "I see you have been acting on some of my suggestions. And I'm glad to see you've got the work done. That's going to help out a lot, for I've got a busy day before me and I want those letters to get off at once."

A little later he came over to Camilla's desk and after giving her several directions about the work that morning, he said in a low tone that could not be heard over Marietta's industrious clicking,

"Good work! I'm delighted! I didn't think it could be done!"

Camilla smiled understandingly.

At noon he sent Marietta out for her lunch promptly, and when she was gone he said to Camilla:

"How about a little relaxation tomorrow night, after all your strenuous labors?"

She turned about quickly and met that engaging smile again.

"I have tickets for the symphony concert and I thought perhaps you'd enjoy going. Could you arrange to get someone to stay with your mother for the evening?"

Camilla's eyes sparkled. She hadn't heard any real music in so long.

"Oh, I'd love it! I'll try. Can I tell you tomorrow morning? I'd have to call up a friend and I'm not sure I can get her till tonight."

"Oh certainly," said Whitlock, and in a moment more he went out of the office.

Camilla went to her concert and Miss York came and stayed with her mother. It proved a pleasant evening for them all, and Camilla went about for days humming bits of melody which she loved. Whitlock had been delightful company, proving to have a fair knowledge of music himself, at least enough for intelligent appreciation. Camilla enjoyed the concert although it must be confessed that her thoughts were a bit distracted when she happened to look toward the boxes and the dress circle where the social leaders sat. The beautiful women, their sumptuous dressing, the flash of a jewel, the deferential bend of an escort's head to his lady's word, all brought back the memory of that one poor little entry of hers into the great world of wealth, and stabbed her with the sharpness of pain to remember certain thrilling incidents that had been treasured, and that she thought she had buried too deep for return. Yet here they were again rearing their heads and mocking at her. Little phrases of Jeffrey Wainwright's, the way he held her coat for her, the way he bent to listen to her slightest word. Just foolish nothings that had no meaning, and yet they haunted her memory and would not give her peace even here in this wonderful music hall amid such heavenly surroundings.

She was thankful that she did not have to do much talking. The music made that impossible, and she could close her eyes to all else and just listen.

During the intermission they went out to walk in the green room and Whitlock pointed out some notable musicians among the throng. It was all very pleasant, only Camilla could not keep her mind from that other outing and that other escort who had made such a happy time for her.

She roused herself to be entertaining, and succeeded in bringing a goodly number of those intimate smiles to the face of her employer.

The next day was a busy one and Whitlock was away on business. Camilla was sorry not to have the opportunity of again telling him how much she had enjoyed the evening, but glad in a way to have the time to think it over unhindered by his personality, which while very pleasant, sometimes troubled her a little by its very possessiveness. It might be good for her resolves to have someone absorbing her time, but somehow it tortured a certain kind of loyalty in her which could not forget. Not that she was in love with *anybody*, of course, she told herself, only that she didn't want her thoughts to be "all mixed up" as she expressed it.

CHAPTER XVI

MARIETTA WAS GOING ALONG NICELY, LEARNING SOME NEW principle every day, and really doing credit to her teacher, whom she still adored. Camilla went home that night feeling that she had earned a pleasant quiet evening with her mother, and was planning to tell her all about the concert and the different people she had seen, who they were, what they wore, and how they looked.

But the moment she entered the house she felt somehow that something had happened, and when she saw her mother's gentle face, with traces of tears on her carefully wiped eyes, and that look of covert anxiety, she knew that it had.

"What is it, Mother?" she cried aghast. "You are not feeling sick again are you?"

"Oh, no, dear," her mother managed a smile, "I'm feeling fine!"

"Then it doesn't matter what else happens," said Camilla with a breath of relief. "Go on, tell me what it is!"

"Oh, it really doesn't matter, dear! It isn't anything very terrible, and of course it's all in the Father's will somehow. It's only that we've got to leave this house! Right away! This week I guess!"

"But we *can't!*" said Camilla aghast. "They couldn't do that to us! We have our lease. The year isn't up yet. They can't put us out!"

"No, dear, perhaps not, but I guess we've got to go anyway. You see the house is *sold—*"

"But the lease provides for that very possibility—" said Camilla insistently. "I'll ask Mr. Whitlock about it. I'm sure they can't put us out."

"But you see, dear—it makes a great difference to them and they have offered to move us and give us a bonus if we'll get out this week!"

"How much?" demanded Camilla, her firm little lips set in a thin line of resistance.

"Well, it's a good deal, dear. You see I told them it was impossible, and they kept on offering more and more until the man said he would refund all the past nine months' rent since we moved in. I really hadn't the conscience to keep on saying no, so I told him we would think it over and let him know in the morning, but he seemed to think there would be other ways of getting us out that we might not like so well if we turned it down, so I really think we better go, dear!"

"But how can we? *This week?*" said Camilla in consternation sitting down weakly on a kitchen chair.

"There'll be a way, dear, if we are meant to go," said her mother smiling. "Come let's eat our supper now, and then afterward we can talk it over. You can't tell what you can do until you try."

"This week!" said Camilla again. "How can we? Why Mother, I can't possibly get off of course to hunt a house until Saturday. Not that Mr. Whitlock wouldn't let me off if I would ask him for he's very kind, but I couldn't be spared, I really couldn't. There is so much to be done!"

"Well," said her mother thoughtfully, "then I guess I'll have to hunt a house," and she laughed. "You know this isn't the most ideal place to live after all, and it isn't in the least likely we shall ever have an offer like this one again, nine months' rent back and our moving free! I thought perhaps we ought to try to get out tonight lest he should change his mind by morning."

"It is wonderful, isn't it, Mother? It doesn't seem real," said Camilla thoughtfully. "And of course we have wanted to get away from this noisy little street before spring comes, but to have it sprung at us this way, I don't see how we're going to manage! If it were only spring we could jump in the car and drive around and look up something."

"There are papers," said her mother hopefully. "I bought two of the little fellow next door who sells them. I've been looking through the For Rents and I've marked several. There are some that look very promising."

"How much?" asked Camilla practically.

"Why, they don't give the price," said the mother looking troubled, "but several said 'low price' or 'reasonable' and some of them sounded very nice indeed. There was one, a flat, that looked interesting, and two bungalows out on the edge of town. That wouldn't be bad for summer, if it wasn't too long a drive for you."

"There are so many things to consider," said Camilla, her eyes full of new trouble, and she sighed.

"Well, dear, this isn't anything of our planning and we must just consider that our Heavenly Father has some good purpose in it for us. And it's likely He had a place for us somewhere."

"If we only had more time!" said Camilla. "Where are those papers? Perhaps there are some advertisements that we could telephone about."

"Yes, a couple gave the numbers. But let's wait till we have finished the dishes and go at it quietly. You mustn't get all tired and excited after your hard day at the office."

"Oh, I'm not tired," said Camilla. "It wasn't an especially hard day. And anybody would be excited to have to move overnight as it were. What day did he say we must be out?"

"He gave us a week at the outside before he 'took other

measures' as he put it, but offered fifty dollars more for every day short of that."

Camilla looked at her startled.

"Well, at least we could afford to pay a little higher rent than we are paying here, then! And things aren't quite so high now as they were when we moved here. That back rent would pay off the doctor and Miss York, too, and we could start fresh. That would be wonderful, wouldn't it?"

"Why of course!" said her mother cheerfully. "Here you put the things away in the refrigerator and I'll wash the dishes. Then we can get to work. How about telephoning Miss York? She gets about so much she might hear of something."

"I would hate to bother her till we are located," said Camilla proudly.

"That wouldn't be bothering her. She might just happen to know of something. Child, that's pride and there isn't a bit of sense to it!"

"All right, Mother! Now go in the other room and get your papers while I put the dishes away."

"Well," said her mother meekly, "all right, only I telephoned Miss York this afternoon, and she's coming over this evening to talk it over with us. I thought she had a right to know in a crisis like this. She's been so interested in us, and so lovely when I was sick."

Camilla laughed with a relieved note.

"Well, I'm glad she's coming," she owned, "and it will be fun to tell her we can pay her everything."

"Be careful," said her mother, "don't talk too much about pay. She's been just lovely, and you mustn't hurt her."

"No, I won't, Mother dear," said Camilla stopping to snatch a kiss as she passed with her hands full of plates and cups, "only it will be so good to feel that the debts are all paid! But what about the incubus upstairs? She hasn't paid us for three weeks, do you realize that? Maybe we'll have trouble with her."

"No," said Mrs. Chrystie with the air of a child confessing her faults one by one, "I've fixed that all up with her. I told her that if she would move out tomorrow we would let the back rent go, and she's gone out to her married daughter's now to find out if she can have a room there for the rest of the winter. It seems she's lost her job and doesn't know when she can pay, so I think she was really relieved."

"But perhaps she's got a disagreeable son-in-law who won't have her," suggested Camilla.

"No, she says he's very nice and has often asked her to come there and live, but she likes to be independent."

"Well, that's a help, anyway. Because, even if we stayed here, and she didn't pay her rent, what would we have done?"

"Yes, I know," said the mother thoughtfully.

"But Mother, even if we had a place to go it might take several days to get a mover. They have to be engaged beforehand."

There was a wise twinkle in her mother's eye in answer to that.

"No, you see I thought of that, and I asked Mrs. Pryor next door if she knew a good mover and she told me of one right in the next street. She's known him a long time and says he's very honest and careful, so I telephoned him and he came over at noon and looked over what we have and said he could move it after five o'clock any day this week, tomorrow if we found a place!"

"Tomorrow!" gasped Camilla, "that would be utterly impossible!"

"I don't see why, Camilla," said Mrs. Chrystie calmly. "I've thought it all out and I can't see wasting the offer of fifty dollars a day. Why, Camilla, if the house was on fire we'd get out on the sidewalk inside of half an hour, and probably save a good part of our things at that. And surely, with a good mover we could do it in a day! And it doesn't seem reasonable for us to lose fifty dollars a day wasting time looking for a house. We can surely find something right away."

"But Mother, how do you know that fifty dollars a day is a genuine offer? The man may be a fraud, and just trying to get us out of house and home for his own interests. I think we ought to find out more about it before we do anything about hunting a house."

"Well," said her mother with another twinkle, "you know I thought so too, so I called up the bank and asked Mr. Baker, and it seems the man is a noted lawyer, and anything he says he'll make good. He offered to put the money in our bank in Mr. Baker's hands, to be delivered to us as soon as we moved."

Suddenly Camilla sat down and looked at her mother with new respect, and then she began to laugh.

"Well, Mother," she said with admiration, "it seems you are able to run our affairs better than I am, and here I was counting myself the dependence of the family! Why, it wouldn't have occurred to me to do all those things and you've got everything practically arranged."

"Yes," said the mother smiling, "your father taught me to be very careful about such matters, and of course staying here all day alone I had time to think it all out. But you're not to discount your own ability, Camilla. I've been proud of you, managing everything so well while I was sick. And I've been glad just to lie back and have everything fixed for me. But I still can do my share occasionally when it's necessary and I thought today, till you came back, it was necessary to act at once, so I acted."

"Well, Mother, what else have you done?"

"Oh, not much else except to call up one or two real estate offices and get a list of houses and apartments for rent. Silcox around on Tenth Street sent a boy around with a list of places with descriptions and prices. I told him about what we could pay. Of course some of them were more than I said. But you can look them over. You'll know locations better than I. I thought Miss York could help in that also. Three agents told me of apartments and gave me descriptions over the telephone. So, you see I've been busy. The lists are over on the desk, and there are three places that can be seen this evening!"

"Well, I should say you've been working pretty efficiently," said Camilla meekly, gathering up the lists and sitting down to study them.

"Then I folded up some of our clothes from the closets and put them in the bureau drawers, and packed some of the photographs and vases and things around these rooms, in the old carved chest there."

"Mother!" said Camilla aghast. "Do you want to get sick again? I just know you are too tired!"

"Oh, no, I've been enjoying myself!" smiled Mrs. Chrystie. "I didn't do much. Just little things that took time and care. I've really been sitting down all day. And it's been such a pleasure to get some things done so that you wouldn't have so much on you. There! That's the doorbell! That will be Miss York! Or perhaps Mr. Glyndon. He said he would come back either this evening or early tomorrow morning to get our answer."

"Glyndon?" said Camilla startled. Things were moving so fast she felt as if she were tied to a runaway horse.

"Yes, he's the man who represents the new owner of the house. He's the lawyer."

Camilla was convinced at first sight of the lawyer that he meant business, and more so when he went away leaving a check in her hands which was a goodly advance on the sum he had promised to pay when they were out of the house.

Miss York had come in while he was there, and slipped through to the kitchen till he should be gone, then she returned, her face full of interest.

"Well, isn't this nice!" she said beaming on them. "I've been so hoping you could get out of this street before warm weather comes, and now it's all planned for you!"

"Now we're going to be able to pay all our debts!" said Camilla rejoicing. "But how on earth we're going to get out in a week is more than I can understand, for I simply can't get off from the office any day till five, and one can't do much at lunch hour even without eating."

"Get out?" said Miss York. "Why of course you'll get out. I don't see why you can't be out of here by tomorrow night! There's nothing to hinder!"

"My dear!" said Camilla protesting, "we haven't even an idea where we can find a house, and how can we move till the house is cleaned. You ought to have seen this house before we cleaned it! It was simply filthy!"

"Nonsense!" said Miss York. "In the first place you don't need to take a dirty place. There are plenty of apartments and even little houses that are perfectly new. Yes, and prices aren't so bad either. Besides, even if you have to pay a little more than you do here, you are making enough to cover it. The quicker you get out the better. What we need to do is find something tonight! It's two minutes to eight now," she consulted her watch, "before ten, Camilla, you and I ought to find something, and tomorrow morning Jinny Wilcox, the colored woman who does my washing, can go right to work cleaning the bedrooms. If you have a clean place to sleep by night that is all that's necessary. You can do the rest after you get in. It won't be such ideal moving as having the whole house cleaned ahead of time, but what's a little thing like that when you are getting fifty dollars a day for tumbling in?"

"But Mother!—She'll work too hard, Miss York!" said Camilla in distress.

"Mother'll have to be reasonable," said the nurse with a look at her former patient that meant business. "We'll make out a program for Mother, and she'll have to take her oath to stick to it or we'll put her to bed in a hospital until the moving is all over."

"Oh, I'll be good," promised Mrs. Chrystie, "I really will."

"Very well, then," said the nurse, "I'll write out the program for you before I go back. My patient's sister is staying with her tonight so I don't have to go back till I get ready, and we can have the time of our lives. Now, first, have you any idea where you *want* to move?"

"Only where we can afford it, and not too far from my office," said Camilla. "Mother telephoned a lot of real estate offices and got a list of places, but I don't have an idea where most of them are."

"Let me see them! I haven't been nursing so long in this city without knowing a whole lot about locations."

Camilla handed over the lists, and Miss York glanced them over.

"You don't want any on that list," she said, giving the first paper back to Camilla. "That's down in the slummy-slums. Vine Street is a tough neighborhood as far down as that, and Third Street isn't much better. It's unhealthy down there in more senses than one, and noisy. Besides it wouldn't be safe for you, Camilla, going out at night. Garner Street might do but it's terribly noisy. Victrolas and radios half the night, and brawls now and then. I nursed down there. Here, this one is better. It isn't fashionable there, but it's respectable. Still, it's desolate. Rows of red bricks like this, only a little larger, but they face a great foundry across the street and the noise is intolerable all day long."

Camilla ran her eye down the prices on the discarded list hopelessly. If these houses cost so much how could they afford anything better?

"Ah! Here is one, Park Circle. That's all right if it isn't opposite the school house! And now here, this last paper is much more possible. Would you think Brentwood was too far out, Camilla? I think you could make it in a half-hour mornings. It's not in the city limits and there are not such high taxes, so the rent seems to be reasonable. These two say 'yard.' Would you like that?"

"Oh, I'd like a yard!" said Mrs. Chrystie wistfully.

"And here is one with a sleeping porch. And two apartments in the east part of the city that might be good."

Miss York was checking them off rapidly with her pencil.

"Here are three that look pretty good," she said, "how about it, Camilla? Can't you and I take the car and run around to these? They aren't so far away and we ought to do all three in a little over an hour."

"*Tonight?*" said Camilla, wide-eyed. "Why, yes, if you have the time."

"All the time there is," said Miss York. "Get your hat on. But before you go, here's an idea. How would you like to take a bit larger place and rent me a room, or even two? I'm a bit crowded where I am, and the woman's married daughter is coming home with her family. Her husband's lost his job. No telling how long they will be there, and she needs all the room there is and then some. She told me about it last night. Said she hated to send me away but she didn't see how she was going to spare the room after they come. So I've got to be looking around, and if you think I wouldn't be a nuisance, maybe we could work out something together that would be nicer and a little bit cheaper than we could get separately?"

"Oh, that would be wonderful!" said Camilla with relief. "You'd like that, wouldn't you Mother?"

"I certainly would," said Mrs. Chrystie. "But you'd never want to live in a plain little house such as we would have to take."

"It doesn't matter about plainness," said Miss York, "and I wouldn't want anything better than you have. Of course certain neighborhoods are better for me than others, but we could easily find the right thing if you'd be willing to have me around. I've been paying—" and she launched into details, showing that she had thought things out carefully.

"If I took two rooms I'd expect to pay more of course, and it would be worth it to me to be with people I like. You know there's nothing like feeling at home, and I haven't had much home in my life. Now, come on, Camilla. There's one other place I have in mind if you don't find these what you want. We'll go see it. It's a lovely location, nice plain substantial neighborhood, little separate cottages with a central heating plant. I don't know what they rent for, but I heard since the depression they've put the rent down. I never saw the inside of them but the outside is most attractive. Now, Mother Chrystie, will you be good and rest while we're gone?"

"I'll be good," said Mrs. Chrystie, "but I'm going to sit in front of the desk and put my papers in order for tomorrow. It isn't hard work. I'll lie down if I feel tired."

"Well, we'll trust you. You're on your honor you know. If you get sick beforehand it's all off. We can't move!" declared Miss York.

So Camilla and Miss York got into the little car and started out house-hunting.

It was ten o'clock before they returned, but in their eyes was a look of satisfaction almost as if they had conquered the world.

"Well, we found a place," said Miss York triumphantly. "Tell her about it Camilla, while I heat up what coffee was left. Camilla needs something, she's too excited to sleep."

"Oh, Mother!" said Camilla, "I really believe we have found a nice place. Anyway it will do for a while till we can look around. There doesn't seem to be anything the matter with it at all.

"It's one of those little bungalow-cottages Miss York was telling about, out in Brentwood, all on one floor and an attic in the peak of the roof for storage. It's really darling. The rooms are fairly large with plenty of windows. It's really a little duck of a house, although the floors are pine, and the porch isn't bigger than a pocket handkerchief. But there's a small yard and a big tree, and there's space at the back of the house to hang up clothes. And Mother, just think of it, central heating! No furnace to tend and no coal to buy! We went next door and asked the people there about it and they say it's very satisfactory, always plenty of heat, and you can turn it off when it gets too hot."

"Why, that is wonderful!" said the mother. "I'm sure I shall like it. Is it located all right for Miss York, and is there a nice room for her? I think the tenant is the best part about this arrangement."

"So do I!" said Camilla with a sigh of relief. "It will be so nice to have her coming home to us sometimes! The only thing I'm afraid of is that she's doing this to help us out."

"Just listen to her, Mother Chrystie, she'd even begrudge me the chance to do a little good deed now and then if I got the chance. But as it happens this time the rooms in this house are a lot better than where I am now, larger and lighter, and the closet is twice as big. There's a closet in every room, all good-sized, and one in the hall. Did you notice that, Camilla?"

"Yes, and a linen closet in the hall, and a towel closet in the bathroom."

"It sounds too good to be true," said Mrs. Chrystie, "I've kept the extra linen in a box under my bed so long I don't know that I'd remember to use a linen closet if I had one. I don't feel that I deserve so much luxury. I'm afraid I've sometimes grumbled at our close quarters."

"Never where anybody could hear you, I'm sure!" said Nurse York. "What I'm afraid of is that I'm not good enough to live in the house with such wonderful people as you are. Ever since I've been here to nurse I've called you folks 'white orchid' people. It just seems to fit you. There are people who remind me of violets, they are so shy, and some are tiger lilies, and some are like weeds, just no account at all, but you folks always seemed to me like royalty in flowers, heavenly royalty at that."

"Mother, she's a poet, not a nurse!" cried Camilla laughing. "Talking poetry like that. I don't know as we shall be able to live up to her. But I think she's got her metaphors mixed somehow. Seems to me I've heard that orchids are parasites."

"There, Camilla, you've said enough!" said Miss York severely. "You go up to the third floor and get done whatever you have to do for the movers tomorrow, while I get Lady Chrystie to bed. Then I'm coming up and get you, so you better hurry. It's going to be my special care to look after you two and see that you keep your health!"

"She's going to be awfully bossy, Mother," laughed back Camilla as she mounted the stairs with her arms full of garments to pack in the trunk up in the attic.

Two hours later she lay in her bed trying to memorize a list of things she must remember to do before she left for the office in the morning. It seemed incredible that this time tomorrow night they would be in another house. It wasn't going to be impossible after all to move in one day. But what a tower of strength Miss York was! And Jinny Wilcox was going to be another tower she was sure, from the brief glimpse she had of her homely face when they stopped to arrange with her about the cleaning.

So, without any memory of her former troubles and perplexities, she dropped away to sleep.

CHAPTER XVII

IT WAS HARD TO TEAR HERSELF AWAY IN THE MORNING. How interesting it would be to stay and look after everything. There seemed to be so many little things she ought to do before she went. Maybe she had been wrong not to ask Mr. Whitlock to let her off for the day. Then she remembered that he might be still away, and that he had been most anxious for certain matters to be finished at once. No, she couldn't trust Marietta to look after it all, not yet! And with a sigh she hurried away.

"Just remember, dear, that I still have my right mind," said her mother smiling as she kissed her goodbye. "I won't let anybody steal our furniture, nor throw the dishes out of the window!"

"Well, but Mother, you've been sick!"

"Yes, but I'm not sick now, and anyway I'm not going to move the furniture personally. Now hurry along. You're going to be late! And don't think about this end of things till five o'clock!"

Camilla had no difficulty in controlling her thoughts that day however, for she was overwhelmed with work and responsibility, and there was no time either for wondering how her mother and the mover would be getting on without her, or for dreaming back into the brief past that had haunted her so long.

To begin with, Marietta telephoned that her stepmother had been taken very sick that morning, "And I gotta stand by, see, till the doctor gets here! I don't wantta, but I gotta! 'Cause she might die, see, and I wouldn't want it ta be my fault, even if she hasn't been nice ta me."

"Why of course!" said Camilla briskly. "You must stay there if you are needed. Have you sent for the doctor? Couldn't you get a district nurse to come? Can I do anything for you?"

"No, thanks! I guess she'll be awright. But she's taking on something awful. Little Ted is all curled up on the couch looking white and sick. He's frightened, hearing his mother scream. I don't know what she's got. I guess it's her appendix. That's what the woman next door says she thinks it is. So ef you can get along without me this morning I'll try and get there at noon. If I can't I'll let ya know."

"All right, Marietta," said Camilla with a sinking of heart. How things were thickening. What a day! And she ought to be at home this minute looking after the moving! It seemed as if everything was all awry. She bowed her head over the telephone for a minute in despair.

"Well," she reminded herself, "Mother always says that when things seem to be in a tangle to us, it's just that God is executing an especially intricate and marvellous pattern in our lives, and we must be pliable in His hands, so as not to hinder. Lord, have Thy way with me today!"

She lifted her head, put down the telephone and went back to her work. She would just rest on that and go ahead.

Many people came into the office that morning, questions came up for her to decide quickly, the telephone rang almost continuously, and finally Mr. Whitlock telephoned that he would not be able to get back until late in the afternoon.

Her voice was clear and steady as she answered his questions, and gave him the messages that had been left for him, writing down his directions carefully. She did not tell him that Marietta was not there. That would not help matters any and would only exasperate him with Marietta. She did not tell him that there had been no time for lunch, and she was going to have a cup of coffee and a sandwich sent up from the restaurant near-by as soon as she could find time to telephone for it. She did not tell him that she was moving that day and ought to be at home. She just went steadily ahead and did her best, determined to let her Lord have His way in her for that one day at least, and not get flurried about it. And she was greatly relieved and surprised to discover as the day went on that she was not as tired as usual in spite of it all. There was something restful in remembering that it was not her responsibility. She had but to go ahead, and leave the working out of things with God.

When intervals of quiet from telephone and patrons came her fingers flew on the typewriter keys. She discovered presently that she was really making progress with the day's work in spite of the many hindrances. Her heart was at rest, and she hadn't time to think of dreams or disappointments. Oh, if she could just keep this heart-rest all the time how wonderful it would be!

Marietta came in breathless about two o'clock, and found Camilla working away so hard that she did not see her enter, writing and taking a bite of her sandwich now and then between pages.

"You poor thing!" said Marietta self-reproachfully. "You been here all alone all day? You didn't have a chance to get any lunch? You go now and get a real good meal and I'll stay till five. They've taken her to the hospital. It was the appendix and they think they've got to operate right off. She's awful scared. I felt real sorry for her. I left Ted with a neighbor. Poor kid, he's scared stiff! If I had known Whittie wasn't here I'd have brought Ted along, but I guess Whittie wouldn't stand for a child in the office, would he?"

"I'm afraid not," smiled Camilla. "Poor child! I'm sorry he has to stay alone. I'd tell you to take him down to Mother this afternoon, but we're moving today and there wouldn't be any place for him yet."

"Moving!" cried Marietta, "then you oughtta be home yerself. You go now and I'll stay here. Ted's all right for this afternoon. He's got some picture papers to read. He likes ta read. You go, and I can do everything. I'll be real careful."

"Thank you, Marietta," Camilla smiled, "that's nice of you, but I couldn't. There are some messages I have to give people, and things that have to be decided when I see what they say. Mr. Whitlock called up. He won't be in till four forty-five, and I'd like to have the work up to the mark. If you think it's all right for you to stay suppose you get to work on those circulars and fold and address them. I'm staying right here till five. We mustn't stop to talk. I hope your stepmother will get through all right, and afterward perhaps there'll be some way I can help. Now, let's get to work!" and Camilla's fingers went flying on.

Mr. Whitlock came rushing in, looking tired and worn, about ten minutes to five. He cast his eyes anxiously over his desk, and looked relieved when he saw the pile of letters awaiting his signature.

"You got them all done?" he said pleasantly. "Well, that's great. Miss Pratt must be improving greatly. I was thinking I might have to ask you to stay overtime and finish them. It is most important they should go out tonight for I find someone else is bidding for the same contract."

"You don't need to give me any credit," said Marietta earnestly, "I couldn't come till about two o'clock. My stepmother was awful sick and I couldn't leave her till they took her to the hospital. Camilla was here all alone most of the day, and she had a lot done before I got here."

Mr. Whitlock raised his eyebrows at Camilla.

"Oh, I'm sorry!" he said. "Why didn't you tell me when I telephoned. I'd have let the rest of the business go till next week."

"Oh, I got along all right," said Camilla, "and Miss Pratt is mistaken about her work. She's been wonderful this afternoon. She did all that pile herself. And she must have been tired too. She's been up nearly all night with her stepmother, and came down here just as soon as they took her away."

Mr. Whitlock cast a kindly glance toward Marietta.

"Well, that was great, Miss Pratt! I appreciate that. If I had known about it I would have told you not to come, even if the work had to go out to a public stenographer for once."

"Thank you," said Marietta blushing scarlet over the unexpected praise and kindness, "but I'm all right. I guess I can get along now. And if you don't mind I'd liketa make up this lost day on Saturday afternoons."

"Oh, that's all right, Miss Pratt," said the employer kindly. "You don't need to make that up. You have a right to an emergency now and then, and you've been doing unusually good work the last week. I appreciate the change in your appearance too."

Then he turned to Camilla.

"You are moving?" he asked. "Isn't that rather sudden, Miss Chrystie?"

"Yes," said Camilla. "The house was sold quite suddenly, and they offered to move us if we would vacate at once, so we thought it would be to our advantage."

"Well, I'm very sorry that you should have had to be here all day."

"It's quite all right," said Camilla. "We hadn't so much to move. I did a good deal last night. The movers will do the rest."

"Well, you must go at once!" he said glancing at the clock and taking some papers from his pocket. "It must have been hard for you today."

"It's been all right," said Camilla brightly, "and they don't expect me till half-past five. I've plenty of time to finish this letter and take some dictation for tomorrow morning before I go."

Camilla could see that this decision relieved her employer very much, though he was gracious about it. So she insisted on finishing the important matters before she left. Marietta, too, stuck faithfully by, working with her homely young face in an earnest frown and her pudgy fingers pounding away on her machine.

It was almost six o'clock when all three finally went down in the elevator together, Whitlock hurrying off to meet a man and take him to dinner.

Camilla was relieved that he did not offer to go with her and help. Somehow though he was kind she did not want him coming into the dilemma of their moving. On the way to the house she tried to reason it out, knowing in the back of her mind that if it had been Wainwright she would have been not only relieved but overjoyed. And yet Mr. Whitlock had been most kind and considerate, and would have been the natural one to help if he had offered, which of course he couldn't do with a dinner engagement on hand. She could sense that these were strenuous times in the office and that he was hard pressed, and she felt all the more obligated to be on hand early and get off those letters he had dictated just now. They should go in the nine o'clock mail, and she would see that they did, even if she had to leave a little earlier than usual to accomplish it.

She had meant to telephone home before driving there, to see if the movers had started away yet with the first load, but she disliked to do it before the others, so she drove home as fast as traffic would allow.

She found the movers just about to leave with the first load.

"Very well, then, Mother, I'll go right along with them. Can I trust you to lie down while I'm gone? No, you're not to go yet till there's a place for you to go right to bed. Have you had anything to eat?"

"Oh, yes," said her mother smiling. "I ate at five o'clock, and I've got the thermos bottle full of hot soup for you. Will you eat it before you go or take it with you?"

"Why, I'll take it with me. That's wonderful! I'll eat it while I'm telling them where to put things. Now, can I trust you to stay right there on the couch till I get back and not lift a finger?"

"What is there left to do?" asked the mother. "But really I don't see why I shouldn't go along now. I could rest on a chair until you got things fixed to your mind you know."

"But you wouldn't, I'm afraid."

"Yes, I would. I'd rest much better if I was right there and the journey over."

"All right, but isn't there anything more here to be done?"

"Not a thing!" said Mrs. Chrystie proudly. "Mrs. Pryor is coming in after the last load is gone and sweep all the rooms. Mr. Glyndon said that was all we need do. He said the new owner would look after all the rest."

"Well, that's wonderful!" said Camilla with a troubled look around to think that all this had been accomplished without her supervision. "All right, Mother, where's your coat and hat? It's pretty cold out."

"Oh, I thought you'd say that so I got out my old fur coat before the trunks left, and I've filled a hot water bottle and wrapped it in a blanket. I thought I might as well fuss over myself as to have you and Miss York do it."

"Well, you have been good," commended Camilla laughing. "Have you got galoshes on? The pavements are icy you know."

"Oh, yes, I saved them out too. Now let's get going. Those men want to get done."

So, for the first time since her illness Mrs. Chrystie went out into the winter world again.

"It's going to snow," she announced as she stepped into the car and sat down. "No, don't worry about me, I'm quite all right. I lay down three times today and I haven't done a thing the last hour but tell the men which things to take in the first load."

Camilla wrapped her mother warmly, put the hot water bag at her feet, and started on, the big van coming close behind.

"Now," said Camilla, "this is the first time you've been out and you mustn't talk in the cold air. Just rest back and relax."

"All right," said her mother, but her bright eyes were watching the streets as they went along, and once when Camilla looked at her anxiously her mother smiled at her happily almost like a child.

"Having a nice ride, Millie, darling!" she said.

"You dear!" said Camilla with a throb of thankfulness at her heart, "I believe you're enjoying this."

"Why surely," said her mother. "Who wouldn't after all these weeks in the house?"

"Well, I hope you like the house," said the daughter.

"Why of course I'll like it! Whatever it is I'll like it. Didn't it bring you money enough to get that debt off your mind, and didn't our Father send it in time for our need? Why shouldn't I like it? I'd like it just because He sends it, even if I *didn't* like it!"

Camilla laughed outright with a child's sudden delight.

"Mother! That's lovely! Do you know, I believe when we get settled I'm just going to take a day off sometime and be thankful for the kind of mother I have. I don't believe I ever before realized what a wonderful inheritance I have, having a mother who can take hard things that way. I wish I had such a wonderful trust as you have. I believe that's what has kept you so young looking in spite of all that you have been through."

"Yes," said her mother thoughtfully, "I guess that has helped me through. Trusting. I couldn't have got through in my own strength I know that. Why, Camilla, you're stopping. This can't be the house, is it? It's all lit up. Do you have to ask the way or something?"

"No," said Camilla, "I don't have to ask the way and this is the house, but I don't understand its being lit up, unless Jinny is still there."

"But, daughter, this is a very pretty little house!"

"Oh, I'm glad it seems nice to you. Now, you sit still, Mother, till I get a chair or something taken in for you to sit on."

"No," said Mrs. Chrystie, "I want to go in with you now. I can sit on the stairs for a while till a chair comes. Or aren't there any stairs? A box then. For pity's sake don't baby me now. Can't you see I'm running over with curiosity?"

Camilla laughed, and let her have her way, taking her arm and carefully leading her where the walk was icy. But when they went up the steps the front door suddenly swung open and a wide path of light poured out, and Miss York with a big white apron over her uniform and a towel pinned over her hair, appeared in the doorway.

"Welcome home!" she cried, bowing low before them, ushering them inside and shutting the door.

"Why, it's warm as toast!" said Mrs. Chrystie looking around admiringly, "and you say there's no furnace to bother with. That will be wonderful!"

Camilla and her mother walked through the rooms with Miss York bringing up the rear. It seemed so wonderful that this was their new home.

In just no time at all they had Mrs. Chrystie established in a big chair in the living room, and the movers were putting up the beds and spreading down the rugs under Camilla's direction. It didn't take long. And Miss York with uncanny accuracy found the sheets and blankets and was making up the bed, while Camilla ate her soup, and gave directions to the movers. Incredibly the house began to be like home with each piece of furniture that came in.

Miss York stayed with Mrs. Chrystie when Camilla went back with the movers to get the last load and close up the house, and soon her former patient was tucked snugly into bed with the light turned out.

"Now, you're to go to sleep at once!" she ordered, "or we shan't let you get up at all tomorrow, and I'll have to give up my job and come and nurse you."

With that threat she closed the door and tiptoed away to prowl around and see what she could do to make the house more liveable.

She found two big baskets of dishes wrapped in newspapers, and set to work putting them on the dresser shelves, putting away knives and forks and spoons in the dresser drawers. The kitchen utensils had come in the first load also, and before Camilla returned Nurse York had the kitchen in fair order, as far as things had arrived, for Mrs. Chrystie with careful foresight had sent in the first load what would be needed first.

Back at the old home Camilla telephoned Mr. Glyndon according to previous arrangement, and before long he arrived, paid the movers, and gave Camilla a check for the rest of the money promised. She stood looking at the check in a kind of daze. It seemed so strange to her that thus suddenly she had been lifted out of the appalling debt that had hung over her and threatened to engulf her, and put into ease and freedom, with a better house to live in, and for her mother the companionship at times of Miss York. She hadn't known how she was going to get along, and now it was all fixed. Of course she wasn't rolling in wealth yet, but it seemed luxury just to be out of debt and have the rent ahead for a few months so that she could have a chance to lay up a little for a time of emergency. How good God had been to her.

Then as she heard the movers coming back to get another piece of furniture she folded the check quickly, put it in her purse, and hurried off upstairs to make sure that nothing had been forgotten.

As she came downstairs again, and looked down upon the emptiness and desolation in the little front hall, a sudden sadness came over her. Something brought back that night that her mother was so very sick, and Wainwright had proved such a tower of strength.

There was nothing left down there now in the living room but a few chairs and the old piano. She could seem to see Wainwright's evening coat lying across the top. And the old Morris chair! She remembered how she had found him that next morning, asleep in the Morris chair in the hall, his long dark lashes lying on his cheeks, his beautiful hair tossed back in disorder from his handsome forehead. How good and dear he had looked to her! And the orchids! Beautiful delicate creatures! And his pleasant grin! It gave her a distinct pang to realize that she would never likely see him again. He would never appear at the door of this house and ask for her! And he wouldn't know where else to look for her!

Suddenly she was appalled to think that she was so absolutely cutting herself off from him, and there wasn't any way she could leave a clue to herself. Her mother had duly written her note of thanks for the oranges but there had come no answer, and she had no excuse for writing again. And even if she had she wouldn't of course. No, he was gone into the unknown world of people, even as he had come, and he would never be in her life again. And it was right that it should be so! But oh, how it hurt! For there still was that sharp sweet memory of the kiss he had given her, the kiss that seemed to seal something precious between them. To think that she, Camilla Chrystie, should have to have a memory of such a thing, a kiss that could still burn and humiliate, and yet could be so precious! She who had always prided herself on her carefulness where men were concerned, her cool reticence, and her ability to protect herself.

And suddenly she realized that she had been counting on his coming back sometime in spite of all. And God knowing that had cut her off from any such possibility! God was helping her against her own weakness. Well, she should be thankful that she was going away where she would not be constantly reminded of him. How unheard of! Just a few days with a stranger, and something had come into her life of which she could not rid herself! She *must!* She *would!*

When she finally locked the door and handed the key to Mr. Glyndon, she felt as if she were shutting the door on one of the brightest experiences of her life, and she was rather glad that Mr. Glyndon was there, saying courteous things about regretting he had had to hurry her, and hoping the new home would be all right. There really wasn't any time to be sentimental about leaving that doorstep, that sordid little grimy doorstep where Wainwright and she had stood together a few short weeks before, and she was glad with a kind of moral approval that it was so.

Back in her car again, speeding ahead of the moving van, she reflected on life. Why did one young man have to get such a hold on her thoughts above all other young men she had ever met? Was it just the halo of romance, meeting him in the street in the dark that way and having his help in her time of need? Was it because of his wealth and position, his personal attraction, his courteous manner, his white orchids?

Why for instance couldn't she be as interested in Mr. Whitlock? He was good looking, too. He probably had plenty of wealth and social position, if one knew the whole story. And he certainly was courteous, and a delightful escort. Perhaps he wouldn't ask her to go out with him any more, but if he did she ought to be glad to put some new thoughts and experiences into her mind. That was probably the matter, she had been too much to herself. She just worked hard and never went anywhere. That must be why the first fascinating stranger held her thoughts so long and so exclusively.

Well, the new home in the new place might give her new friends and erase morbid longings for something that was never really hers.

So she arrived at the new house, and realized that she was terribly tired. Such a long day with so many responsibilities. She just must stop thinking about herself and give herself to the duties before her. She had to direct the placing of all the rest of the things before she could think of getting to bed. And there was the kitchen. She ought to get things in shape for a breakfast.

So she drove into the tiny corrugated iron garage at the back of the tiny lot, and shut her car in for the night, thankful that there was a garage and she didn't have to leave the car with its new paint out in the open, for it looked as if there was going to be more snow.

But when she opened the door there was Miss York still holding the fort, and the dishes in shining rows in the dresser. A sense of comfort and peace came upon her.

"I brought over my electric toaster," said Miss York indicating her arrangements on the shelf of the locker, "you can make toast in no time in the morning, and you're not to get up any earlier than usual. Jinny is coming over in the morning to work and see that your mother doesn't. I found the bread box had a loaf of bread in it, and I hunted the coffee. Also the woman next door put a note in her milk bottle to ask her milkman to leave you some cream in the morning. I started some oatmeal and it will keep cooking a little all night on the pilot light in that double boiler. If that isn't breakfast enough for you the first morning you can get more in the city."

For answer Camilla flung her arms about Miss York's neck and gave her a kiss.

"You dear angel-guardian!" she cried. "What should we have done without you!"

"There, there, now, no sob-stuff!" said the nurse, turning pink at the caress. "Hurry up and get done with those movers so I can tuck you into bed before I go."

"But it's almost eleven o'clock. You ought to go home at once! I don't like you running around so late alone."

The nurse stared and then laughed.

"Don't you know I've been used to taking care of myself for thirty years? Don't you worry about me."

"Well, if you're going to worry about me," declared Camilla, "then I'm going to worry about you. Come now, please put your hat on and go, and I'll promise, honor bright, to get into bed the minute the movers are gone."

The movers were not long in getting the last load placed. They had their pay and were anxious to get home to their beds. But Miss York managed to stay around until they were gone. She was used to having her way.

So presently Camilla found herself sinking away to sleep and feeling like a traveler just set sail upon new seas toward strange unexplored lands.

CHAPTER XVIII

STEPHANIE VARRELL WAS READING A DAY-LETTER JUST RE-ceived from her lawyer.

She sat on the end veranda of the hotel that looked off toward the sea, but she did not see the water. On her face was the smile of the cat who has just licked the cream off the pan of milk, or the frosting off the sponge cake. The telegram read as follows:

"Have opportunity to sell at good advance the property on Vesey Street acquired for you last week at your suggestion. Tenants moving out to-day. City Gas Company offers great inducement if sale can be completed at once. They are putting up new plant in same block and wish to acquire the whole unbroken. They are tearing down and rebuilding. Time a factor. Can get unusual price if you are willing to sell. Chances are they would be able to get building condemned, and commandeer it at their own price, if you refuse now. Wire instructions immediately.

R. R. Glyndon."

Stephanie read it through several times carefully, the cat-and-cream expression still on her face. Then she took her little gold pencil out of her purse and wrote rapidly on the back of the telegram:

"Am willing to sell on condition the building is torn down at once, this week if possible. Otherwise nothing doing. Ultimatum!

S. Varrell."

When Mr. Glyndon received that message he smiled amusedly.

"The divine Stephanie must hate somebody pretty badly just now," he said to himself.

Stephanie had sent that message on its way and then had left the view of the leaping, dancing, golden sea and searched diligently until she had discovered Jeff's mother, in one of her usual knitting haunts in a windless corner where her marcel would not be disturbed. Stephanie dropped down to exclaim over the beauty of the knitting she was doing.

Madame Wainwright gave her a keen glance and ignored her, and presently Stephanie in honeyed words asked about Jeff.

"He's having a wonderful time, isn't he?" she gushed. "They say that trip is great if you can stand the insects and the serpents."

"There are a good many kinds of insects—and serpents," remarked Jeffrey Wainwright's mother dryly, but gave no further information.

"But I thought he told me he had to be back in the north before this," lied Stephanie with narrowed jacinth eyes on her victim.

"Perhaps he did," said Jeffrey's mother calmly. "He probably changed his plans."

"He went with his younger brother, didn't he? I don't blame you for being nervous about the little fellow down in an awful place like that, although it must be perfectly fascinating."

"He went because he chose to," said Mrs. Wainwright calmly, beginning to count her stitches. "There was no reason why I should be nervous about Sam. He's quite capable of looking out for himself, even if there hadn't been a competent man in charge of the boys."

"Then you think Jeffrey may return in time for the tennis tournament Saturday?" cunningly asked the girl. "It would be too bad for him to miss that. He's practically a champion now, isn't he?"

"I really don't know what my son's plans are, Miss Varrell," said Jeffrey's mother coldly.

"But at least you don't think he'll go back north yet, do you?" persisted the girl.

"That will depend entirely on whether his father needs him," said the woman haughtily. "Excuse me, I've got to count these stitches again. I think I've made a mistake."

But Stephanie had found out what she wanted. Jeff hadn't gone back north yet, that was pretty sure. She had been afraid he had slipped away home already, but she had taken a chance and caught his mother unaware. Women like Mrs. Wainwright could evade, but they didn't deliberately lie. Jeffrey was still in the south, and if Mr. Glyndon did his duty, there would be no house left on Vesey Street when Jeffrey got back home. She walked to the other end of the veranda and looked off to sea, and her jacinth eyes glinted gold with triumph. She would win out for a few more days anyway, perhaps. She meant to crush that other gold-haired deep-eyed girl like an eggshell under her foot if she got in her way again. And perhaps the longer Jeff stayed in the forest the quicker he would forget the other girl, and whatever it was she said to him that night they had all met.

Meantime, there were other pleasant things she could do besides worry over her hates and desires. There were other fish in the sea as good as those that had been caught, or nearly caught, and she was pretty sure that Jeff was safe for a time. Why not enjoy herself?

So she garbed herself scantily and dropped down to the beach with her best golden lure.

Twenty-four hours later workmen arrived at one-twenty-five Vesey Street and began to roll up the tin roof of the little old shabby house like a scroll, and unbrick its wall, and pull out its windows like old teeth, and tear up the cheap worn floors, and the two stubby wooden steps where Camilla had stood to say good-night to Jeffrey Wainwright the last time she saw him. And surely if intangible things can haunt, the ghost of that kiss he laid upon her lips that night must have fled the neighborhood in utter rout.

So trifling souls, even those with jacinth eyes, are sometimes used to mould history and change destinies. This time the whims of a spoiled girl with a heart full of hate for anything that came in her way, even unwittingly, decided a much mooted question of whether the City Gas Company should expand on its south side or on its north side. It was a question of which block they could soonest get possession, and Stephanie Varrell's cryptic telegram swung the balance.

CHAPTER XIX

IT WAS LATE IN THE AFTERNOON IN CAMP. THE BOYS HAD just come in with the fish they had been catching that day, a fine lot of silvery shining fellows. They were proud of the day's catch. A certain detachment of the company were cleaning the fish down by the water, and the low swinging sun made ruby paths across the lake making the tall pines stand out almost black against the glow. Another detachment were making the fire and getting the mess

plates out on the rude table. Still a third were preparing
the corn bread, washing lettuce and getting out the butter,
salt, pepper, and other condiments. There was a huge pile
of oranges in the centre of the table for dessert.

John Saxon, after giving his orders to the young workers, had swung himself in a hammock stretched between
two coconut palms, and Wainwright, more weary with
the day's march than he cared to own, dropped silently
into another hammock and lay still with his eyes closed
and his arms stretched above his head. He was thinking
how good it was merely to lie still, how pleasant the
smell of jessamine, and the odor of the frying fish that
was beginning to mingle with the perfume of the flowers.
How hungry he was. He couldn't remember ever to have
been as hungry in his life before. It was good to be tired
and hungry, and to anticipate plain food so eagerly. The
very smoke from the pine fire was restful and pleasant.

If he looked out across the blood red path on the water
there was a strange picture, quiet, restful; the slipping
away of the sun so silently. And presently while they ate
it would be gone without notice and they would be left
to finish by the firelight.

He opened his eyes now and then and watched the
progress downward of the ball of fire that was the sun.
There were no gold lights in it now to remind him of
golden hair, but there was a quiet darkness in the shadows
of the woods that made him think of her eyes, darkly
troubled when she had said she was not of his world.

What had she meant? The old question back again as
soon as he had nothing else to occupy his mind! She was
right, too, he was beginning to realize. Hitherto he had
always thought of but one world, with workers to make it
go smoothly. Now he saw there were other worlds, each
different. Each complete in itself. Yet somehow he suspected that somewhere there must be a point of contact.
And it was that point of contact which he was out to
find.

He turned his eyes toward John Saxon, lying across
there in his hammock, one arm swung up over his head,
the damp brown curls snapping back from his bronzed
forehead, his face so strong and yet so sweet sometimes,
and withal so stern and almost forbidding at other times.

John Saxon was of another world from his also. Was

he perhaps of Camilla's world, he asked himself searching-ly? Perhaps. Was there no bridge? No bridge but that strange inscrutable sentence "ye must be born again," that John Saxon had read that first night in the woods?

He lay watching the other man between the half-open fringes of his eyes. He had come to love and admire him during the few days they had been wandering in this strange tropical world together with these kids. Yet always at night when the Bible was read and he heard the strong tender voice in prayer, John Saxon seemed like another man, a man he only half understood. The best part of him seemed hidden behind a mystery that he could not penetrate.

And why was he so interested in that little worn Testament that he carried everywhere, even fishing, and brought out on any occasion? He wished he dared ask him. Somehow he had not yet come to the point where he felt free enough to do so.

Suddenly he followed an impulse and spoke, quietly, in a voice that could not be heard by the boys at work.

"John,—"

They had come so far in friendship as to call one another John and Jeff.

"I wish you'd tell me what it means to be born again."

John Saxon looked up with a quick light of joy in his eyes, his face kindling with that strange tenderness that Jeff had seen there before several times and wondered at. It was almost as if John had recognized in him a kinship which he had not before suspected.

"I guess the best way to understand that," he said thoughtfully, "is to think what it meant to be born into this world the first time. You did not exist in this world, you know, until you received the life of your parents. Then you were born and became a citizen of this world, gradually growing in the knowledge and privileges of it."

Jeff was watching him eagerly, weighing every word.

"In the same way," went on John Saxon, "you do not exist so far as the spiritual world is concerned until you receive the life of God. Then He says you are born spiritually and can begin to grow in the knowledge and blessings of the spiritual world."

Jeffrey was almost breathless with eagerness to grasp

every word as he heard again of that distinction between "worlds" that Camilla had mentioned.

He sat up in the hammock and put both feet on the ground, his arms widespread grasping the meshes of the hammock.

Then Camilla had not meant just the difference between wealth and poverty, between social position and the lack of it! He had been sure all along that there was a deeper meaning to her words than he understood!

"How does one receive the life of God?" he asked earnestly, his eyes looking straight into John Saxon's eyes. "A child in coming into the world has no say in the matter."

"No," said John Saxon, "a child of this world is born at the will of its parents, but a child of God is born by willingly accepting the gift of God's life. To do that you must first realize that you need it. That you are a sinner, helpless to make yourself fit for God's presence, deserving nothing but His righteous judgment of eternal banishment from Him. If you don't want that banishment, that separation forever from God, if you do want to be with Him and be like Him, you will accept the gift He offers in undeserved kindness—the gift of eternal life which He purchased for you by shedding the life-blood of His own Son instead of yours."

John Saxon's voice was full of awe and wonder as he added:

"He paid that much for me, too!"

There was silence then for a long minute while Jeffrey studied his friend's fine strong face, a trifle puzzled perhaps. He couldn't quite see what John Saxon could have done that should make him so deserving of eternal punishment. His own gay thoughtless life, filled utterly with his own pleasant self, fulfilling its wishes, nothing very bad perhaps, but still a life lived apart from God, *might* deserve punishment perhaps, though he had never considered the matter before, having always felt that he was a pretty good sort of fellow as the world went. But John Saxon. What could he have done to feel himself such a sinner, that the redemption of himself should bring such awe and adoration into his face? There must be more to this than appeared on the surface, and Jeffrey felt himself to be a babe in this new study in which he had engaged.

He was about to ask a question about this matter of being such a terrible sinner when you hadn't done anything much at all, when suddenly the boys came whooping over to announce supper ready, and to drag John Saxon from his hammock like so many officers of the law. Little Carlin came to Jeff, too, and slid a grubby little skinny claw into his own confidingly pulling him up and over to the table.

Jeff put a strong arm about the slender shoulders of the little loveless child, gave him one of his most bewildering smiles, and called him "Little Pard!"

Jeff was more than usually quiet during the evening. He joined to a certain extent in the games the boys were playing, but John Saxon noticed that he was deeply thoughtful, and when at last the camp was quiet for the night, John Saxon came and sat down beside Jeff. He was reclining by the fire gazing deep into the night where a tired late moon was making ragged ripples of silver in the blackness of the lacquered lake.

"What's perplexing you, Brother?" said John Saxon, sliding down beside him, cross-legged in the sand, and picking up a small stick which he began to break into tiny splinters and throw one by one upon the fire.

"I can't quite see this sin business," said Jeff looking up gratefully. "Now, you,—I can't undestand that look in your eyes when you spoke of a great price having saved you. You were never a great sinner, I'd wager that! And I, while I'm no gilded saint of course, I've had a good time and not worried much, but I've been as good as the average I'm sure and a lot better than most. I've been clean, and fairly unselfish—! Where does the sin come in?"

Then did John Saxon unfold to him the story of sin, beginning in heaven when it was first found in Lucifer, son of the morning, the brightest angel of heaven, when pride made him want to be worshipped like the Most High.

John Saxon took out his electric torch and read snatches here and there from his Bible as he talked, till Jeff heard the whole amazing story of sin in heaven, and on earth, causing the fall of man.

Jeff had never heard it before. Any phrases or references to a devil, or to the fall of man, he had always taken as jocular, whimsical language and had never stopped to question what might have been their origin. He listened with deep attention, asking now and then a question.

"And since then," finished John Saxon, "everyone is born with a dead spiritual nature, and cannot see the kingdom of God until he is born again."

It was very still all about except for the snapping of the flickering fire, and the far call of some night bird. Presently, John Saxon took up the story again, of the love of God for fallen man, and told in clear, graphic words of the shedding of blood that was necessary to satisfy God's justice and vindicate his righteousness.

"There you have the story," he said. "It's not lying and stealing and murder, nor even uncleanness that makes us sinners. Those are only the result of our being sinners. It's turning away from a love like that! But a sinner can be made righteous in the sight of God by accepting Christ's death as his own. Do you understand now how we are all sinners, and have come short of the glory which God intended for us when He made us?"

"I think I do!" said Jeff reverently, slowly, sorrowfully. "I never saw that before. I've been greatly guilty. I've lived utterly for myself, cleanly, morally, cheerfully, kindly, perhaps, but utterly forgetful of God. I think perhaps you've led me to what I came out to these woods to find. I knew there was something I had to find before I went back."

"Praise the Lord!" said Saxon softly.

A little later the two bowed their heads beside the fire and prayed together. Perchance the angels on the ramparts of heaven whispered together, "Behold he prayeth!"

CHAPTER XX

IT HAD BEEN SNOWING HARD ALL DAY, GREAT WHITE HEAVY flakes, and when Camilla came downstairs from the office she paused in the doorway in dismay. She hadn't realized that the snow would be so deep. She was glad she had worn galoshes, although she had hesitated about doing so, for when she started from home there seemed to be only a few lazy flakes, and she thought the storm would not last.

She stood there a minute wondering if she kept close to the buildings whether the snow was deep enough to get inside her galoshes, and then just as she was about to plunge in she heard a step behind her and a hand was laid on her arm.

She turned about startled and there stood Mr. Whitlock with his nice protective look, smiling down into her eyes.

"How are you going to get home?" he asked, as if he were responsible for her welfare.

"Oh, I have my car around at the garage. It isn't far," she answered gallantly.

"Well, I'll take you to the garage then," he said. "My car is parked just outside here. I knew I wouldn't be upstairs long, and it's too stormy to go around much without it. I can't have you getting pneumonia you know," and he gave her another of those pleasant smiles that were so almost possessive.

"Oh, thank you," she said with relief. "That will help a lot. But I have galoshes you know."

"I'm afraid they won't do much good in this depth of snow. Here, where's the janitor of this building? Joe, where are you? Joe, just get a shovel and run out a footpath to my car, won't you? You ought to keep this walk clear you know."

"Yes sir," said Joe, "I was just going out again, sir. Seem like I can't keep up with this snow, nohow."

So Camilla walked dry-shod to her employer's car and was taken to her garage.

"Have you chains on your car?" asked Whitlock.

"Why, no, I've never really needed them. I guess I'll be all right. I drive very carefully."

"Put some chains on that car!" ordered Whitlock to the man at the garage, and then he insisted on paying for them himself although Camilla protested.

"That's all right," he smiled, "it's to my interest you know that you should be protected. You'll need them in the morning if you don't now. And I think I'll just drive along with you a ways and see that you get through all right. This is some weather. Is your windshield wiper in good order?"

When they were ready to start Whitlock said he would go ahead with his heavier car and break the way in case there were streets where no traffic had been, and so in spite of all that she could say he escorted her to her door, made her get out at the house, lifting her across the deep drift by the steps, and himself put her car in the garage. Then he came in for just a moment, he said just to meet her mother.

But Mrs. Chrystie had been worrying all the afternoon about how Camilla was going to get home, and she was so grateful for Mr. Whitlock's escort that she insisted he should stay to dinner. So he stayed.

Camilla went flying around in the kitchen helping her mother to get the dinner on the table, and wishing in her heart that Mr. Whitlock's first visit to their home could have been under more favorable circumstances. Somehow she didn't feel as free with him as she had with Jeffrey Wainwright. There was something rather formal and dignified about Mr. Whitlock. She recalled the quiet dignity of the old inn, the perfect service, the immaculate table. Of course Mother's table was always exquisitely clean and lovely, but it happened this night that there was a darn in the fine old tablecloth right where it would show. It seemed too bad when Mother did have lovely things put away that she could have put on if there had been time. But dinner was all ready and could not wait. Camilla did manage to place a lovely doily of beautiful drawn work and set her mother's little fern on it, but there were no flowers of course for the table, none of the accessories that Whitlock gave the impression of being so particular about. She did get out some of the best napkins however, and put a dish in front of the darn, and it had to go at that.

Whitlock was very pleasant. He seemed to enjoy the home-cooking and took second helpings. He enjoyed the homemade bread, the little white creamed onions, and the pumpkin pie which was the dessert. He praised the coffee, too, and said few people knew how to make good coffee.

When the meal was over, however, he did not go into the kitchen to help with the dishes as Wainwright had done. Camilla gave him no opportunity. She shut the door sharply and decidedly on the dining room and kitchen, and led both mother and guest firmly into the living room. Somehow she didn't want Mr. Whitlock to help in that intimate way. It didn't seem fitting.

However he showed no desire to help. He seemed to take it as a matter of course that they were done with dishes for the night, and he sat for a couple of hours talking with Camilla and her mother, most interestingly, telling incidents of a trip abroad, describing pictures and statuary he had seen, giving details of his visits to historic places of interest.

It was almost like attending a delightful lecture and both Camilla and her mother enjoyed it, yet when he rose to go a little before ten o'clock, Camilla felt relieved. It had somehow been a strain, for while he was there it seemed as if every flaw and crudity of the little house stood out like a sore thumb.

"Well, he's very nice," commented her mother as they watched through the snow-blurred window and saw him drive away. "I'm glad you have a good clean-minded man like that to work for. It makes me feel safer about you when you are away. It certainly was kind of him to come all the way out here to protect you."

"I didn't need protection," laughed Camilla, "and I was scared to death to have him stay to dinner lest it was hash night. How did you happen to have chicken tonight, Mother dear? It isn't a gala night. I never expect chicken except on a holiday."

"Well, the egg man brought it," said her mother smiling, "and the day was so snowy and forlorn I thought we'd have a little good cheer. It didn't cost much. And besides, Miss York telephoned earlier in the day that she thought she might get off tonight and take dinner with us, but about five she called again and said the snow was so deep she guessed she wouldn't venture."

"She'd have had to walk," mused Camilla, "and the snow is almost a foot deep. It's a good thing we got moved before this blizzard came."

"Yes, isn't it? We have a great deal to be thankful for."

Then after a minute of silence, while Camilla was gathering up the dishes and making quick work of clearing off the table:

"Camilla, where does this Mr. Whitlock live? In a hotel? Or has he people? He isn't married is he?"

"Why, no, I think not," said Camilla looking startled. "No, of course not!" she said. "He certainly wouldn't be taking me out to dinner, and to a concert would he, if he were married?"

"Some men do such things," said Mrs. Chrystie thoughtfully, "but I remember the people at home spoke well of him. And he seems a fine quiet sort of man. He was very interesting, wasn't he? I enjoyed his description of those cathedrals."

"Yes, he can talk well. And now I remember hearing him say that he lives at his club. It's one of the best ones down town. I forget the name."

"Well, he seemed like a lonely man to me," said Mrs. Chrystie, "and once he spoke of his mother's death as being quite recent after a lingering illness. He's probably one of those men who have devoted themselves to an invalid mother, just as my girl is beginning to have to do for me."

"Mother! Don't talk that way!" said Camilla with troubled eyes, "you're not an invalid any more, and I'd rather be devoted to you than to anyone in the world!"

"You're a dear child!" said her mother laughing. "But I'm glad you've got such a kind employer. He's really much younger than you led me to suppose."

"Young?" said Camilla with a dreamy look, "why, Mother, his hair is gray all around the edges!"

"You don't like him much, do you Camilla?"

"Why, of course I like him!" said Camilla. "Why shouldn't I? I'm not in love with him, if that's what you mean. I doubt if I shall ever love anyone that way. Mother, why will you persist in thinking every man that speaks to me wants to marry me?"

"Oh, child!" said her mother, in a shocked tone, "I don't! What a thing to say! But I do want to know all about anyone who shows you the least attention of course, and I do want you to have some nice friends of your own kind."

"Well, he isn't my kind," said Camilla quite crossly, "he's much older than I am. Oh, he's nice and interesting all right. He doesn't bore me, if that's what you mean. He talks of books and art and music, and is quite intellectual, but I don't know that he's of my world any more than anybody else I know."

"He spoke of a church which he attends," said her mother speculatively.

"Everyone that goes to church nowadays isn't a Christian, by any means," said Camilla as she turned out the kitchen light.

"No, of course that's true," agreed her mother.

Camilla got up early the next morning, wrapped herself in warm garments and went out with the old snow shovel. It had stopped snowing, but the sky was still lowering. Camilla attacked the front walk and the path to the house. Luckily they were short or she could not have managed them, for the snow was heavy and deeply packed. But she cleared the walks, made a shovel-wide path to the garage, and came in with glowing cheeks to breakfast.

"I'm glad it's stopped snowing," said her mother, "I shouldn't have let you go to the office if it hadn't."

"Mr. Whitlock said I was not to come if it was still storming," said Camilla. "He's really very kind."

"Yes, he is," said her mother. "But I wish you'd telephone me when you get to town. I'd feel a great deal better about you."

Camilla promised and went away happily.

Mr. Whitlock was in the office when she got there. He looked up from his desk to welcome her with somehow a freer, more intimate air about him than he had ever worn before. Marietta hadn't come in yet.

He greeted her pleasantly, and then added:

"You have a very interesting mother, Miss Chrystie. I enjoyed my chat with her very much. I shall avail myself of your invitation and repeat my visit of last night often if I may."

They were casual words, lightly spoken, but something warned Camilla that they had a deeper significance than was on the surface. It was as if he were preparing the way for an intimacy, and it came as something she was not sure she wanted. He was her employer, and it seemed fitting that she should keep him as such and not make a playmate out of him. The memory of it hung around her all the morning unpleasantly, yet when she thought it over frankly she couldn't understand why she should feel that way. She couldn't go around alone all her life and never go anywhere nor see nor hear anything, and if Mr. Whitlock was the key to a little recreation she ought to be glad that he was willing to take her places and call often to see them, making the home life cheerful for Mother also.

When she searched her mind for a reason for her hesitance to take Mr. Whitlock into their home circle, she found that deep in her heart there was a reluctance to have anybody blot out the memory of Jeffrey Wainwright and the few beautiful days when he had come in and out among them. And when she realized this, she became suddenly most cordial to Whitlock, who developed an interest in her home and relatives, and asked questions about her father and where and how she was brought up. If Whitlock came often to the house and they grew intimate, perhaps in time she would get over this insane habit of recurring to the thought of the young man who seemed to have obsessed her with his brilliant personality. Maybe she could get interested in Mr. Whitlock and forget Wainwright. Of course Mr. Whitlock was distinguished looking, even if he did have a bit of silver in his hair. And he had nice kind eyes when he was not thinking about business.

So Camilla answered him cordially, and presently there grew up a kind of intimacy between them, comfortably friendly, yet such as could easily be set aside when business hours came.

But before long the look in Whitlock's eyes when he

turned them toward Camilla had something more than just friendship in them, and Marietta was quick to see it and react.

"Gee!" she said one afternoon after he had gone out, "he's got an awful crush on you, hasn't he? Gee, if he'd look at me with that 'drink-ta-me-only' look in his eyes, I'd fall in my tracks. I positively would!"

"Oh, for pity's sake, Marietta, don't talk that way!" said Camilla sharply. "What a silly idea! You see he knows a lot of my father's old friends and he's just being kind to me for their sakes."

"Oh, yeah?" said Marietta with a grin, "I heard that old 'friend-o-my father's' gag before. He's got it bad! Me, I know the signs! I haven't ben watching other folks get courted all these years for nothing! You're too innocent! That's what gets me. You never use one bit a 'come-hither' at all,—though you got plenty you could use if you was a mindta,—and they come rushing ta yer feet. Oh, I haven't got any feeling about it, Camilla. I never expect ta have anybody taking me places, but I liketa see you have it. I do honest. I just love you, and I wanta have you have anything you want."

"You dear thing!" said Camilla trying to put away the annoyance she felt. "You'll have attention yet, sometime. But don't get notions about me, please. And by the way, Mother's making some more gingerbread boys for Ted tomorrow. You might tell him if you like."

"Say, that's great!" said Marietta flushing eagerly. "Ted will be awfully pleased. And say, I meant ta tell you yesterday only Mr. Whitlock was here all day, how I been reading the Testament you gave me ta Ted, and he loves it. And my stepmother listens too, sometimes. You know she's back from the hospital now, and can't do much all day but just lie still. She's a lot different since she was so sick. I guess she was scared, and sometimes she's real kind to Ted, talks kind of motherlike to him. Gee, that gets me. I don't care what she does to me, so she's good to him. And he seems so pleased, poor kid!"

"Oh, I'm so glad!" said Camilla. "You know, Marietta, it may be the Lord has put you right in that hard place to lead both your stepmother and little brother to know Jesus."

"I was wondering about that," said Marietta. "Do you

suppose He'd trust me ta do a thing like that? If I thought I could, gee, that would make up for me being so plain and homely. I'd like ta try."

"I certainly think you may be just put there for that very thing," said Camilla eagerly. "And don't you know, Marietta, one can grow beautiful by being with the Lord Jesus every day and trying to please Him? If you let Him live in you, there is a beauty of soul that will shine through, the beauty of the Lord Jesus living in you and moving you to every thought and action. You can live Jesus, even when you have no words you can speak that people will listen to. They can't help listening to your life."

So the days went by and Marietta grew in the finer things of the Spirit, and in the knowledge of God's Word, and Camilla worked hard, praying God to conquer for her the longings and desires that were not of Him.

And Whitlock more and more fell into the habit of asking Camilla to go to lunch with him, or driving out to her home with her for dinner and an evening talk, and as spring drew nearer he began to talk of places he wanted her to see when the warm weather came.

Mother Chrystie, looking on, puckered her anxious brows and sighed sometimes, and wondered if this was God's best for her beloved Camilla? Wondered if Camilla understood how great a thing it was to choose the right mate for life, and how wrong it was to be hasty about it. Wondered if Ralph Whitlock was not perhaps in his way as worldly as the dear bright youth who came no more to see them, nor even wrote to enquire; sighed and wondered if she ought to warn her child, yet held her peace a little longer lest she precipitate something she feared and dreaded.

And Camilla went on gaily, sometimes breathlessly, trying not to think. Trying to take the good times that were handed her and not question the morrow. Looking at her employer more and more in the light of a friend.

And Whitlock came to assume more and more the attitude of one who expected sometime to be even more than a friend. He assumed a kind of friendly dictatorship over Camilla, bringing her books to read, ordering her what newspaper to take, and instructing her in all things pertaining to life, almost as if he had already the right to say how she should live and move and have her being.

And yet, there was a certain point beyond which Camilla would not let him go. She would not let him grow sentimental, or very personal, and she would never let him touch her, always withdrawing her hand if he took it in too close a clasp, always keeping him just a little at his distance. She did not herself know just why. She was not ready yet to ask herself questions about it. And strange to say this attitude on her part only seemed to make him admire her more. It suited his conventional, somewhat formal character to have her so.

Camilla had attempted to probe her admirer concerning the things of life that meant most to her. She had asked him point blank one day if he was a Christian, not realizing that her question had been half answered before she asked, by the very fact that she had to ask him, and he answered her quite readily:

"Oh, certainly! I joined the church when I was not more than fourteen, and I've been fairly faithful in my attendance ever since. Of course many things that I believed in those days have been greatly modified as I grew older and wiser, but I have always maintained that man needs religion, and that the church is a valuable influence in the world and should therefore be supported by all thinking people. I have not been quite as active in the church organizations the last few years as I was when I was a lad, but of course a business man has less time than a youth, and in spite of that I have gone out of my way to accept positions on boards and so on. Just now it happens that in addition to being a trustee in the church where I hold membership, I am taking time on a special committee to work out a plan whereby our church shall be able to pay off its entire mortgage, and make out a full budget for the coming year."

With this vague explanation Camilla had to be satisfied. She wished she dared ask him what he meant by not believing all that he had as a child, but there was something about him that prevented questioning of his ways. He did not suffer criticism nor suggestion, and somehow every question that Camilla tried to formulate seemed almost like a criticism of his Christian methods, so time

went on, and she was still vague about his definite beliefs.
Still of course, he owned he was a Christian, and he often
asked the blessing at the table when her mother asked
him to; it sounded a bit cold and formal perhaps, but still
it was phrased in language that was familiar and had the
right ring. She could not possibly feel that he was out of
her class when he owned to being a Christian.

But sometimes Camilla wondered, and a great oppres-
sion came upon her young soul. She hadn't known him
long, yet he was taking things for granted so rapidly that
sometimes she was breathless and troubled.

And one night after he had gone, after having spent
the evening describing at length a trip he had taken but
two years before, in which he saw gay Paris on its most
sophisticated side; an evening in which Camilla had sat
almost silent in the shadow of a great lamp shade, listening, looking almost troubled, her mother looked at her
keenly.

"Are you going to marry that man, Camilla?" she asked
suddenly.

"Oh, *Mother!* What a question! Why! Why— I don't
even know that he would want me to marry him! Why,
I'm not thinking about marrying people, Mother!"

And suddenly Camilla burst into tears and buried her
face in her mother's neck.

Loving arms went about her and loving lips were laid
against her hot wet cheek.

"There, there, dear!" soothed her mother gently, "I just
thought I ought to remind you that it is a woman's
business to be aware of such things and not let a man go
too far, if she does not intend to go all the way with him!
It looked to me as if he was expecting a lot of you, my
dear, and I wondered if you were ready to choose him
for life,—if you were really satisfied with him? He is a
good man I guess, but—I wondered if you were *sure*,
sure beyond the shadow of a doubt, that he is the one
you want? You know a woman should be *sure!* That's the
only thing that makes marriage happy, it's the only thing
that makes it tolerable!"

And Camilla clung to her mother, trembling, quivering
in every nerve, shot through and through with question-
ings and doubts, and trying not to remember a kiss that

had gone deep into her soul. She thought that if it only hadn't been for that kiss she might have been able to think more clearly.

CHAPTER XXI

The plaything that Stephanie Varrell had found on the beach that afternoon had proved to be more than usually interesting, and before Jeffrey Wainwright's return to civilization she had used her jacinth eyes to such an extent that she was wearing a strange golden stone on her finger with a curious fire in its heart, set in workmanship of the far orient, and there was much gossip abroad, for Stephanie and her "Count" were seen constantly together.

Yet it had not been a part of her plan to have Jeff come upon them just where and how he did.

She had been accustomed to use certain tactics with Jeffrey that she found always worked. Invariably she had been able to bring him back to her feet whenever she wished, and she had never let him drift quite so far away before.

But something had happened the night of that dinner of hers that she did not understand, and she was playing high stakes now to undo what she had dared to do in inviting Myles Meredith. There was nothing like rousing jealousy in a man's heart to bring him to terms, Stephanie firmly believed, never having read aright the fine soul of Jeff. She had never sensed that instead of being merely jealous for himself, he was jealous for her reputation, and his ideal of her which he had made himself and cherished for genuine.

But Jeff came home just after the sun had dropped the velvet curtain of night down upon golden Florida and driven the guests of the hotel to their rooms to dress for dinner and the evening.

Then Jeff came down late to dinner, escaping a good
many people whom he wasn't in a hurry to meet. He
took a walk on the veranda after dinner with his mother.
He sat for a while with her in the softness and darkness
of the evening, talking, telling her this and that about his
experiences on the trip, telling her some things about his
brother Sam he thought she ought to know, of how the
boy was developing character and an interest in certain
studies that should be fostered. He kept feeling around
and wondering how he should tell her of his new experience. Was it the right time? Would she understand? In all
his life he had had very little real heart converse with his
mother. She was a cold reticent nature, taking certain
things for granted, ignoring certain other things. He had a
feeling that perhaps she would not approve, might perhaps think he was going off on a tangent. He greatly
desired, when he did tell her, to do it so that she would
be impressed with the deep reality of his new experience.

"Mother," he said at last after a long silence broken
only by the regular sound of the sea breaking on the sand
not far away, "I've been thinking things out while I was
away in the woods and I've made some decisions."

His mother stopped rocking in the big willow chair,
with a short sharp little sound of quietness as if she had
feared something and thought it might be coming now.
She wondered if it was that yellow haired girl with the
queer sly eyes? Or was he wanting to go and kill lions in
Africa? Some new sensation of course!

"The most important decision," he went on, "is that
I've become a Christian!"

He had thought it all out and had decided that this was
the best way to express it to his mother. She wouldn't at
all understand if he should say he had been born again.
She might even resent it, as if his first birth had not been
good enough for him. She had a strange deep pride of
family. The word Christian he felt sure she would
understand to a certain extent, and it was still, of course,
perfectly respectable. As the world, her world, counted
respectability.

His mother was still, holding the rocker motionless for
a full second while she thought it over. Then she
answered calmly:

"That's all right with me, Jeff, just so you don't make it

a fad. I'd hate to have a child with a religious complex. Of course a little religion doesn't hurt anybody if it's kept within bounds."

Jeff sat silent for a long time after that realizing just how little his mother would be in sympathy with his new life, yet feeling that he had no further word for her at present.

Presently Mrs. Wainwright drew her soft wrap about her shoulders with a little shiver and rose. Suddenly leaning over her son she patted his dark head with an unaccustomed caress and said:

"You always were a good boy, Jeff!"

Then after an instant, "Come, I'm going in. There's too much breeze out here for me."

He escorted her into the hotel where she settled down among a group of her kind, and with a graceful good-night he left her and sauntered out to the piazza again, stalking down the full length and across the sea end.

The great ballroom was that way, down along the north side of the building, and dancing was going on inside, but a glance showed the piazza entirely empty just then, a long stretch of darkness broken by the rectangles of light from the open windows, and lighted not at all except by one single lamp at the far end. Jeff strolled on, keeping out near the railing. He did not want company just then. He had some serious thinking to do. He would just walk by and glance in the windows, and see who of the old crowd were there. He was suddenly beginning to realize that life was going to have some very decided changes for him in the near future. His old world was not going to recognize what had happened to him. They were not going to understand. They were not his world any more. He had been born into a new world.

He walked slowly, quietly, the sound of the beating waves, and the throb of the orchestra covering his deliberate footfalls.

Pausing an instant to glance through a window, he was startled to hear a light familiar laugh coming from out the shadows quite near him, and turning sharply he saw one of the great glider seats with which the place abounded, drawn slantwise into the shadow so that the occupants could get a full view of the ballroom without themselves being very visible to those inside the windows, and there they sat quite oblivious of any but themselves. They had evidently not heard his approach, for they were absorbed in each other. He could see the gold of the girl's hair, crowned with a sparkling jeweled tiara, the lifted face with the offered lips, the gleam of her white arm as she threw it about the neck of her companion, a tall man who bent a comely head above her and embraced her passionately. Stephanie! And he had just been thinking about her!

He had just been considering that in some sort he was entangled with her, or he had at one time asked her to marry him. True she had not answered him, had put him off time after time laughingly. But she was capable of making trouble about it if she chose. He had been perplexing himself over it, wondering what was his duty now. For he understood himself well enough to know that she was not for him. He had been hoping that she might have gone back north, but now here she was not three feet from him, and lying in another man's arms! If Jeffrey Wainwright had any of his former illusions left about Stephanie Varrell, they were dispelled at once. Her whole attitude, her soft honeyed purring tones, the caresses she was showering upon the man, made it quite plain that Stephanie was not in love with Jeffrey. And suddenly his heart leaped with a thankful throb. Here at last was absolute evidence. He had feared that perhaps after all he had misjudged her, and that her association with other men against his protest was really as innocent as she had always declared. He did not wish to be unjust. But here was the evidence of his own eyes.

Well, what should he do now? Get away without their seeing him of course, if it could be done. But could it? The music had stopped for the moment.

He made a quick stealthy movement with one foot, to back away, keeping his eyes upon the two on the couch. But he did not realize that someone had piled a couple of chairs in a rocker, just behind where he was standing. His foot came in sharp contact with the point of the rocker, and the rocker being set in motion, the two smaller chairs came crashing down to the floor noisily.

It was all over in an instant. The two people in the porch seat sat up sharply, staring at him, and Jeff came out of the darkness and came up to them at once with a grave bow.

"Sorry to intrude," he said with his easy courtesy. "I did not know that anyone was here. Don't let me interrupt!" and with a significant glance at Stephanie he turned and walked deliberately away. As he went he carried the memory of Stephanie's eyes, jacinth eyes, gleaming in the dark like cat's eyes.

He had almost rounded the sea end of the piazza when he heard a scurrying sound behind him of feet running, and the two were upon him, Stephanie's light heartless laugh ringing out.

"Jeff! Oh, Jeff! Wait!" she called, and reaching his side slid her arm within his own, as she had so often done before, with that soft little confiding air that had at one time meant so much to him.

"I want to tell you the news and introduce you to my fiance," she said eagerly. "This is Count Esterhoff, Jeff, and we were just engaged tonight! He knows all about you of course. And I want you to see my wonderful curious ring! There isn't another like it in all the world."

Jeff paused politely in the light of the next window to acknowledge the introduction and to survey the weird ring whose setting of strange serpents curiously intertwined with uncanny symbols smacked of aged pagan worlds. The new-made fiance who hadn't known his fate and standing with the siren until that moment, stood there blinking, and staring at the girl who had just so unexpectedly become engaged to him.

"Congratulations!" said Jeff, with a delighted grin. "That's splendid news. Delighted to meet you, Count. And say, that's some ring! An heirloom I take it. A most unusual setting, isn't it?"

He lingered a minute or two chatting, adding a few more polite phrases and then excused himself from the scene lest his overwhelming relief become too painfully obvious. He hurried away and disappeared by a roundabout route to his room.

He had been calmly sleeping for what seemed to him many hours when his telephone roused him, and Stephanie's voice, amazingly meek and tearful called him from his pleasant dreams.

"Jeff, is that you? This is Stephanie, Jeff, and I'm *so* unhappy—!"

There was a silence during which Jeff got awake enough to visualize once more the scene he had witnessed on the north piazza a few hours before.

"Isn't that too bad!" he said at last, a note of mocking in his voice.

"Now, Jeff, if you knew how unhappy I am you wouldn't try to be unkind," reproached the markedly humble voice at the other end of the wire.

Jeff was still, trying to think hard. Then he spoke in his clear firm voice, with finality in its very fibre.

"I'm not trying to be unkind, Stephanie. I'm just puzzled to know what I have to do with all this. It can't be many hours since you told me you were engaged to another man, and I should think this matter of your unhappiness would be referred to him."

"But Jeff,—*darling*—!" she spoke the word in a tone that always used to move him deeply and he marvelled that it no longer stirred him in the least. There were sobs in her voice now and unmistakable tears. He frowned in the darkness and drew a deep breath of annoyance.

"Suppose—Jeff—" sobbed the voice softly, "that I've found I've—made—a terrible—mistake!"

"Then I should think that would be entirely up to *you!*" he answered crisply. "I certainly haven't anything to do with it."

"Yes—you have—Jeff—!" went on the pleading voice. "Have—you forgotten—Jeff, I know you haven't—that you asked me—to—*marry* you once? Jeff, I've seen my mistake—and—I want to tell you—b-b-before it's forever —too late! Jeff, it's *you* I love. And I'll marry you, Jeff darling,—tonight, if you'll take me! I could be ready in half an hour. There's an airplane lying out on the field that I've been learning on. I've chartered it, and we could go on that, and then all my troubles would be over! I should be—ecstatically—happy! Oh, Jeff—darling—will you go tonight? You are such a comforting person—"

"Nothing doing!" said Jeffrey Wainwright, "that was all off the night of your dinner. You chose then between me and that low-lived villain, Meredith. And if I had needed anything else, tonight would have been the finishing touch. You'll have to go elsewhere for comfort, Stephanie. I'm going to sleep, and I don't wish to discuss this matter any further, either now or at any future time. Good-night!" and Jeffrey Wainwright hung up the receiver and turned over in his bed.

But he did not go back to sleep. He held a court and judged himself. He had learned while out on that camping trip that if we would judge ourselves we should not have to be disciplined by God. So then and there he held court and found himself guilty. He looked back over his young manhood and saw himself a selfish time-waster, a chaser of every new fancy, a lazy spendthrift, and good-for-nothing, a spoiled child of luxury playing with every toy that came his way. Of course he had had certain standards and adhered to them fairly well, but within limits he had been determined to have whatever his fancy chose. And Stephanie had been one of those things.

That she had been dangerous he had known from the start. That she had been full of deception he had often suspected. That she could do about what she chose with him at one time he had rather enjoyed. He had always known that she was not the kind of woman to bring into his family. That she would have to change before his mother, whom he was fond of, would ever accept her as a daughter, and before his father whom he greatly revered and loved, would honor her. But he had blindly gone ahead, determined that she should somehow be made to conform to the Wainwright standards, convinced that when she was his, and he flung his love about her and enthroned her in his home, she would be everything that he would ask her to be.

He had known for a long time now that he was a fool to believe any such thing. The first time he saw Camilla he knew that the look in her eyes was the one he had been so long hoping to see in Stephanie's eyes. The night he dared to lay his lips to Camilla's in that precious kiss he knew that this was something rare and fine in love that he had never found in his infatuation for Stephanie. To-night down on the hotel piazza the last shred and vestige of respect for Stephanie had vanished.

He lay a long time considering his present situation. Suddenly he snapped on the light and looked at his watch. Then he hunted a number in the telephone book and called it.

"Is that you, John Saxon? Are you still up studying? I hoped so. Well, this is Jeff. May I come out to your place tomorrow morning early and help you spray orange trees or whatever it is that you went home to do to them? I don't know how, but I'll learn, and I've got a few questions I need to ask you."

"That's great news, Jeff," came back over the wire. "Bring on your questions! Wear your old clothes and be prepared to sleep in a hammock. I'll be waiting to welcome you at the head of the lane with open arms."

Jeff wrote a note to his mother.

"Dear Mother:

"I'm leaving early in the morning for a few days with a friend. You can reach me by phone at the above number, but please don't inform *anybody* else.

"If Dad wires let me know at once, and if you need me I can be back in less than an hour.

Yours,

Jeff."

Then he turned out the light and went to sleep again.

Quite early the next morning before any stray damsels were abroad, Jeff arose and went on his way to see John Saxon.

CHAPTER XXII

Miss York duly moved in bag and baggage as soon as the last big snow of the season was melted and gone, and though she was still engaged on a case and was able to be there very little, it gave a comfortable family feeling to have the extra room furnished and ready for use whenever she should be able to get off for a night.

She turned up the very night after Camilla had cried on

her mother's shoulder, and announced that she had come to stay over the week-end.

They had a cheery little supper together and were anticipating a real home evening, leisurely laughing and talking as they did the dishes, and suggesting how the furniture could be arranged in Miss York's room to best advantage.

And then right in the middle of it Whitlock arrived.

He had been away in New York and had attended a great political meeting and met some interesting people. He wanted to tell about it. He enjoyed telling things, and liked an attentive audience.

Camilla felt a disappointment as she opened the door and saw him standing there. She had supposed he would be gone over Sunday. She was arrayed in a plain little old dress, expecting to help Miss York put up her curtains.

She invited him in, a constraint upon her because of what her mother had said the night before, but Whitlock was full of his experiences and did not notice any lack in her.

"Well," he said taking off his overcoat and hat and hanging them on the hall rack as if he belonged there, "it is good to get back. Where's your mother? Aren't the dishes done yet?"

It was characteristic of Whitlock that he had never attempted to go into the kitchen and help, though he had several times been a guest to a meal.

"Why, yes," said Camilla, "the dishes are done. Mother, here's Mr. Whitlock. Miss York, won't you come in and meet my employer?"

Camilla was a little startled at herself for calling him that. She had of late avoided calling him anything. He had told her once that his name was Ralph, but he hadn't made a point of it, and somehow she had hesitated as if the use of it committed her to something intangible for which she was not quite ready.

"Miss York?" said Whitlock with an annoyed frown. "Who is she? What's she doing here?"

"Why, she's a member of our family, that is when she is not out on her job," said Camilla with heightened color, "I guess you haven't happened to meet her before have you? She has her room here and comes when she is not on a case."

She looked up and there stood Miss York in the door-way with Mrs. Chrystie just behind her.

"Mr. Whitlock, this is our dear friend, Miss York!"

Miss York stood for an instant looking at Whitlock with a sudden startled gleam in her eye as the man rose and faced her with a puzzled frown. Then the nurse spoke.

"Good evening, Mr. Whitlock, we've met before, haven't we? I've heard Camilla speak of her employer but I hadn't an idea it was the same Mr. Whitlock."

Miss York was entirely at her ease and spoke with assurance. But Whitlock looked at her blankly.

"Miss—York did you say? Your—ah—face does seem somewhat familiar, but—I'm afraid—I can't place you. I see so many people of course in the day's work."

"Yes, I suppose you do," said Miss York pleasantly, "but you'll remember me when you know who I am. I'm the nurse that took care of your wife when your baby was born. A little girl, wasn't it, and a very pretty baby if I remember rightly? I know its mother said it was the image of you, and you were as pleased as could be!"

Mrs. Chrystie gave a soft little exclamation and looked at Whitlock, and Camilla in the shadow of the hall doorway gave a startled glance at her mother, and then turned to watch Whitlock, her own face still in shadow.

Over Whitlock's face had come a strange and subtle change. Every vestige of color had drained away leaving him severely gray and tired looking, yes, and old. Camilla was startled at the change. He seemed fairly haggard. He faced them all with miserable, cold eyes.

"Yes?" he said in his most official voice. "It seems to me I do recall a nurse. One doesn't always register faces at a time of crisis." His voice did not encourage further conversation, but Nurse York seemed not to notice. She gushed on pleasantly.

"No, I suppose not," she said. "One wouldn't be ex-pected to remember a mere nurse at such a time. But do tell me how your wife is? She was such a sweet dear little woman. I really fell in love with her, and that baby was one of the sweetest I ever saw. Dorothy, wasn't that her name? Dorothy Rose Whitlock. I remember thinking how well the names went together. I suppose she has grown to be quite a girl by this time, hasn't she? Is she as pretty as she promised to be? I thought her hair was going to curl."

Mr. Whitlock fixed Miss York with a haughty stare and answered in tones so cold it is a wonder that they did not freeze into icicles.

"Miss York, I have not seen my wife for over five years now. We are separated! And I do not know anything about the child. She is with her mother!"

"Oh," chirruped Miss York blithely, "what a pity! I'm sorry I spoke of it."

He turned from her abruptly addressing Camilla quite formally.

"I came out to see if you would mind letting me run you in to the office for a few minutes. There are a couple of letters that ought to get off tonight. I'm sorry to bother you, but they ought to be typed, and, if you're willing, why, you can go that much earlier tomorrow you know." He tried to finish with a light laugh but his voice sounded harsh and shaken.

Camilla caught a troubled look in her mother's eyes as she turned to answer.

"Why of course, I'll be glad to do the letters," she said heartily, "but you needn't take the trouble to drive me in to the office. I have my own typewriter here you know, and it just happens that I brought several extra sheets of the letterhead paper out with me the other night when I brought home some of the work to type."

Camilla wheeled out the little table containing her machine, drew up her stool that fitted under it so nicely, and was ready for work.

She could see that Whitlock was not much pleased with the arrangement, but there wasn't anything he could gracefully do about it, so he dropped into a chair and began to dictate in his most impersonal office voice. Miss York and Mrs. Chrystie drifted back into the kitchen, talking cheerily and moving about putting away things.

The letters proved to be very commonplace affairs and Camilla suspected that they were a mere excuse to get her away from the house. It wasn't of course especially pleasant for him to be around Miss York after what had been said, but she typed away rapidly and soon had both letters written, addressed and sealed.

"There!" she said brightly, "that was a great deal easier

than going away down town and opening up the office for just those few minutes, wasn't it?" and she smiled a bright tense little smile. The very air seemed charged with electricity, but something had been lifted from her heart that made it lighter. She didn't stop then to question what it was, she only knew that a great relief had come upon her.

"Yes, that's very nice," said Whitlock in a dry tone, that did not sound at all as if he thought it nice.

He took the letters and held them a moment looking at them. Then with a glance toward the kitchen where cheerful voices were still to be heard, he lowered his voice and said:

"You wouldn't like to come out for a little drive, would you Camilla?"

Camilla's breath came quickly, but she managed a bright smile.

"I couldn't, tonight, really Mr. Whitlock. Miss York can only be here for a short time and I promised to help her put up her curtains this evening."

He stood looking at her thoughtfully for a moment, his brows drawn in a frown. Then he lowered his voice and stepped nearer to her.

"Camilla, I want to talk to you. I have something very important to tell you. I really came over partly to tell you tonight."

"Why, of course," said Camilla feeling her heart suddenly coming up in her throat, but trying to seem brightly sympathetic. "We can sit right here and talk. Nobody will bother us. They are busy getting Miss York's room fixed up. Won't you take this big chair?" and Camilla indicated the most comfortable chair in the room, well in the far corner in the shadow, and herself dropped into a small straight chair opposite.

Whitlock's lips were set in an unpleasant line but he accepted the chair and sat down rigidly on its edge, but he did not speak at once.

Camilla was holding herself firmly in hand. She found a tendency in her hands to tremble, but she would not let it get the ascendancy.

"It's about Marietta, I suppose," she said breaking the silence. "Poor Marietta! I had hoped you felt she was doing better. But I suppose it is hard to put up with her."

She felt that she must put off embarrassing topics if possible.

"No, it's not about Marietta," said the man brusquely. "She's doing very well, far better than I supposed possible. It's all due to you of course, and so long as you are willing to keep her on as a pupil I'm willing to put up with her. It must be hard on you, but you are most unselfish. Camilla, you are the most unselfish person I know. That is why I have been so attracted to you."

"Oh, no, I'm not unselfish," said Camilla quickly, "I'm just sorry for Marietta." She laughed lightly, hoping to avert further personalities.

But Whitlock sat gloomily across from her and looked at her, saying brusquely:

"Well, it's not of Marietta I was about to speak. I was going to say that I should have told you long ago of my wife, perhaps. But I was hoping to delay—until—something decisive had been done—something in the way of—divorce proceedings. Of course it is all a very painful topic to me!"

"Of course!" said Camilla quickly in a sympathetic tone. "Please don't feel you must tell me anything more. I quite understand that it must make you very unhappy to speak of it. I am sure Miss York would not have spoken of it if she had known."

Whitlock wasn't so sure of that, but he did not say so. He paused again painfully and then said:

"No, I would rather tell you. Now that you know of her existence at all you should know all about her."

"I don't see why, Mr. Whitlock. I am just your secretary. It isn't customary for business men to tell their private affairs to their secretaries."

She tried to turn the matter off lightly, but Whitlock persisted in watching her gloomily and went on.

"You are far more to me than a secretary, Camilla," he said feelingly. "You surely know that. You cannot have failed to see that. You must know what a comfort you have been to me in my loneliness—"

"Oh, Mr. Whitlock!" protested Camilla, deeply troubled by his tone, and endeavoring with all her might to refuse to understand his meaning, "I'm glad if I have helped at all. I was only trying to do my duty. One doesn't know how those about are suffering, of course."

Whitlock gave her a quick keen glance. Was she really as dull of comprehension as she seemed?

"You see," he said dropping his glance for a moment and placing the tips of his fine long fingers together, "my wife was a spoiled child. That was about the truth of the matter. She was determined to have her own way in everything. She had been petted and humored and she expected me to do the same by her that her parents had done."

Something in the black look that came over his face at the memory gave Camilla a swift revelation of what it might be to live under the domination of this man, who could be so gentle and fascinating when he chose, and yet so overbearing when the whim took him. She shuddered at what might have been her fate if she had gone on a little longer. Even if there had been no wife in the offing, his nature would have been the same. But aloud she only said:

"That was hard for you both!"

His face hardened at that.

"It was certainly hard for *me!*" he said uncompromisingly.

"It must be very hard when a home is broken up!" moralized Camilla, loathing herself for the smugness of the remark, yet unable to think of anything else appropriate to say.

"Get rid of the idea that she was a martyr," said Whitlock brusquely. "She had her own way. She's living with her father in his palatial mansion. She has everything she wants. I am the one that is cast out. I have done everything that I could to make her see where she was wrong and make her come back to her home and her responsibilities and she has refused. Now I think it is time to think of myself. I have refused to get a divorce, feeling that she might weaken, but my life is going and I am alone. There has been no one to understand me, no one to cheer me when I come back from a hard day!"

He paused a moment and Camilla gazed at him in troubled silence.

"Until you came, Camilla—!" his voice softened and he gave her suddenly one of those deep possessive looks, those smiles that had puzzled her often before, and now filled her with a new kind of alarm.

"Oh, please,—" she said in a distressed tone, "I'm glad if I have helped in any way. But I'm not the one to do anything much of course. If someone—something—could only bring you two together again! It must be so very hard for all of you. In spite of disagreement, it can't be happy for any of you to be apart! You belong together! It's what God wants—*expects* of you! And—your little girl! How dreadful for her not to have any father, and for you not to see her every day and watch her grow up! My father was so much to me. I wouldn't give up the precious memory I have of him for anything!"

The man almost squirmed away from her words.

"Yes, of course, there's that," he said almost roughly, "but then she's having every luxury, more than I could give her. She isn't really missing anything. It's I that am starved for human sympathy—until you came, and—and then I began to feel that there might still be a little brightness left for me on earth—if—"

Suddenly Miss York appeared in the doorway, and her pleasant hearty voice boomed into the atmosphere so tense and strained, seeming to clear away the morbidness and bring a fresh breath to Camilla.

"Well, I just looked in to see whether you two were done with those letters. If you are I wonder if I could get your help for a minute or two, putting up this awkward old picture. I can't seem to hang it alone. Mr. Whitlock, you used to be handy about the house I remember, would you mind lifting the picture while I twist the wire to shorten it? These ceilings are so low that the cord is too long."

Whitlock arose stiffly, severely, and followed the nurse into the room across the hall, doing what was asked of him without a word, his face like a thundercloud all the while, and then when it was done, he turned to Camilla.

"I'll say good night," he said stiffly. "I must get these letters into the mail!" (Although Camilla knew quite well those letters weren't important at all.) "I'll see you on Monday about the rest!" he added significantly, and taking his hat and coat departed, without a word or even a glance in Miss York's direction.

"H'm!" remarked that good woman significantly. "Grumpy as ever, I see!" and then added, "He had the sweetest little wife I ever saw, and he treated her like the very dust under his feet. I'm not surprised she couldn't stand it. But I guess he can be nice in the office, can't he?"

"Yes, he can be nice," said Camilla thoughtfully. "He has really been very kind to both of us girls in the office."

Miss York eyed her keenly and said no more, and they spent a very happy evening getting Miss York's room settled, but nothing more was said about Mr. Whitlock's affairs.

Camilla, however, was much disturbed in mind, though she managed an eager interest in Miss York's room that well covered her troubled thoughts. But when Monday morning came she went down to the office in great trepidation.

Whitlock however gave no sign of anything out of the ordinary. He was gravely courteous and quiet during the morning, with even more than usual of his brusque abstraction. Marietta sensed it at once when she came in, and snapped into her work with a frightened vigor that warmed Camilla's worried soul.

It was not until noon when Whitlock sent Marietta out for her lunch that he unbent and spoke to Camilla.

"Now," he said looking up with a relaxing of his grim dignity, "I want to talk to you Camilla. Thank goodness we shan't be interrupted here, except by the telephone, for nearly an hour."

Camilla swung her swivel chair about from her desk, a startled look in her eyes, although she had been quite expecting something all the morning.

"Move your chair over here near me where you always take dictation. I don't want to have to talk very loud."

Camilla moved her chair to her usual place, innocently carrying her pad and pencil as she usually came for dictation.

She tried to look up composedly, but met one of those possessive glances that had come to seem so frightening.

"Camilla," he said, "I have been utterly miserable all night." His eyes certainly attested his words. "I haven't been able to sleep. I have thought and thought until I am nearly crazy. I felt that we should talk it over and decide what we ought to do."

"We?" said Camilla opening her eyes wide in alarm.

"Yes, Camilla, I felt that you had the right to make the final decision."

"Decision? I don't understand, Mr. Whitlock."

"Why, decision as to how we ought to move, you and I. You know of course that I have been loving you all winter! And I thought that I had reason to believe that you felt the same way."

He reached out his hand and covered hers with a warm soft tender grasp. Camilla started out of her chair aghast and drew her hands quickly from under his clasp.

"Mr. Whitlock!" she exclaimed in no uncertain tones. "You had no right to love me! How could you have thought that I had any such feeling? How dreadful! How perfectly *terrible* for you, a married man, to feel that way!"

There were tears in Camilla's eyes and her face was white and drawn. She turned away from the desk and stood over by the mantel.

But Whitlock got up and came over beside her.

"Don't speak that way, Camilla! Don't weep. I cannot bear to see you suffer too. You don't know how it tears my heart! You little beautiful lovely darling. Oh, I love you, love you, *love*—!"

"Stop!" cried Camilla. "It is disgusting to me to hear you say that! It is unholy! You humiliate me!"

"No, Camilla, you mustn't feel that way, dearest. You don't know how I love you, how I long, oh how my hungry arms long to hold you close! Just once, Camilla, let me feel your heart against mine. We have a right to that! Just to put my lips on yours—"

His arms went out to embrace her and there was passion in his glance, but suddenly Camilla sprang away from him and went and stood over by the door.

"Don't you dare to touch me!" she cried, and her eyes flashed fire. "Mr. Whitlock, I didn't think you were a man like this! I never would have come here to work if I had known that you would dare to talk to me like that! My mother would never have invited you to dinner. We thought you were simply being kind to us for the sake of our old friends at home. I thought you respected me!"

Whitlock stood white and shaken across the room from her, looking at her sternly.

"You misunderstand me," he said hoarsely. "I mean

you no disrespect. I want to marry you as soon as I can get a divorce. When I said I wanted to discuss the matter with you, I merely meant whether we should go on for awhile and keep our love between ourselves or whether I should come out in the open and ask my wife for a divorce. I can easily do that you know, for it was she who left me."

"Mr. Whitlock, I don't know what you mean, keep our love between ourselves. I have no love for you, and you have no right to love me, nor to tell me so. And even if I could ever care for you that way I would *never* marry a divorced man. It's not right!"

"Oh, now, Camilla," he pleaded, "don't say that! It is all right and quite respectable for people to remarry after divorce. Everybody is doing it today."

"Not Christians!" said Camilla quietly. "Not born-again ones. It would not ever be right in my eyes, and I do not believe it would be in God's eyes. He has given but one cause for divorce and not any for remarriage as long as both husband and wife are living. But we do not need to discuss that. Even if you had never been married and did not need a divorce to set you free, I could never marry you. I do not love you and never did. And the fact that you could say what you have just said to me this after-noon has almost made me hate you."

"What have I said, Camilla, that has made you so angry?" he pleaded, giving her a self-righteously innocent glance.

"You have confessed an unlawful love for me!" declared Camilla her eyes flashing anew at the memory. "A love you had no right to even recognize in your heart, much less allow and foster. Oh, if I had had any such idea when you first began to show me kindness I would never have looked at you again."

"Forgive me, Camilla," he said almost humbly, "you do not know the heart of a man when he loves."

"Well, I hope I never may know then, if it is unholy like that. A good man would have torn it out and up-rooted it and fled from anything that would have reminded him of it!" Camilla's tongue was sharp and her tone was hard and bright. How she despised the man, and yes, despised herself too for not having foreseen such a possi-bility and guarded herself and him against it. Even if he hadn't been married she had never really seriously considered him in the light of a lover. Not even when her mother warned her the other night had it seemed at all possible that such a thing could be. She had been to blame perhaps in going out with him those few times, in welcoming him to the house, in using him as a sort of mild entertainment to keep herself from thinking of another man whose bright personality had been obsessing her! Oh, how wrong she had been! She hadn't meant to play the game of hearts the way the world was playing it.

Suddenly she lifted honest eyes to his angry mortified ones.

"If I have inadvertently done anything to lead you on to this," she said earnestly, "I most humbly ask your pardon! I did not dream that you meant anything like this in the kindness you showed me. I am ashamed that you could even think I had cared for you that way. I *never did!*"

He was still so long that she wondered if she would have to speak first, and then he lifted his eyes again to hers.

"You didn't, Camilla," he owned. "You are a good girl. I appreciate your goodness. But you are somewhat fanatical in your ideas about divorce, you must own that. It's not your fault of course. Your mother has trained you that way, and of course she's not so much to blame. It belonged to her day and she has lived up to what she was taught. But the world has made progress today. It has gone far from narrow-minded precepts that did well enough for a former generation. What kind of a God would it be that condemned two people utterly unmated, hating each other, making each other miserable, to live their lives out together?"

"Living their lives out apart is one thing," said Camilla with conviction, "and either of them marrying someone else is another. Mr. Whitlock, the world may change and progress as you call it, but God is the same yesterday, today and forever, and God's principles never change in spite of the world's fashions. But I can't discuss this with you any more. I wish you would go back to your work and let me go back to mine, and forget all this awful hour—if we can!"

"Yes,—if we *can!*" said Whitlock bitterly. "Camilla you

could not talk so severely of right and wrong if you loved me as I love you. You see this is the first time I have ever really loved a woman. I have seen in you the ideal woman of my life and I have laid all at your feet. You could not treat me this way if you loved me as I hoped you did."

"Perhaps not!" said Camilla, "but you see *I don't*."

He watched her furtively from beneath his half closed lids, as she stood with her hands gripped fiercely together, her young brows knit in trouble, and her eyes dark with indignation.

Suddenly he raised his head with that motion that his young office force knew so well when he was hurried or troubled and was giving some command about work to be done, and said in a voice that was low and determined.

"Well, I'll *make* you love me!" he declared. "I swear I will!"

Camilla laughed suddenly, a slow amused laugh.

"That would be quite impossible!" she said in a low controlled tone. "Not even if you were free, and all things to be desired, I wouldn't love you!" and something faraway like the memory of a dream danced in her eyes and made them laugh.

And Ralph Whitlock stood and watched her grimly, helplessly, and suddenly knew that he had lost.

"Camilla," he asked after a long, long silence, "why? Is there someone else? Is there, Camilla?"

She looked at him steadily for a moment, startled anew, then turned her face away from him toward the window where the sun had suddenly shot out from behind a cloud, and a smile dawned in her eyes.

"Yes," she said quietly, in a clear voice, "there is!"

CHAPTER XXIII

IT WAS GROWING LATE FOR THE FLORIDA SEASON, AND MRS. Wainwright was beginning to talk about going home.

There had been no word of her husband's coming south, and she was beginning to realize that he hadn't really expected to be able to come at all. And now that the season was about over and so many flitting to their homes, it didn't matter so much after all. She talked idly with her friends of "business" and of how hard her husband had to work in these times, and rocked and knitted. She was distinctly glad that Stephanie Varrell had at last given up bombarding her with questions as to where Jeff had gone, and was about to leave the hotel. Rumor had it that she had had a quarrel with her latest fiance and he had departed hastily. But recently a new adherent had arrived, a darkbrowed foreign-looking stranger who walked the piazzas with her and seemed to order her about as if he had the right. They were off now in an airplane, sailing over the blue sea, into the bluer sky, looking like a mosquito on a field of blue. Jeffrey Wainwright's mother profoundly hoped she would sail so far that she would never come back into her range of vision again.

Jeff meanwhile had been with John Saxon, doing actual physical labor and learning profound truths from the Word of God. Such fellowship and joy had come from this friendship as he had never had before, and a vision of what heavenly lives could be on earth, even in a little old ramshackle shanty in the midst of a lonely Florida orange grove, waiting for the oranges to mature and pay for ordinary necessities.

One night, sitting under the great Florida moon Jeff told John Saxon about Camilla. Told him too that he was worried because she had not answered his letter.

John Saxon listened quietly, read between the lines, studied the speaking face of his friend, and then spoke in a tone of deep brotherly love.

"Man! If you've found a girl like that go back and get her promised before someone else carries her off! There aren't many of them these days. Jeff, I'll be missing you, but—I'll be praying for you, old man!"

Jeff went the next day.

He found at the hotel a summons for him from his father. He would come down for a week with the mother and bring her home, if Jeff would come back at once. So Jeff sent a wire and went.

His first day in the office was a busy one for his father had left detailed directions, and Jeff carried them out conscientiously to the letter. It was late and he was tired when he got through, but his heart was singing. He was going to see Camilla in a few minutes. God grant no other man had found her yet and carried her off. What a fool he had been to leave without telling her something, getting some definite word from her, and yet, how could he? She had definitely put a barrier between them which he had to find out how to cross. Thank God he had found the way and crossed it, and now was free to go and tell her.

So he ate a hasty dinner and drove down to Vesey Street.

But when he reached Vesey Street it wasn't there at all! Something had happened. It was gone entirely, dropped right out of the world. It seemed as if he were living in a fairy tale and a bad fairy had woven an enchantment. Of course he had made some ridiculous mistake and it was there somewhere, but he couldn't find it.

He drove up a block and down a block and round several blocks and came to a standstill again right where he had thought it was, but Vesey Street had departed.

He consulted a policeman new on the beat who informed him that there were portions of an intermittent Vesey Street located erratically here and there in the neighborhood and he canvassed them all to no purpose. One hundred-and-twenty-five Vesey Street had vanished off the map.

Stephanie Varrell sailing trackless skies to strange lands with her dark foreigner would have laughed with the gaiety of the underworld if she could have seen his face, utterly baffled, and so easily, by a couple of summary little telegrams. Sometimes in her thoughts she exulted over having wiped that block of Vesey Street from off the face of the earth. She wondered what had become of the girl, and whether she was by this time forgotten? Whether the letter too, in ashes, had done its work. She felt, if she had no other satisfaction, at least she had that. For she hated that girl, of whose likeness to herself more than one man had dared to tell her that night.

But Jeffrey Wainwright came back at last to the heap of bricks and plaster and glass and tin that composed that portion of Vesey Street and searched till he found a boy who used to live in the row and who remembered a family by the name of Chrystie. He used to serve them papers sometimes, he said. But they had moved away. "Suddenly," he said. "Maybe they couldn't pay their rent." He didn't know where they had gone, perhaps a long way off. "People did sometimes when they couldn't pay their rent."

So Jeffrey Wainwright went his troubled way. He tried to find out who had done the moving, but the boy didn't know. He wasn't on the spot at the time. He was serving papers on his beat. His brother might know, but he was gone away to his uncle's on a farm.

Long evenings Jeffrey Wainwright searched for Camilla, coming back each night to the empty place where Vesey Street used to be, and asking anyone who passed, but nothing came of it.

He even searched out the postman on that beat, but the postman, though he remembered the Chrysties said they had left no forwarding address. He said they never got much mail anyway, just a letter now and then from the west. But he couldn't remember the name of the town, so that came to nothing. And the bricks and débris of Vesey Street grew daily less and less as the ground was cleared and prepared for the great building that was to go up for the Gas Company. Even the old wooden step where Jeffrey had stood with Camilla that night was carried away, gone, utterly gone. Only the memory of that precious kiss was left.

That night he wrote John Saxon a brief anxious letter asking him to pray hard!

One day Jeffrey Wainwright remembered Miss York. Why hadn't he thought of her before? And he drove to the house where he had gone for her on that memorable night in the winter.

The snow was gone, and the grass was growing green. There was a scraggy row of daffodils blooming in the little side yard of the house where he had found the nurse, but when he knocked at the door nobody answered, and looking at the windows he found there were no curtains, no sign of inhabitant. A query about the neighborhood brought out the fact that the folks had gone to live with their daughter instead of her coming to live with them, and the house and daffodils were for sale or rent, but no one knew what had become of the nurse!

It was a strange set of circumstances, as if some evil minded power were playing a trick on Jeff. He thought of the kind old doctor next. He would know his patients, the Chrysties, and what had become of them. He would surely know where Nurse York was at least.

But when he went to the doctor's house where he and Camilla went that first night they had met, he found crepe on the door. The doctor had had a stroke and died two days before, and no one about the house knew or cared where a Nurse York lived, and they had never heard of patients named Chrystie.

All day Jeffrey worked in the office, every evening he searched for Camilla. He occasionally met acquaintances here and there in the city who invited him to their homes, asked him to go out with them, but he declined them all. He was too busy. It got about that he was at home and the telephone rang incessantly when he was there, but he told his man to say he was going out. If Stephanie Varrell called or did not call he did not know nor care. If she was in the city it made no difference to him. What did make a difference was that Camilla had vanished as completely as Vesey Street, and his heart was crying out to find her. The kiss upon his lips was real now, and came back to him in his dreams and thrilled him. Where, oh, where was Camilla?

CHAPTER XXIV

MATTERS AT THE OFFICE HAD BEEN MOST TRYING EVER SINCE that Monday talk that Camilla had had with Whitlock.

He had been in and out of the office, working hard and silently, answering everybody shortly, glaring into the telephone as if it were a human being, most irascible even to Camilla. And as for poor Marietta, she was getting in these days all the discipline of life that she had missed when she was a child.

Camilla had time now and then to look at her proudly, and encourage her with a smile, for really Marietta was showing some of the fruits of righteousness which hard trials often bring. She was neat, she was respectful, even in the face of faultfinding, she was humble, she did not answer back nor chew gum nor read novels, and she did her work well and more and more rapidly.

"If I should have to leave," thought Camilla, and she thought it many times a day in these days, "Marietta could almost take my place!"

Camilla had not told her mother her fears. Time enough when the blow fell if it did, but she knew enough about human nature to understand that things could not go on continually as they were doing.

But wise Nurse York was watching and whenever she came over to the house for a few hours, which she did as often as she got a chance, she watched Camilla keenly, and she asked casual wise questions to find out whether Whitlock was as frequent a visitor as he used to be. She had pretty well convinced herself that the Chrysties had not known about Whitlock's wife until she let it out. She did not mean to say any more about it unless she had to, to save Camilla from making a mistake, but she was taking no chances. The Chrysties were thoroughbreds and would not show their amazement, would not want her to think there had been any attention that a married man should not show. They would keep their thoughts to themselves, but nevertheless Nurse York would watch. She so loved Camilla and despised Whitlock that she would not let things go too far.

She noted the strained look about Camilla's eyes at night when she came home, yet was satisfied that it was not from heartbreak at least, and when the next weekend passed and there was no further sign of Whitlock she drew a breath of relief and took heart of hope.

One day Whitlock came into the office about noon with a strange desperate look on his face. He sent Marietta off to her lunch summarily, and Camilla wished she dared rise and go too, but Marietta was scarcely out of the way before Whitlock came over and stood before her desk.

"Camilla, I'm desperate," he said, "I can't stand this any longer." Camilla lifted up her heart in swift prayer for help and guidance. "Oh, I'm sorry," she said quickly, gently, "I know myself there are times when it seems as if there was not a soul to go to but God. But I know too, that He can always help us through hard places."

The man looked at her strangely, his head down, his eyes lifted, piercing through her very soul as if he would probe her to find out if she was really meaning all she said, as if he would find some weak place in her armor if he could.

"How could God help me!" asked the man in a tone of scoffing.

"Nothing is worth while in which God cannot help," said Camilla. "You told me once, I think, that you were a Christian."

"Oh, yes I told you that I was a Christian. I suppose I was, perhaps, I don't know. I joined the church, but it hasn't done me much good, has it? Look what a rotten deal I've had. A marriage that was a failure, and a love that came to nothing—the only woman in the world that I could ever love telling me practically that she hates me! Would you call that a fair deal? Would you want a God that treated you that way? Come, tell me what *you* would do about it?"

His under jaw was out and his eyes were flushed and angry, desperate eyes. They almost made her shudder to look into them. Camilla if she had followed her impulse would have turned and fled from the building and never gone back any more. But something, perhaps it was the challenge from the lips of the man who was usually so calm and conservative, so absolutely correct in everything he said, made her stay and answer.

"Come, what would *you* do?" he urged. There was something in his eyes, like an angry bull about to charge.

Quietly she answered.

"I think I would look into my own heart first, before I blamed God, and try to find out whether any of the trouble had been my own fault."

"What? *My* own fault?" he lowered. "What do you know about it?"

"Nothing," said Camilla calmly. "You asked me what I would do, and that is what I think I would do first. I would get down on my knees—on my face—and ask God to show me myself utterly. And if facing things honestly that way I found any of my trouble was my own fault, and if there was anything left to be done that I could do toward righting things, no matter if it cost me all my pride, I'd *do* it!"

He scowled down upon her and a wave of memories rolled over him, each one bringing a deeper frown.

"Right it? What do you mean, *right it?* Right my love for you?"

"Why, yes," said Camilla thoughtfully, "I suppose it would right that too, for that was only an effect of the other, not a cause. There was something back of that or it would never have come. The first wrong was far behind that. I don't know when it came, but if you had been loving your own wife, and living with her in unselfishness and happiness, you would never have fancied you cared for me. It was not a natural right love, it was abnormal, and I suppose God may be trying to make you understand that."

He looked at her out of his bloodshot eyes as if he could not believe his ears.

"But I couldn't love my wife," he said, "and I don't want to live with her in happiness. There's no happiness where she is concerned."

"You thought there was when you married her," said Camilla calmly. "Perhaps I'm all wrong, and of course I

don't know the circumstances, but there's usually wrong
on both sides when things like that happen, and they
never can be righted until both are willing to own it. I
couldn't advise you, really. I'm too young and inexperi-
enced. But I should think you'd talk with the Lord about
it, and then you'd go and try to make up with your wife,
and get your little girl's arms around your neck, and see
how it feels to have her lips kissing you. I don't believe
you're going to find relief in any other way. Only God
can make you want things right in your life. No love that
isn't right could ever bring you anything but more trouble. And now," said Camilla with a throb of great relief,
"I hear Marietta coming and I think I'd better go to
lunch. I've told you everything I know to say, and if you
would like me to leave the office after you have thought
this over, if that will help you to do right, I'll be glad to
go."

The door opened and Marietta walked in, giving a
furtive glance at the wild-eyed master, and wondering if
Camilla was fired at last, and if *she* would come next?

But Whitlock snatched his hat and coat and hurried out
of the office. Camilla smiled at Marietta out of tired
brave eyes and went out to her lunch. She didn't feel
equal to answering Marietta's questions just yet.

CHAPTER XXV

JEFFREY WAINWRIGHT PARKED HIS CAR NEAR THE EXCLUSIVE
flower shop where he had been used to purchase his flowers. The last time he was there he had bought white orchids for Camilla to wear to dinner with him. He had a
yearning now to see if they had any white orchids. He
did not quite know why he got out and went up to the
lovely window with its marvellous display of flowers. He
had a vague idea of sending his mother some Parma
violets. His mother loved violets and he had no one else

now to whom he cared to send flowers. It just seemed pleasant to go there, that was all, to remember how he had gone that other night that now seemed so long ago, and sent the orchids.

He locked his car and stepped across the pavement, weaving his way among the people who thronged the way always at the noon hour. It was foolish his coming there then, he could just as well have telephoned for them and saved his trouble.

He did not notice the people who stood beside the window. He stepped up and looked over the head of a woman, and there sure enough in the centre of the window were some lovely specimens of white orchids, their delicate forms standing out as rare faces will sometimes amid a throng.

A group of three women who had been exclaiming over a bank of brilliant yellow flowers moved on and Jeffrey took their place, where he could look more carefully at the flowers down in front. Yes, there were violets, and they looked like his mother's favorite kind. He gave one more wistful glance at the white orchids. It seemed to him he had never seen such lovely ones before, and then he turned to step behind the other window-gazer and go into the shop to order his flowers. But the woman turned also, and they were face to face each trying to go in opposite directions. He lifted his hat apologetically and looked down, and then he saw her as she looked up.

"Camilla!" he cried joyously, his face lighting with a great joy, "Oh, Camilla! My Dear!"

And then and there he placed a hand reverently on each of her shoulders, and bending down he laid his lips upon hers. Right there in the throng of the street!

"Oh, Camilla, I have found you!"

And then he reached down and caught her little fluttering hands.

People turned and looked, and one woman who always explained everything she saw to any companion with her said:

"It's her husband! He's been away, don't you think, and he didn't expect to meet her just there? My! He looked happy, didn't he? I wonder if he'll take her in there and buy her some flowers! Wouldn't that be nice? My, I like to watch people, don't you? Yes, he's taking her in. I wonder what he'll buy her? I'd like to stop a minute and see, wouldn't you?"

"He's not her husband if he's buying her flowers!" said the other woman sourly. "They don't! She'd better enjoy them while she can. There won't be many more after they're married."

"Oh, now you don't know," said the first woman wistfully. "See, see, I believe he's going to buy those white orchids for her. Isn't that wonderful? White orchids are awfully expensive, aren't they?"

"Yes, I guess they are. I wonder what she'll do with them," said the sour woman. "She is dressed dreadfully plain, though she's pretty. But she looks tired and worn out. She's likely his sister and he's buying orchids for his girl. Come on, we can't stay here all day."

"No, she isn't his sister," said the first woman firmly, "didn't you see how he kissed her? It wasn't a brotherly kiss, not that one. It was real I tell you," and she turned away with a wistful backward look through the window.

But Camilla stood within that flower shop and watched Jeff as he bought the flowers, those very white orchids for her, and pinned them on her shabby old coat that was ten times more shabby than the last time it had white orchids pinned upon it. Camilla with her cheeks glowing rosily, and her eyes alight. Camilla trying to realize that it was herself and not a girl in a dream! Camilla with that precious kiss stinging sweet upon her lips, and the feel of Jeff's hands upon her shoulders, the hungry feel of his arms, that had restrained themselves, for the sake of the world that was looking, from taking her close to his heart. Somehow she felt it, knew it, without a word being said about it, without the thought being even formed into phrases. It was just there, a great wonderful knowledge.

And it was all a part somehow of that word she had said just a few minutes ago in the office when Mr. Whitlock had asked her if there was anyone else, and she had answered, with such amazing quickness, knowing on the spur of the moment that it was true, "Yes, there is!"

Somehow out of the chaos that had separated them for so many weeks, that Yes had called him quickly to her side.

And the strange part about it was that she had no

doubts, no fears, no protests about his being of another world. Why was it that her soul was so at peace?

They went out of the shop with the lovely white orchids pinned upon her breast, and her hand drawn within his arm, his eyes down upon her like a great light.

"Where do we go now, Camilla?" he asked, pausing in the doorway to the immense delight of the first of the two women who had lingered before a bargain window of silk underthings just for the sole purpose of getting another glimpse of romance. "Is your car parked somewhere near, and do we have to retrieve it, or can you go in mine? And is there somewhere you must go first or do we drive right home? And *where* is home?"

She laughed at the torrent of questions, and he laid his hand upon hers with a close loving pressure.

"I never take my car out at noon," she managed to answer, though his eyes were looking wonders into her own. "I can go in yours if you will be so good. It isn't far. I've had my lunch. But I must be back there in twenty minutes. My lunch time is almost over. I just came around this way—to—see—the flowers!"

She bent low to look at the lovely ones she was wearing and her face grew more rosily red than ever, for she knew by his smile that he understood that she was loving those orchids when she stood there alone window-gazing. And she knew in her heart as she looked at the delicate petals that she was also loving him, though then she had never expected to see him again. But the glorious knowledge that she loved him had so thrilled her as she acknowledged it to herself that she had had to come and look at the orchids to bear the joy of it.

All this her eyes held and she lowered them from his gaze lest he should read it there, too soon.

"Office!" he said, frowning above his smile like a sun-shower in April. "I can't spare you to an office. How long does it last? Must you go today when we have just found each other?"

"Oh, yes, I must go." She laughed happily. "It lasts till five o'clock."

"Then I shall park outside the door and watch everyone who comes out. I'm running no risks of losing you again. It's been agony these last weeks since I got home and found you'd gone and taken your street away with you, root and branch."

"Oh!" said Camilla softly, her eyes glowing, and then: "Oh,—what do you mean, 'taken the street with me'?"

"Didn't you know the street was gone? Here, I'll show you. It won't take long, we'll drive around that way so you can understand what I've been up against. I even wrote a letter and mailed it to an address that wasn't any more, hoping somehow the post office would find you, though they had said you had left no forwarding address, and this very morning it came back to me from the dead letter office! It made me feel sick to look at it. I thought I had lost you forever. Camilla, *why* didn't you answer my letter that I wrote from Florida?"

"Letter?" said Camilla looking up amazed. "Did you write me a letter?"

"I certainly did," he said, "and I watched every mail for an answer. I thought you had forgotten me. But you haven't, have you Camilla?" He looked earnestly into her face.

"No,—I haven't forgotten you," she said softly, "but I never got any letter, though—I often—wished—for one."

"You *dear!*" he said with that tender wonderful look in his eyes. "Even though we were of different worlds? You looked for a letter?"

He was driving with a royal disregard of traffic laws, but perhaps because the traffic was too dense to let him go very far at a time, or because the traffic officers were looking the other way, nothing happened, and now they whirled into the open space where Vesey Street and its surroundings used to be, but neither of them realized it, for they were looking into one another's eyes, and only the angels must have guided and protected that car as it moved along in its own sweet way, certainly Jeff did not.

"But that's all over now," said Jeff with a lilt in his voice, "because, Camilla, I've been born again!" And suddenly he stopped the car and bent over and kissed her for the third time. Right in front of where the old house at number one-twenty-five Vesey Street used to be! And neither of them knew it!

Not till suddenly Camilla came to herself and realized that people were passing and looking at them.

"Oh!" she said, her voice full of her great joy, "Jeffrey,

we mustn't, not here! People will see us! Where are we?"

"I don't care if the whole world sees us!" he laughed, "they can't spoil our joy anyway!" Then he looked about him as he drew his arm away from about her.

"Why, we're at Vesey Street, don't you see? And Vesey Street isn't at home! But I don't care any more, do you? I've found you and that's all that matters!"

Then did Camilla sit up and look around. Vesey Street? It couldn't be Vesey Street! It wasn't anywhere! And she had to look around several times before she finally identified the old church on the next street with its solemn old clock chiming out the quarter-past hour.

"Oh, I'm late!" exclaimed Camilla. "I must go at once!"

"What will they do to you, darling? Make you stay after school?" Jeffrey's eyes were laughing as he started the car.

And then he would insist on getting out and seeing her up to the office.

"I've got to know your haunts you see," he said seriously, "how do I know but you've a way of making the office and the building and all disappear too? Such enchantment as you carry might do almost anything. And tell me, quick, before that elevator comes, what is your new address? I'm not going to run any risks at all till I have you safe and fast for my own!"

He said these last words in a low tone in her ear just as the elevator door clanged back to let them enter, and though Camilla's cheeks were very rosy and her eyes most bright, there was no other opportunity to answer.

Whitlock stood in the hall opposite the elevator as they arrived at the office floor, his face drawn and anxious, his watch in his hand, and a look of relief came to his face as he saw her step out of the elevator.

"Oh!" he said stepping to her side, "I was afraid you were not *coming back!*"

And then he saw Wainwright standing smiling beside her,—and then he saw the orchids,—and Camilla's brilliant cheeks, and his face went blank suddenly.

"I'm sorry to be late," chirped Camilla blithely, "it was—rather—unavoidable! Mr. Whitlock, let me introduce my friend Mr. Wainwright!"

Whitlock turned and looked at the other man, searching his face intently, and Camilla saw that her employer's face was deadly white and stern, but he put out his hand and greeted Jeff like one who acknowledged the championship of his rival.

Then suddenly, with another look at the orchids, Whitlock raised his eyes to Camilla's, an almost humbled look of homage in them.

"I just want to tell you," he said in his usual business tone, "that I've decided to take your advice about that matter we were discussing, and I'm leaving at once. Do you think that you could get along for a few days without me in the office if I am detained?"

Camilla's face lighted up, though it had seemed before that that it wouldn't be capable of shining any more brightly than it already was.

"Oh, yes," she said joyously. "I'm glad! I hope you will be most—successful! I'm quite sure it's going to be—all right!"

He was gone and Jeff looked down after the elevator as it slid away, and said in a pitying tone:

"Poor bird! I'm sorry for him. He doesn't know what he's about to lose! But I guess he can get another secretary, and I couldn't get another Camilla in the whole wide world. She's the only one!"

Camilla laughed softly, with something moist and tender in her eyes. Sometime, perhaps, she would tell Jeff everything, but it didn't seem to matter just now, only her heart took time to be a little glad that Whitlock was going back to find his wife.

Marietta sat working away intent upon her business when they entered the office, but when she looked up and saw Camilla with those gorgeous orchids pinned to her coat, and her face shining, she sat and stared, oblivious for the moment of the tall young man who loomed behind her. But when Camilla introduced him and he bowed and smiled at her, she was entirely overcome, utterly speechless.

Jeff didn't stay but a minute. He said he had an errand and would be back at five o'clock, would come up to the office and get her.

"We'll drive home in your car, shall we Camilla? And I'll have mine sent up later. I want to see what kind of a job they made of the car."

And right there before the wondering eyes of Marietta he had the effrontery to stoop and kiss Camilla on her happy lips, and say "Good-bye, Camilla, till five o'clock!"

Marietta remained speechless until the door had closed after him and Camilla had turned toward her smiling. Then she said:

"Oh, Camilla! Isn't he *swell*? Does he really *belong to you*?"

It was hard for both girls to do any work that afternoon. Marietta was fairly bursting with questions and Camilla could not keep her thoughts from wandering back to her joy. But five o'clock came at last and Jeff was exactly on time.

They filled Marietta with everlasting gratitude and joy by tucking her into the car and taking her home before they went on their way, but at last they were out and alone, and could talk. Camilla at once became dumb. She couldn't say what was in her heart. She could only smile and look at Jeff's dear face.

But Jeff wasn't dumb.

"Camilla, I've been thinking a lot while you were up there in that office. How soon can we be married? I simply can't wait a long time! We've wasted a lot of weeks already. And I've been making plans. I have a gorgeous piece of land out on the Ridge, and I thought perhaps we'd like to build and have our house just the way we plan it? How about it? Would you like that?"

But Camilla could only gasp and smile and exclaim.

"We'd want it specially arranged so that your mother could have a little suite of rooms, sitting room and boudoir and bath and so on you know, right on the ground floor. I wasn't sure but we'd have the whole thing built long and low so we could all be together. I know it isn't good for your mother to do much climbing of stairs."

Camilla glowed. It didn't seem that any of this was real, only a dream, and therefore no answers were required of her.

"And then I was wondering if we couldn't get hold of that nurse you had. Wasn't her name York? And just get her to live with us and kind of look after us all, and be someone to stay with Mother when we had to be away a few days. I thought if we arranged the rooms right it might be very pleasant, and she would take a lot of responsibility off you if any of us were sick. She seemed such a nice sort of person. Would you like that?"

On and on he went with his wild lovely plans, and they were at the house before they realized.

Jeff insisted on going in the back door straight from the garage with Camilla.

"I want to begin to be at home right away," he said grinning.

And then in he walked and took Mrs. Chrystie right in his arms and kissed her gently on both cheeks.

"Here I am again, Mother Chrystie," he said with his nice grin. "And you might as well make up your mind to like me for I've come to stay. I'm going to be your son just as soon as I can pry Camilla loose from that job of hers and we can get married. I hope you don't mind for I love you a lot already!"

"And where do I come in?" said a voice from the dining-room door, and there was Nurse York just come in for a few minutes to see how they were getting along.

"Why, you come right in on the ground floor, of course," said Jeff heartily. "Camilla and I were just talking about it. We were wondering whether you would be willing to give up what you're doing and be our official nurse? We're building you a special room just as you want it, if you will, and we won't take no for an answer!"

After dinner was over and Nurse York had gone back to her patient, they sat together talking it over joyously.

"But Mother," said Camilla, "I don't see how we're ever going to have the right kind of wedding in this tiny house with our resources. Marietta has been telling me all the afternoon what swell relatives I'm acquiring, interspersed with clippings to prove it from the newspapers, and I'm afraid they'll feel uncomfortable here. They couldn't all get in, either. And we haven't a church around here that we know well enough to feel like getting married in. I wish people could just go quietly to a minister and get married. Very poor people do that. Why can't we?"

Her troubled eyes turned toward Jeff, who met hers with a perplexed but not at all worried look.

But it was the mother who solved the problem.

"Oh, that will be easy, dear," she said sweetly. "We'll just go back home to Burbrook and you can be married in the church where your father and I were married. The same minister is there yet. He was a young man then, he's old and retired now, but he could marry you. Then you can have a little reception right there in the church afterward, that's often done. And you know there's a new apartment hotel there now, a lovely place they say. That would make plenty of room for the guests who stayed over night. It's not so far away, only a hundred and fifty miles. Wouldn't that be all right?"

"That would be great!" said Jeff. "And now, Mother Chrystie, how soon do you think it could reasonably be? Camilla has so much devotion to that office that I can't quite trust her decision, for I'm in a hurry, I'm telling my father and mother tonight, and I'd like to announce the date. Also I want to bring them to call tomorrow."

The wedding was fixed for June and very simply planned. Camilla went round in a daze of joy and couldn't believe it was anything but a dream, until the wedding presents began to come in and then she was almost in a panic. How could she ever live up to those wedding presents? They more than filled the little house and were more wonderful than any dream she had ever dreamed.

She said something of this to Jeff one day, and he put his arm about her and drew her close.

"You don't have to live up to them, sweetheart. They are only things of this world," he said, "and you and I have been born again into another world, thank God!"

But there was one wedding present that filled Camilla's heart with thanksgiving,—not because of its intrinsic value, though it was beautiful and rare and costly enough, —but because of the card that accompanied it,—though it was only a plain engraved card. It read: "Mr. and Mrs. Ralph Whitlock," and down in the corner in a woman's fine hand was written, "In Gratitude."

The wedding was charming and the bride very lovely in her mother's wedding dress of fine embroidered organdy, with bits of real old lace. John Saxon was there of course, and Marietta too, the trip and a new dress being a gift from the bride.

All Jeffrey Wainwright's rich relatives were present and called the old church "quaint" and "darling" and said the bride was "rare," and wasn't it nice that she was willing to wear Jeff's grandmother's wedding veil?

It hung about her like frost work of old silver, and Jeffrey said it made her look like an angel. She wore real orange blossoms that John Saxon had brought. But the bridal bouquet was of white orchids!